D1125801

Presented To:

_____

From:

_____

Date:

_____

# THE
# UPPER
# ZOO

# THE UPPER ZOO

### MICHAEL ROBERT WOLF

DESTINY IMAGE® PUBLISHERS, INC.
P.O. Box 310, Shippensburg, PA 17257-0310
*"Promoting Inspired Lives."*

This book and all other Destiny Image, Revival Press, MercyPlace, Fresh Bread, Destiny Image Fiction, and Treasure House books are available at Christian bookstores and distributors worldwide.

For a U.S. bookstore nearest you, call 1-800-722-6774.
For more information on foreign distributors, call 717-532-3040.
Reach us on the Internet: www.destinyimage.com.

ISBN 13 TP: 978-0-7684-4098-0
ISBN 13 Ebook: 978-0-7684-8868-5

For Worldwide Distribution, Printed in the U.S.A.
1 2 3 4 5 6 7 8 / 15 14 13 12

# DEDICATION

Dedicated to Logan, Nathan, and Asher,
who are each wise in different ways.

# ENDORSEMENTS

A slice of life from the 1960s. You will not be able to put this refreshingly entertaining book down.

Sid Roth, Host
*It's Supernatural!* Television
www.SidRoth.org

*The Upper Zoo* is an exquisitely written novel that will tug at your soul. Those who enter its world will find it deeply affecting and poignant.

Jonathan Bernis
Jewish Voice, President

*The Upper Zoo* captured my attention from page one. I became immediately locked into the story. Jonathan became the young boy inside me and I needed to know what was going to happen to him.

Don Finto, The Caleb Company

# FOREWORD

I COUNT IT AN HONOR and privilege to be invited to write the foreword to this remarkable work of fiction, *The Upper Zoo*, by Michael Wolf. Michael has been a close friend for over 30 years. He is a gifted speaker, songwriter, and screenwriter. Having said that, I had no idea that he was capable of writing such a remarkable piece of fiction. When he first asked me to write the foreword, I accepted more out of friendship than excitement for the book. Of course, in order to write an informed foreword, I needed to read the book, so I sat down with a heavy sense of obligation to become familiar with the story, its characters, and its plot.

Almost from the onset, I felt myself being pulled into the storyline and its unusual cast of characters. The more I read the more excited and engrossed I became. The storyline is unusual and unpredictable. I can honestly say I had no idea where the plot was going and could not imagine the twists and turns the author created.

The story revolves around a young Jewish boy, Jonathan, who experiences a severe personal crisis as he enters the eighth grade. Because he did not make his seventh grade education a priority, he finds himself in the humiliating position of being placed in a "special" class of purported "under-achievers." *The Upper Zoo* is filled with colorful and diverse characters that live interesting but for the most part sad and tragic lives.

There are two "special" remedial classes he describes as the "upper" and "lower" zoos. Both are remedial, but the Upper Zoo (he believes) is for the *smarter* slow learners. He consoles himself with the belief that at least he has been placed in the Upper Zoo...a small and unconvincing consolation. From there a cast of classmates, parents, and others is developed as their unique lives unfold and intertwine in the most surprising and interesting ways.

In the end, Jonathan achieves the great triumph of extricating himself from the Upper Zoo, but even more importantly doing so in the midst of a life that is filled with great challenges.

When I finished *The Upper Zoo*, I said to myself, this is not just a great book, but perhaps a classic for the enjoyment and edification of many generations. I also believe *The Upper Zoo* may find its way to movie houses all over the world...it's that good. Congratulations Michael and congratulations to you the reader for you are about to enter the strange and wonderful world of *The Upper Zoo*. Enjoy!

—Joel Chernoff

# CHAPTER 1

THE NIGHT BEFORE THE FIRST day of eighth grade, Mom stood with folded arms and blocked the TV set.

"Turn off Bonanza, Jonathan. I need to talk to you."

I didn't even like Bonanza. For one thing, it served as a reminder that our TV was black and white and not color like our neighbor's, Robert Rogers. Nevertheless, I didn't budge. I just sat there next to Billy waiting to see what Hoss and Little Joe would do next.

"Now!"

She glared at me and aimed her finger directly my way. Even as I complied, I tried to look around her so I could get another glimpse at the screen. Billy stayed on the couch. I figured he thought he could avoid my fate and keep watching after we left. But she went over and slapped the on-off switch. The picture shrunk to a little dot. Finally, Billy sprung up too.

"Not fair! Why can't *I* watch?"

"No TV! School starts tomorrow."

She folded her arms again and tapped her toe. That meant the jig was up. Billy realized he had no choice but to leave. He stalked out, hands outstretched in unwilling surrender. She sat down and slapped the seat next to her like she had the on-off switch. That meant "sit there." Then she looked at me with those piercing brown prosecutorial eyes. I had no choice but to take a seat right where she had slapped.

"We need to talk about school. Martha Rogers next door says if you don't do well in eighth grade, chances are you won't be a good student in ninth grade or all through high school. She read it somewhere."

Mom stood up and started pacing, throwing her hands up in the air like a lawyer driving a point home before a defendant.

"Of course *her* kids are all A students; Robert, in your class...*top student;* Scott in Billy's...*another top student."*

She pointed toward the ceiling, and Billy's room. "Not that Billy isn't holding his own. He's up there with Scott."

I hated that phrase, "holding his own." How secure could one be just holding one's own? Still, my brother Billy was safely stowed in fifth grade, so he could hold his own and get decent grades...but not me. Mom knew that I seemed not only to be not holding my own. I seemed to be letting go altogether.

"Okay, Mom."

"...on the honor roll."

"I know, Mom."

She stopped pacing and stood still. She was wearing one of her collection of calf-length, flowered dresses. She shook her head in a no direction, her brown, permed hair staying in perfect place the whole time. Then she added the finger of death.

"I don't understand what you do in your room all night."

"Sleep."

She didn't flinch. She just stood there, finger extended.

"We've gotten you personal tutors. Nothing. Take your last report card, for example."

"Yes, Mom."

Then all at once I saw a hint of tenderness in her eyes, like I was the rare defendant in which she saw something redeeming.

"Of course I don't believe it. It's not true. What Martha...what Mrs. Rogers said isn't true. You *will* straighten out," she half declared and half decreed. "And I just can't wait till you get past this stage."

I also hated those two other popular phrases: "straighten out" and "past this stage."

"You know what the teachers always write. 'Jonathan is such a bright boy, but he's not living up to his potential. He needs to work harder and do much better.'"

Another popular phrase: "not living up to his potential." I'd heard it often, especially the year before. She didn't have to remind me that my seventh grade year hadn't been great. The break between my 1961–1962 single teacher elementary school world and my 1962–1963 junior high world of shuffling between classes was a shock to my pre-teen system. I didn't adjust well. Everything distracted me; the various teachers with various temperaments, the load of textbooks with long chapters that built on ones I hadn't read, the six periods a day.

Mom sat back down in the same spot. When she did that, it meant something important was coming. She looked at me with a hint of both softness and sternness. Then she put her hand on my shoulder.

"I have to tell you. You will be taking special classes this year."

"Special classes?"

Nothing could be worse. I couldn't believe it. Some afternoon when everyone else was out playing, I'd be cooped up in some musty old schoolroom with three other kids and an impatient tutor. I already had Hebrew School two afternoons a week. Would I never get the fresh air teachers and parents say growing children need? Or maybe I'd miss gym class or playground time. That would be just as torturous.

She looked me in the eye and leaned forward as if to make sure I understood the news.

"I just wanted you to know. The special classes start tomorrow."

"But..."

She closed her eyes. That always marked the end of a conversation.

"It'll help you. Well…it's time for bed. You have to be up early tomorrow."

She kissed me on the forehead and walked out. "Special classes," I said to myself out loud. "Great."

I awoke the next morning at 6:30. I reached one limp hand over and felt for the alarm of my clock radio. When I found it, I almost rolled over and went back to sleep. But when I opened my eyes for a split second, the darkness of the early morning hour jarred me. I hadn't seen 6:30 since early June. Then I realized what day it was.

After dressing while still half asleep and stuffing a school note on my bureau into my pocket, I walked like a zombie down the stairs of our little house, the tail of my brown knit shirt sticking out and my brown, curly hair uncombed. The kitchen light was blinding compared to the darkness outside the window over the sink. I practically didn't see Billy or even Mom, who was running around juggling cereal and bowls like she was racing against the clock in the *Beat the Clock* game show.

I sat down at the old, laminated yellow kitchen table and stared at Tony the Tiger. There was no time to read the back of the box, like I had all summer. Billy was making an effort to do just that with the back of the Rice Krispies box while he shoveled the crackling grains into his mouth.

I only got a half a bowl of Frosted Flakes down before I looked at the thin, black hands of the big round white clock over the sink. It read 6:50.

I kissed Mom unceremoniously on the cheek while she stood there in her flannel robe. She gave me a quick hug.

"Good luck."

"Thanks," I mumbled.

Then I threw on my light gray jacket and left the house with barely a peep, like a chick being ejected from its nest. Billy followed close behind. The bus was rounding the corner on the way to the bus stop.

The ride was bumpy…I'd forgotten how bumpy. There was Robert Rogers from next door, with his combed hair and eager, shining eyes. I leaned against the window that wet my face with its cold condensation.

As I entered the familiar school hall, I pulled out the piece of paper I'd stuffed in my pocket earlier. On it was written a room number…122.

The first thing I noticed when I entered the classroom was that Robert Rogers was missing. Where had he gone? Maybe he was in the bathroom combing his already-combed hair. Or maybe he got moved up to an elite class in an undisclosed part of the building. But that was a crazy thought.

Then all at once, I noticed that *none* of the students in my seventh grade class were around. The students I *did* see looked resigned to being together. But I'd only seen a few of them before, probably from the hallways of seventh grade. I recognized by name only Robey Romero, a tall, lanky, imposing boy with a shock of straight thick black hair. Robey had a straight Roman nose like the kind I'd seen on a bust of Caesar in the art museum. He was legendary. Everyone in my seventh grade knew who he was and how to pronounce his name…it rhymed with Moby, as in Moby Dick. I knew that there were several legends connected with him. One had to do with two-dozen stolen Dixie cup ice cream treats from the cafeteria that mysteriously ended up in his freezer at home. The story went that he sent a thank you card to the principle containing a crisp ten-dollar bill. It wasn't an apology, but a thank you note. That made it a legend.

As I stood there alone among strangers instead of my familiar classmates, an anxious tightness swept up from my belly and radiated through my arms. I was in the wrong class, time was passing, and the teacher had just entered. He was a tall, thin man with a thin tie, a no-nonsense face, no-nonsense blue eyes, and a patch of straight, blond hair. I had never seen him before. The bell rang, the clock was ticking…and my eighth grade class was starting without me. My heart beating anxiously; I walked up to the teacher.

"I…I think I'm in the wrong class."

He was writing something in a spiral notebook, and he didn't even look up. I repeated myself.

"I think I'm in the wrong class."

"Name?"

"Jonathan Richman."

He pointed to a piece of paper on his right without even looking at it.

"You're right here."

I glanced at the sheet. There I was. And there was Robey Romero. I noticed that the size was about half of the normal class, maybe fifteen students. I had thought students were just late.

"But no one in my seventh grade class is here…"

"This is 8H, Mr. Richman. Please take a seat."

"But…"

"Please sit down."

8H. Where had I heard that before? It was infamous somewhere. But where? The tightness increased, but a different kind of tightness… not the kind associated with turning the wrong way into the wrong class, but rather with turning the right way into a place where something wasn't quite right.

It began to dawn on me that Robert Rogers didn't go *up*. No. He remained where everyone else was. Instead I went *down*, left behind, yet still somewhere in the vicinity of the eighth grade, as if stuck between floors in an elevator.

Then it hit me like a sledgehammer. This must be the "special classes" Mom was talking about. It wasn't an after school class at all, or something in place of gym or playground. Then on the heels of that revelation, came another more ominous one. Maybe I was in the…the…it wouldn't come out. I couldn't even *think* it. In seventh grade the words floated aimlessly like a distant legend from far away, even more exotic than the Robey legends. Only what was a folk tale was now literally before me. This must be it…it must be…I finally let myself think it…*the Zoo*.

But weren't there two zoos in the legend, an Upper Zoo and Lower Zoo? Yes, there were. I was never clear what that was all about. I stood there only slightly recalling that the upper one was bad…and the lower one was worse. Or was it the other way around? No, the lower was definitely worse…perhaps. So which was it? How low had I descended? Which Zoo was I in, if I was indeed in the Zoo? I had to know.

The teacher got up from his desk and tapped a pencil on his palm as he introduced himself.

"You are in 8H. I'm Mr. Garner. You will be instructed by myself and one other teacher, a Mr. Schott, whom you will meet after the lunch break. Yes, two teachers…and only two. He will teach English and social studies, and I will teach math and science. It's as simple as that. 'What are you doing here?' you may ask. Perhaps you are here for one of a number of reasons, but it all really boils down to one thing. You have not applied yourselves. You have not performed to your potential. We've done the testing. We know that."

It seemed this guy was all business. His gray suit told the story; very neatly pressed. I wasn't sure I wanted to spend every morning with him. But what choice did I have?

"Call it laziness, aimlessness, or too much recess…that's going to end this year. You *will* study and you *will* learn."

His poem was dryly entertaining. And he certainly confirmed that I was in a special class, as Mom promised. *Yes, this must be one of the Zoos,* I admitted to myself. But I was still processing, thinking *Which Zoo am I in? And exactly what's the difference between them?*

There was a break between the start of class and lunch. I could hear shuffling and banter in the hallways. Robert Rogers was somewhere out there earnestly focusing on the next class. But our class was not allowed to leave the room. We stood around in the back, silent, awkward. I approached one girl with stringy hair who seemed to cover half of her face, including her eyes. She wore a frayed, light brown hand-me-down dress that looked kind of like a brownie dress with the award patches removed.

"Hi. My name's Jonathan. Yours?

She hesitated, looking down toward the floor. Finally, after what seemed like five minutes, she said, "Gwen."

I half whispered. "So what is this, Upper or…or Lower?"

"What?"

"You know. Which is it? Upper or Lower?"

I couldn't bring myself to say Zoo.

"I don't know what you're talking about."

She turned and slowly walked away. There was definitely something strange about her. I glanced past her. There was Robey, his head protruding above the others. At least I already knew his name. I walked over to him. He was turned away from me, just gazing at the door. Hesitatingly, I reached up and tapped his shoulder. Time was short, and I had to know where I was before class started again.

"Yeh?"

"Robey…"

"Yeh? What is it?"

He scarcely turned toward me. He seemed agitated, upset about something. I repeated myself.

"Umm…Robey?"

"That's my name. Don't wear it out."

"Could you just let me know? Umm…is this the…the Upper or… the Lower…(then very quietly)…Zoo."

"That's a dumb question. Maybe you should be in the lower one with that question." He answered without turning around.

"So it's Upper then?"

He started to walk away.

"Good. You can stay. I guess you're not a retard like they are in the Lower Zoo."

So the Upper Zoo was bad, and the Lower Zoo was worse. And we were in the Upper Zoo. At least I knew that much.

# CHAPTER 2

I SPENT THE TWENTY MINUTES on the bus ride home wondering how to break the news to my parents. The window, no longer wet with condensation, had become my friend. I leaned against it, as if pressing to escape life, including the inevitable questions from my mother about my first day. I averted my eyes from all the other students on the bus. They were joking, bragging, talking about their teachers and books and homework. And I was pressing my head on the glass window, now with my eyes closed so I didn't have to see Robert Rogers or anyone else. Scenarios about my impending meeting with Mom and Billy presented themselves before me for consideration. The top one consisted of going straight to my room and staying there until bedtime.

At the stop, I sat up. Then I hung back, letting Robert Rogers pass me. I walked past the laughing and joking and boasting and got off. As soon as I stepped onto the street, I could see Billy and Mom standing in the yard. After a day with eighth graders, I noticed how short Billy was. His slightly too big, horn-rimmed glasses caught the fall sun. As was his habit, he poked them onto the bridge above his nose with his finger. I wanted to pass them both by and enter the house, but Mom demanded my attention. She got in front of me, blocking the front door like she had the TV. Her hands were on her hips. I knew she was waiting for a report; and like a criminal being interrogated, I was bound to give it.

"I got a call from the school office. They said the class is called 8H. Well?"

I couldn't get past her. My strategy had been sabotaged. I sighed and gave in to her glare.

"Yes. It's 8H. That's the class." Then to Billy, "What are you looking at?"

It seemed like he was trying to keep a straight face. I wished he would just laugh and get it over with.

"Nothing."

Mom beckoned to me with her right hand. She pointed to the door with the other hand.

"Do you want to talk alone, Jonathan?"

"Not really. I just want to go in and get something to eat."

I wasn't hungry, but it was a good excuse to get me past them. They both followed me in like detectives. I pulled a banana out of the refrigerator. Mom followed me back into the kitchen. Billy had gone upstairs. She pressed the matter, her eyes intensely focused on mine.

"Can we talk about it?"

I only had one question in response.

"Does Dad know about the…special classes? What did he say?"

She hesitated. She had that look she got when she was trying to convince me Dad *really* cared about me. It was as if a thin, foggy veil came over her eyes. And at the same time, she slightly cocked her head to the side, completing the impression that she didn't fully believe the very thing she wanted to comfort me about.

"He knows you're in a class to help you catch up and do better."

"Okay…it's not a *class*. It's like…the whole eighth grade year. And he's not upset?"

Her eyes got less convincing as she tried to make them look more convincing.

"No. He only wants to see you get help."

Suddenly, Robert Rogers popped into my mind. I asked without hesitating, "And what are you going to say to Martha Rogers?"

"What should I say? You're getting some help and you'll be as good a student as Robert when it's all said and done."

"Hmm."

She sighed and closed her eyes in that end-of-the-conversation mode. She clearly didn't want to talk about Dad or Mrs. Rogers. But I had one more thing to ask.

"Do you know what they call it? What everybody in the eighth grade calls it?"

"No. It doesn't matter what they call it. It's a special class to help bright children meet their potential."

Despite her effort to brush my answer aside, I could see she was bracing herself for my answer. She looked off to the side and sighed again, trying to appear impatient to move on to another point.

"They call it the Zoo. The Upper Zoo. That's what they call it… the Upper Zoo."

She froze, her eyes now fixed on me. I thought I could detect the hint of genuine pain in them, like she had been slapped in the face. She collected herself and inhaled, mounting up like a cat on the defense.

"Well…you're *not* an animal. You're my son. *You're my son.*"

We stood there for a few more seconds. Then she turned on her high heels and walked into the living room. I sat down to eat. I could hear her continued sighing even in the kitchen.

That night in my room I lay on my bed. I had no books, unlike all the other kids on the bus. There was nothing to do but just lay there listening to the sounds in the house. The walls were rather thin, and I could hear my father enter through the front door and slam it shut.

"So tell me about this flunky class Jonathan is in."

"Shhh. He'll hear you."

Then they lowered their voices so I couldn't hear them. But I could just imagine my father running his hand through his prematurely balding salt and pepper hair, then tucking both hands in his pants on either side of his slightly paunching stomach. He was a man of few words, and in a minute or so he'd finished speaking and walked into another room.

The next morning, Billy entered the kitchen while my Eggo was toasting. We were even later than the day before, and there was no time for cereal and cereal box reading. Mom was still upstairs. Billy grabbed his own Eggo and threw that into the little chrome toaster on the green Formica counter. We were both silent until mine popped up like a jack in the box. I grabbed it with a napkin and shook it at him threateningly like a dagger.

"Wait until you get to eighth grade. They'll put you in a class just like this. Maybe even in seventh grade. You're not even in school yet. You're in a playground with a door."

"Did I say something?"

He was about to mount a further defense, but his Eggo popped up and he turned and grabbed it, dropping it on a plate. I wouldn't let him off that easily.

"I know what you're thinking."

He sighed and tried a gentle approach, one I wasn't about to let him get away with.

"I know you're not dumb. You're smart. I'm your younger brother. I should know. You're just a different kind of smart and they don't understand."

I pointed the remainder of my Eggo at him like a switchblade and continued defending myself against his approach while he picked at his breakfast.

"What's that supposed to mean? Are you trying to act smarter than me? Huh?"

"I just know you're very smart. Maybe smarter than me."

"You're right. I am. So just remember that."

"Can we play this weekend?"

"Maybe."

I felt like I just kicked a puppy. But it felt good even as it also felt wrong. I put the rest of the Eggo in my mouth and walked out, shutting the door behind me. My second day hadn't started so well.

# CHAPTER 3

THE MORNING, AS IT TURNED out, went better than I expected. Mr. Garner, for all of his serious warnings the day before, ended up being a pretty enjoyable teacher. He explained number systems by using cavemen and piles of bones and actually kept my attention. There were little plastic bones on his desk, and he picked them up one by one and tried to explain what he called the binary system. The whole thing seemed like a foreign language to me. But I was beginning to vaguely understand it.

He became more animated as he continued. In fact, he got so excited that he started juggling with three of the bones. No teacher in seventh grade had done anything like that. I looked around to see whether anyone was smiling. It seemed like they were as surprised as I was. They just sat there and stared. Mr. Garner flipped one high in the air and caught it with his hand behind him. Then he smiled, as if to make up for the lack of smiles in the class.

"Well, what do you think of that?"

There was silence, so he gave up on the entertainment and continued teaching. After a repeat of zeros and ones, he gave us a break, during which I stayed to myself. I tried not to look anyone in the eye. I wasn't sure I wanted to make any friends in the Upper Zoo.

After the break, Mr. Garner taught us science. He used a model of a molecule for a chemistry lesson that looked like a tinker toy. He actually told a joke. It was a pun that confused atoms with Adam of the Bible. A few laughed awkwardly. I heard Robey laugh loudly above the others. It seemed like he always stood above the crowd, whether in stature or laughter. Mr. Garner's smile broadened, apparently pleased with Robey's response. Perhaps that put him in a good frame of mind when he gave us our first homework assignment, because it consisted of merely going over the table of contents in our math and science books "so we would get the big picture." Not bad.

Lunch, which was usually something to look forward to, was harder than class. There was no way of avoiding the fact that the boy who disappeared from his regular eighth grade class the first day had appeared during the second as part of a strange group of losers who had Upper Zoo written all over their sorry selves. Demeaning looks were directed our way, as if we all had third-degree burns on our faces. And the whispering that accompanied the looks just rubbed salt on oozing wounds. I was a boy out of space and time. Like that elevator, I was stuck between floors. And I had no choice but to sit trapped at a *special table* with my new *friends* and eat my unappetizing lunch that passed for beef stew.

Though I might have wished we were quarantined somewhere in a separate lunchroom away from prying eyes, I decided to make the best of the situation by initiating some polite conversation through the clatter and din around me. Next to me was a chubby kid with a round flat face. He seemed innocuous enough.

"Garner's pretty cool."

"What?"

"I said Garner's a pretty good teacher."

I was hoping I'd found at least one person to make some small talk with. But he screwed up his face into a grimace and separated his lips like he was about to spit at me. That concerned me because he was chewing a mouthful of food, which didn't stop him from sharing his opinion and making a request.

"He's a jerk. Are you gonna eat your chips?"

I slid my plate his way.

"No. Here."

"What about the pudding?"

"Yeh, I am."

The bell rang. I waited until my old class moved through the door along with everyone else. Then I slowly got up and threw out the pudding in the corner trash can. Slowly, the cafeteria emptied. A kitchen worker seemed to come from nowhere with a rag and began wiping the tables, starting from the side of the room where the Upper Zoo had been sitting. As she quietly worked, her silence stood in contrast to the clacking of dishes and clinking of silverware in the distance.

I looked around the now empty room, whose walls seemed to reflect pure loneliness. They were an ugly neutral color, hard brick with a shiny coat of some sort. The lights above were a dull incandescent yellow encased in old-school style, marshmallow-shaped, opaque glass globes. As I looked around, tears of deep shame and loneliness began to fill my eyes. I slowly walked out into the greenish halls and headed for the Upper Zoo class.

Mr. Schott wore horn-rimmed glasses…but unlike Billy's, his fit. He plastered his dirty blonde hair down with the ever-popular Brylcreem. His face was decidedly Germanic, with a square jaw and beady brown eyes, and he wore a three-piece suit with a white shirt. Like Mr. Garner, he was a trim man in his thirties. Unlike Mr. Garner, he spoke in hushed tones. I never heard him raise his voice. Sometimes he almost whispered. And it always seemed like he spoke slower when he got angry.

Everyone was standing in the back of the class, as usual. So far I had talked to three of the fourteen. I wondered, as I watched them trying to make small talk, just what each one's story was. When did their failure in school first become apparent? How many were smarter than me, and how many dumber?

Already, I could see the social patterns forming among them. I wondered if everyone else in the room sensed it. I was sure I was outside of it. Yet I took my place among them by just being present and standing by myself. And I knew it. There in the very back was Robey, holding court by merely standing and slouching and doing whatever else he did. Boys and a few flirtatious girls surrounded him like iron filings to a magnet, some closer than others. Two iron filings were closer than the others. I hadn't noticed those two boys before. They seemed to be hanging on his every word. Gwen and chubby boy were outside this circle, in smaller circles of their own.

Mr. Schott struck a ruler on his desk, which rang out above the conversation like a gunshot. That was followed by a quiet appeal to be seated. Slowly, one by one, each student headed for his or her desk. This was staggered. The first one to sit down was what, upon first glance, appeared to be the prettiest girl in the room. She was well-dressed in a bright yellow dress and was well-developed for thirteen years old. I couldn't help noticing that. And she had carefully combed long, shiny brown hair that looked like a Prell shampoo commercial. But I noticed that she had an obviously crooked nose that leaned left. I had never heard her voice up until then. Now suddenly she let out an enormous shriek that made the ruler crack sound like Mr. Schott's whisper. Everyone jumped, not knowing what that was all about. Then a short, skinny boy sat down. He shouted out a certain four-letter word, causing Mr. Schott to slowly respond, "Mr. Maaaangusss!" Dragging Magnus out almost endlessly. Shrieks came forth all around me. It was a minute or so before it became obvious that some person or persons had put thumbtacks on various seats. Realizing this, Mr. Schott began going up and down the rows of desks collecting the tacks. He then stood silently in the front, scanning the seats like an oscillating fan.

As he began to speak, his quiet voice kept getting slower.

"Let me make this clear. This—is—not—a—zoo. This—is—a—class—for—learning."

That was the first time I heard the word. Then even more slowly...

"We will sit here until the perpetrators raise their hands. We can stay until suppertime…or…beyond."

Suddenly I realized there was no tack on my seat. Why? I had several minutes to consider that question. Mr. Schott was either a very patient man or a very stubborn one. He just stood there scanning the class, now like a beacon at a prison camp. Five minutes went by. *Ten.* Most teachers would decide that precious class time was passing by and table the investigation until later. Not Mr. Schott. *Fifteen.*

Finally, after seventeen minutes by the oversize clock above the blackboard, Robey's hand slipped up. After that tense ice breaking moment, his two henchmen followed him like obedient iron filings and raised their hands also. Mr. Schott walked deliberately over to Robey while talking even more slowly, slowly.

"You—think—you're—smart. I'll—show—you—smart."

He reached out one large, muscular hand and grabbed Robey by the front of his collar, violently pulling him out of his seat and onto his feet. He looked up at him, but he might as well have been looking down at him. He proceeded to shake Robey's body from side to side like a limp doll. Robey seemed to just stay loose and let it happen, wearing a thin smile like he was actually in control the whole time. Then with a sudden crisp crack as loud as the ruler on the desk, Mr. Schott slapped him across the mouth, causing an immediate red welt to appear.

"Wipe—the—smile—off—your—face."

Robey made a valiant attempt. Speaking in a barely audible whisper, but at a more regular clip, Mr. Schott continued.

"Listen carefully. You and your two friends will sit on tacks for five minutes…now. Come on. Here are the tacks. Right now."

He distributed the tacks to the three violators and gestured to them to sit on them. I had no religious education to interpret what I observed next, being part of a Conservative Jewish home and having little exposure to Roman Catholic theology. But as I watched Robey out of the corner of my eye, it seemed like he took the punishment very seriously…as if he was doing some sort of penance. I knew that word from an old Bible movie I'd seen on TV, and it came to mind. He sat directly on the tack and gritted his teeth. There was something that seemed almost military about it, like he was John Wayne bucking up and taking it.

Then, just as the whole episode started with a sudden scream, it ended with a sudden subject change by Mr. Schott. It was as if the last half hour never happened. He calmly asked us to open our composition book and paced the teaching roughly like Mr. Garner had, which I liked. There were no jokes, but there was a story about two boys during the depression. He read the whole thing, complete with exclamations and laughs, which felt a little like kindergarten. But I enjoyed listening. Something came alive in me as he read. The tripping sound of the words and the melody of his unfolding tale telling stirred part of me I hadn't been aware of. Something about the special gift of being alive and growing up was in the reading of that little short story. And then it was over.

The homework consisted of reading a two-page story before the next day. I could definitely handle that.

The bell rang just as he finished, and Mr. Schott just slowly walked back to his desk. It was break time. We moved to the back of the class. Suddenly, Robey walked up to me and made eye contact.

"I like you, kid. I don't put tacks on the seats of people I like."

Then he sauntered away like John Wayne at the end of a movie. Robey Romero wanted to be my friend. Maybe things wouldn't be so bad in the Upper Zoo.

# CHAPTER 4

I HAD TO ADMIT, AN overture from Robey Romero felt a little dangerous. But I couldn't get his penance out of my mind. It was a little crazy, but also courageous. *He might make a good friend,* I thought. Still, I decided that since he made the first move, I'd let him make the second.

It was unusually quiet at dinner. As always, Dad was working late. The only sound was Billy's slurping. And as he slurped, he kept is face down, directed at his soup bowl. So much so that I thought his glasses might slip off his nose and fall into the bowl. Obviously, something was bothering him. Maybe he was nervous about starting up a conversation with me since we'd talked at breakfast. What did he mean when he told me I was a different kind of smart? At any rate, his silence was fine with me. I was in no mood to discuss that or the thumbtack affair.

Mom had been putting up with the silence. But her sense of good manners prompted her, and she put her soup spoon down and addressed Billy.

"Billy, stop slurping and sit up straight."

Billy looked up and gave me a quick angry glance. So it *was* about me. At least we could focus on something else besides the thumbtack affair. Mom, having straightened out Billy, turned to me.

"I heard you had quite a day."

"What do you mean?"

"Your teacher called and told me about the thumbtacks. He wanted to make sure no one got infected."

I couldn't believe it. Apparently, Mr. Schott must have called all of the parents. Of course, Billy's eyes grew wide with curiosity behind his oversize glasses.

"What didn't get infected," he said.

"Nothing." I turned my back to Billy and faced Mom, trying my best to ignore him.

"There was nothing on my seat."

"I see. Do you know who did it?"

She was already shaking her head no with incredulity, combined with that disapproving scowl that always made me feel all the world's problems were somehow my fault. I didn't want to answer, but I had to say something.

"Yes. Everyone does. The kid owned up to it."

"Well, he's one to stay away from."

Billy's eyes got even bigger as he figured things out.

"Someone put thumbtacks on your seat? I guess it really is a zoo!"

"I'm not taking this."

I banged both hands on the table, which made them both jump. It was my way of playing the victim of circumstances and cruelty. But Billy took the role away from me with a slight whine.

"Sorry. I was just curious. I wasn't as mean as you were this morning."

I grabbed whatever food I could hold in my hand and left the table for my room.

Mom called after me, "Jonathan, you get back here!"

"I want to be alone," I shouted as dramatically as I could. "I'm going to my room."

"Fine, stay there until your father gets home."

That *was* fine with me. I knew he wouldn't get home until I was asleep, and there was no place I'd rather be that night than alone in my room. I entered it and slammed the door just loud enough to make a point, but not so loud that Mom would comment from the kitchen.

I looked around at the dark tan walls, the Beach Boys poster, the model 1958 Impala with the sloppy robin's egg paint job, the single bed with the itchy, brown cover, the AM tube clock radio that buzzed constantly, no matter what station it was tuned to. I sat on the edge of my bed and picked up my books off the floor. I glanced at the table of contents and the two-page story for about ten minutes while I ate a roll and a few French fries. Then I got undressed and went to bed.

The next morning I woke up fifteen minutes before the clock radio went off to the rhythm of rain on my bedroom window. After dressing, I avoided Billy and even Mom as I came downstairs and all through breakfast. There was a bit more time than the last two days for Billy to read the same cereal box he'd been reading all summer and for me to eat my Frosted Flakes. But it went quickly. As I was about to run out the door, Mom reached over and gave me a quick hug, planting a kiss on my forehead just under the ridiculous checkered cloth hat meant to protect me from the rain.

"I love you."

"Love you too, Mom," I mumbled back, intending for only her to hear. I was actually glad she did that. It prepared me for contact with the world again.

On the way to school, rain poured against the bus window, making it even colder and wetter. But the hat shielded me from the condensation. As I got off to enter the school, I almost collided with a boy from my seventh grade class in the poor visibility caused by the rain and the hat. John Parker…the shortest kid in the class, who never said five words to me the year before…looked up at me.

"Zoo boy."

I glanced away and walked on, trying to pretend I didn't hear. But his words shook me. I had to get away from everyone, if only for a few minutes. There was no better place than the bathroom, where boys never make eye contact.

I stared at the bathroom mirror. At least I had a few seconds to be by myself. Suddenly Robey appeared next to me, like an angel or demon from another world. His shiny black hair was drenched and slicked back. He was too cool to wear a hat. He combed his hair while I looked at both of our reflections. I couldn't have looked more different from him, at medium height with rings of curly brown hair, which I tended to curl even more between my fingers when I was nervous. I had baggy pants with cuffs and brown oxfords. He had tapered cuffless black pants and thin pointy Italian shoes. I glanced at him in the mirror as he towered over me. He looked back at me.

"You know where the Lower Zoo sits during lunch, Richman?"

"No, not really."

He pointed his finger like a gun at my reflection in the mirror.

"Meet me during lunch. We have to make it clear that we're the smart ones."

"Sorry, but…"

"Lunch."

He pointed his finger again for emphasis and then walked away. I left the bathroom and headed for class, as troubled by my encounter with Robey as I was flattered by it.

The morning was a blank. I was too anxious to focus. This is what happened to me in seventh grade and even before that. There was always something to worry about. Sometimes it was Dad, sometimes it was the test I wasn't prepared for. Now my mind began to wander into a trance-like meditation on Robey's words. "We have to make it clear we're the smart ones." I was disrupted by a demanding adult voice.

"Richman! What's the sum of this equation?"

Mr. Garner was pointing at the blackboard. I was as clueless as I had been in seventh grade. What a way to start the school year.

"Get your head out of the clouds!"

He turned to Gwen, the girl with the curtain of hair over her eyes. I tried to play catch-up, concentrating on the math problem on the board and in the book, looking back and forth from one to the other, trying to untangle the meaningless numbers. I started curling my hair. My mind drifted again.

Part of me wanted nothing to do with Robey, and part of me wanted to be his best friend, closer than his iron filings, more real, a peer. But what did he mean when he said, "We're the smart ones"?

The bell rang. I waited until everyone left. Then I walked out and toward the cafeteria. Maybe he would forget the whole thing and I could eat quietly, in peace, and as alone as I could possibly get in the cafeteria. As I walked through the door, a sharp pain struck my upper back, causing shock waves over my whole body like I'd been shot. It was Robey. After he slapped me, he draped his arm around me, putting the weight of his tall frame on me.

"Richman, this…is Ted and this…is Mike."

There they were, the iron filings. They stood motionless like robots.

"We'll sit here. Get your lunches."

He motioned to us to follow him. We got in the line, received our scoops of shepherd's pie from the sweaty kitchen help, and came back to the table. He leaned over the table like an umbrella casting a large shadow over us.

"Ted, Mike, eat your food."

He didn't seem to care whether I did. At least he didn't suggest it, and I hadn't started. I wasn't hungry.

"Jonathan, let me be straight with you."

He looked directly down into my eyes.

"You see these other kids all over this room? They think the Upper and Lower Zoo are the same thing. Did you notice their looks, their whispering? Eh?"

I slouched down, silent. But inside I was saying, *Yes! Yes!*

"We have to show them the difference. Capiche?"

I'd never heard that word, and I had no idea what it meant. I still didn't respond.

"Eat boys. Eat! I'm trying to explain things to Richman. Boys, get to know Jonathan Richman here. Capiche?"

There was that word again. At Robey's command, Ted and Michael rushed to quickly consume their food as robots might. The utensils went mechanically in and out of their mouth, almost in unison. Ted finished first and smiled as a child might when finishing a chore for his father.

"All right. Time is short. We have to treat the Lower Zoo like everyone treats us. That's what the Bible teaches, right?"

I had no idea.

"You see that table over there?" He pointed. "The dumbest kid in the Lower Zoo is there."

"So?"

"Mike, tell Jonathan what we're gonna do."

Mike snickered into his napkin and finished swallowing the last bite even as he spoke.

"We're gonna go over and let everyone know they're the *Lower* Zoo, and we're not."

Robey was pleased with the answer.

"Good. Okay Theodore Cleaver Teddy, anything to add?"

He shook his head no.

"Good. Let's go. Come on Richman. Our teachers aren't gonna explain it. Who else is gonna tell everyone what's going on? Hmm?"

I looked over at Robert Rogers across the room. He was in the process of looking at me and looking away. I didn't want to call attention to myself, but something told me that in this case staying seated might bring more attention than getting up. So I stood up even before Robey and the iron filings. Robey stepped in front of me and led the way. I was glad to be hiding behind his tall frame, thin as it was.

We arrived at a table of maybe ten kids sitting there eating. Some of them *did* look like they had some sort of problem. As we approached, I could hear a tall, gangly girl slurring her speech as she talked. A boy next to her had what looked like three quarters of a sandwich in his mouth, and since his mouth was open the whole time, it wasn't hard to verify. Robey waved his hand over them like a lawyer presenting evidence.

"Everyone around here thinks we're *them*. Isn't that right, Clarence?"

Clarence looked up at Robey towering over him. I was surprised that Robey knew his name. He had straight, brown hair in a bowl haircut like Moe's of the Three Stooges, a round pasty face, a head that was a little too big for his body, eyes that seemed to dart everywhere at once, and a habit of rocking to and fro constantly like my Orthodox uncle when he prayed in his synagogue. He quickly scanned back and forth and up and down even while he was in mid-rock. Then he eyed Robey for an instant.

"What...what...what...what...what do you want...what?" he asked in a strange shaky yet quite loud voice.

Apparently he knew who Robey was, just as Robey knew who he was. Robey leaned over and whispered in his ear, but I could hear him clearly.

"You're dumb, right?"

"Yeh, yeh, yeh I'm dumb...dumb...I'm..."

"Tell everyone."

His rocking got faster.

"Tell them."

"I'm dumb...dumb...du...du...dumb."

"Louder."

Robey got louder even as he insisted Clarence speak louder. He pointed with his finger like a puppet master.

"Louder!"

"I'm dumb. I'm dumb...I'm...I'm...really...really dumb."

"Louder!"

At this point Clarence, still rocking, put his hands over both ears like they were earmuffs. Then he emitted an eerie screech of some sort, which was somewhat swallowed up by the din of the cafeteria. Some at adjacent tables giggled, but no one at this table. They sat like targets of a hunter's rifle, looking petrified with fear. Even the boy with the open mouth stopped chewing. Clarence's darting eyes jumped around like a pinball until they landed on mine. I detected pure terror. Robey just stood there waiting. Then, when the screeching finally stopped, he whispered like Mr. Schott.

"Remember that."

The two iron filings, preceded by Robey, took turns picking some of Clarence's French fries from his plate and dumping them unceremoniously into his soup. They floated in the tomato broth like dead worms in blood. Suddenly and without warning, Clarence started flailing his hands wildly and whimpering. He banged on the table. Then he rocked twice as fast as he had been. Robey turned around to face the tables around us and spoke clearly, like he was one of the adult monitors.

"See? These are Lower Zoo retards."

A real monitor seemed to come from nowhere to challenge his pretender in mid-speech.

"Romero, all of you...get back to your seats...now!"

As quickly as it started, it was over. I went back and sat next to Robey and his friends. He had a huge smile on his face, as if to say, "mission accomplished." The bell rang, and once again I waited until the room emptied before slowly walking to Mr. Schott's English and social studies class.

# CHAPTER 5

THE SECOND DAY IN MR. Schott's class was much calmer than the first had been. Now he could teach, unhindered by disruption. And he did a remarkable thing. He didn't tell jokes or use models like Mr. Garner did. Instead he read poems, and he read them just like he had disciplined the class…quietly and very slowly during the more dramatic parts. I never cared much for poetry. But I enjoyed listening to Mr. Schott read "Die not, poor Death, nor yet canst thou kill me," separating each word with an eternity and pronouncing each one like he was examining a diamond. His mouth moved like he was eating a delicious chocolate fudge cake. He tasted every word even to the last morsel. If he'd been loud or even spoken at normal volume, the class would have been distracted and unruly. But his method of reading was hypnotic, even exciting.

I looked around to see how the other students were responding. Some were actually listening, sitting completely still in their chairs, held by the force of Mr. Schott's whispers. I locked eyes with Robey. He pointed at his head with a nod of approval and then gave two thumbs up.

As soon as I turned back to the front, I remembered what we'd done to Clarence. I felt like an accessory to a crime. Guilt grabbed me by the throat and wouldn't let go. *He must hate me*, I thought. *I don't even know him, and he must hate me.* The look in Clarence's eyes followed me through the rest of the class and all the way home. Every time I closed my eyes, I could see the look. Fortunately, he didn't ride on my bus. I never wanted to see him again. I looked out the window at the rain as it cleansed the sidewalks and poured into the gutters and leaned my head, cloth hat and all, against the pane of glass.

Finally home, I threw my wet jacket and hat on the closet floor and grabbed some Oreos from the cupboard, heading for my room. There was Billy in the hallway.

"What about Saturday?"

"What about it?"

His eyes pleaded with me behind the oversized glasses.

"You want to go to the movies? They have *Twenty Million Miles from Earth* at the Fox.

"I don't know, Billy."

"Please…I mean they *don't* give you homework."

My eyes communicated steel as I rose up in response.

"What's that supposed to mean?"

The pleading seemed to flee, replaced by feigned innocence.

"I don't know. You'll have the time. That's all."

"You trying to say I'm in the stupid class?"

He pressed the glasses to his nose bridge nervously.

"No. I told you…"

I pointed in his face, almost pressing on the glasses myself.

"I saw somebody stupid today. You want to see somebody stupid? This kid Clarence is stupid. I'm not stupid. And as a matter of fact I've got a lot of homework, and I'll be busy doing it all day Saturday. I'm going to my room."

"Something's wrong with you, Jonathan. I'm in the fifth grade, and even I can see you've got a problem."

"Shut up you brat," I whispered like Mr. Schott as I left. I didn't know if he heard me or not.

I used to teach Billy how to build models and fly them, or throw a ball and toss a Frisbee. Now it was all turned around. He was trying to teach me. Everything felt backward. It wasn't right.

As I sat in my room eating cookies, I couldn't imagine going back to school the next day. Just the thought of it made me nauseous. Maybe I was too sick to go. That's what I kept telling myself. I kept repeating it until I was convinced. *Maybe I'm too sick. Yes, probably I am.*

Of course, to my mother, the all-important test was my temperature. If it wasn't up, I couldn't pass the test, and no matter how sick I told myself I was, my temperature was normal. It was clear to me that I needed an extreme measure to deal with the extreme situation of being sick with no fever. I knew what I had to do. It was just a question of how.

There were two approaches. One was the matchstick method. But this had its downside. If Mom smelled the match, she might guess that the temperature was artificial. The other method was hot water. I had used this once before with great success, and though the judgment day of an unwritten paper finally arrived, it was forestalled for two whole days. That was in seventh grade, and the reason for using the hot water method was very different. I had gotten behind. In 8H I wasn't behind. Billy was right. We got very little homework, at least not so far. In this case, I was just sick...sick of Robey, and Clarence, and Robert Rogers, and everyone at school. And I just wanted to spend the next day in bed.

I walked quietly into the bathroom and took the thermometer out of the medicine cabinet. I held it like a secret weapon in my hands, a powerful tool able to bring time to a halt and alter the events of next day. I ran the water until it began to get hot. I had learned from experience not to allow it to become too hot. If I adjusted the tap and the length of time the thermometer was under the water just right, I could produce a reading of one hundred degrees. This was perfect. By combining this with a hot washcloth applied for a moment to my forehead, I could create a believable fever that would be my passport to a day off. And that was reasonable. After all, I *was* sick, just not sick with a fever. I accomplished the task in the privacy of the bathroom. Within five minutes I was back in the kitchen. I chose my words carefully.

"Mom, I don't feel so well."

Mom looked at me with some skepticism and some concern. She started with the medical questions even before she reached out and touched my forehead. And I knew she had to do that soon or I would cool off.

"What's the problem?"

"I...I don't know. Umm..."

"Yes?"

I had to work fast. I folded my arms and attempted to shiver.

"I...I think I have a fever."

She reached out her seasoned hand and touched my forehead. It remained there as she assessed the situation with skill akin to when she tested melons at the supermarket.

"Hmm."

Her natural suspicions were overcome by the empirical evidence, which was slowly fading but still remained.

"I think you *do* have a little fever."

She probably added the word little to comfort herself that I would be okay. I could see she was worried. I had passed the first test. But the second one would be the greater challenge. I had to put the thermometer in my mouth before she could check it and shake it. This took the finesse of a card shark.

We had two thermometers in the bathroom. I had carefully placed the dummy one in eyesight on the sink. That was the one she would have to check, sterilize, and shake. The other one was in my pajama pants pocket.

As we went into the bathroom, everything was proceeding according to plan, and I would not be going to school in the morning. Mom, her apron still tied around her flowered dress from having washed the dishes, grabbed the thermometer on the sink and began checking and shaking. She popped it in my mouth, tenderly checked my brow again, and left for the kitchen. I quickly switched the thermometers and put the other one in the bathroom closet behind some bottles.

The deed was done, and I was certifiably sick. Within a half hour I was under a hot, itchy blanket with two aspirin in my stomach. They helped me sleep and blunted any vestige of guilty conscience I might have had. By the morning, with a 6 A.M. short repeat in the bathroom, I was resting comfortably on the living room sofa. I heard Billy leave for school. I was free and clear.

As I lay there later that morning watching the Tide commercials wash in between *I Love Lucy* and *The Price is Right,* I was fully aware that this temporary solution was no solution at all. I could hear Mom in the kitchen cooking up some soft-boiled eggs for me. I knew it gave her comfort to nurse her suffering son, which increased my guilt all the more. The aspirin had worn off and without medication to blunt the edge of my "illness," I was left only with my conscience and a mother who was being too kind. She entered with the comfort food.

"Mom. We need to talk"

"About what?"

I proceeded to tell her everything…about Robey and Clarence, the thermometer…everything. I knew it would end forever my use of the extreme measure. She stood up and slapped one hand over her eye like she was taking an eye test. The other eye looked unflinchingly my way.

"Is this what you did last year?"

Busted, but I had to admit it.

"Yes. But…but…"

"Jonathan, you *lied* to me."

"No. I do feel sick…sort of."

She freed her eye and threw both hands in the air.

"What do you mean sort of? You are or you aren't. I should drive you to school *right now.*"

"Please, Mom. No. I need your advice. Please help me."

I assumed a beggar's pose, with both hands together. But I really meant it. I saw a crack in the door as she gingerly entered the supportive mother mode.

"About what? Just tell me. Then we'll go."

"About what to do. I can't go back to school. I just can't"

She shook her head no in her inimitable way.

"Don't be silly. You have to go back to school."

"I know that. Okay. I don't want to."

Her head stopped as she looked directly into my hesitant eyes.

"But you have to."

This was going nowhere. I had to appeal to her wisdom.

"Please...what do I do about Robey and Clarence?"

She sat down next to me like she had the night before the school year began.

"Okay. Listen to me. Clarence is someone to feel sorry for, not to spend time with. When you grow up, you will meet many Clarences. You can give to organizations that help feed and clothe them. Or you can visit them from time to time in their institutions. But you can't be friends with them."

I felt like fate had tossed Clarence and me on the ash heap of junior high world, and Mom was doing her best to pull me out of the ash heap and leave him there. But we were both stuck there, for better or for worse—no matter what Robey said about the difference between the Upper and Lower Zoo. I wanted to tell Mom I'd do what I wanted. I even had a strange desire to defend Clarence, though I hardly cared about him or even knew him. But I didn't say anything. She continued as she put her motherly arm around me.

"Those friendships are not good for you. They would drag you down. You should be friends with people who are normal and are good students, like for instance Robert Rogers."

He always came up sooner or later.

"He's not in my class, Mom. I don't see him that much."

She had a comeback, as she always did. She tilted her head forward and looked pityingly in my eyes.

"I understand. Well, okay. But there has to be some nice boy in your class who takes school seriously and stays out of trouble. Make friends with *him*. And stay away from that Robey boy. *He's* trouble."

"Okay, Mom."

I gave up trying to get any advice. But I still needed to insure my freedom for one day.

"I'll look for a nice boy tomorrow. Can I stay home today?"

I could see that she had moved totally to the supportive role side… almost.

"Please?"

She put her hand to her chin and deliberated silently as if she was deciding whether to pardon a condemned man.

"Well…all right. I'll write a note saying you were under the weather. Children can be under the weather in many ways."

I leaned over and gave her as much of a bear hug as I could while sitting next to her.

"Thanks, Mom!"

She smiled and kissed me on the cheek.

"Be careful. I could catch what you've got," she snickered.

She was funny when she wanted to be. I liked that. But of course I was at the same place I had been the day before, except that I was out of extreme measures.

Like a guilty man on the way to his execution, I spent the bus ride to school the next day with eyes closed and my head leaning once again against the dirty glass window, absorbing the vibrations of the worn spring suspension. I accepted this torture as justice for my deception, just has Robey had the thumbtack.

But justice was deferred. The first period was actually pleasant. It occurred to me sitting there that these two teachers must have been hired to keep the attention of poor students like me. And it was working. Between Mr. Garner's science museum-type lectures and Mr. Schott's dramatic readings, we were sufficiently entertained. Mr. Garner continued with a one hour Bell Telephone Science film, complete with little cartoon characters.

I kept my eyes away from Robey. I didn't even know whether he was in the darkened room. The whir of the sprockets on the projector and Dr. Frank Baxter's grandfatherly voice on the soundtrack calmed me. I liked being in the dark and watching a movie. It was a great way to hide from everyone and everything.

Navigating lunch seemed just as pleasant. I went back to the old seating arrangement with the fat boy on my left. I was far from Clarence and at least a table away from Robey. I looked down at my plate. Even the creamed chipped beef on toast looked better than anything I'd had so far that year, even though it was terrible. Maybe it was the company, or lack of it. No one was asking anything of me. I could eat in relative peace.

I turned to my other side. There was Gwen. In the middle of a bite of chipped beef, she tapped me on the shoulder very lightly. I almost didn't notice it.

"You want me?" I asked.

"You okay after the tack prank?"

"Okay, I guess."

I didn't want to tell her there wasn't one on my seat. And it turned out there was none on hers either.

"There was only one tack on a girl's seat, you know. I wonder what they had against her."

It amazed me how meticulously Robey had planned the whole thing. She continued.

"I hope you're okay. I wouldn't want you to get sick or anything. I noticed you were out yesterday."

Was this the same girl who wouldn't or couldn't answer a simple question the first day? I had to admit I liked the attention. She was so much less threatening than Robey Romero. Her stringy hair was still unsightly, but for the first time I was close enough to almost get a good look at her face. What I could make out of her features looked exquisitely perfect. I gradually realized that through that curtain of hair she was beautiful, much more beautiful than the girl with the crooked nose. Through the fog of tangled hair, I thought I detected a brunette version of Sandra Dee, complete with electric blue eyes, an adorable perfect nose, and exquisite pink lips. And I had a very deep crush on Sandra Dee. I had seen all her movies. I had only recently forgiven Bobby Darin for marrying her in 1960. Could she be sitting before me now…a vision of loveliness like Sandra Dee in the person of this girl Gwen?

I had only one question, but I had no intention of asking it. Still, I thought it. *What caused her mother to send her to school with stringy hair and faded old dresses?* While I was pondering that, she looked down toward the ground and spoke in a gentle whisper.

"I like that you're sitting here. Will you sit next to me at lunch tomorrow?"

I was taken aback.

"I…I guess. I don't see why not."

She turned back without saying a word and started eating her creamed chipped beef on toast. She kept that up for several minutes, daintily taking morsels one by one from the outside in. I couldn't think of anything to say. We sat in silence. Then without warning she jumped up, her lunch half eaten, and quickly walked away. *Great,* I thought, *a crazy person. And I just told her I would sit next to her tomorrow. I should add her to my mother's list of people to avoid.* Then suddenly subject to avoid number one sat in her place as she had morphed into him.

"Hey, bright boy. What are *you* doing here?"

I was irritated, and I let it show.

"I'm with the class."

"We're sitting over there at that table."

He pointed toward Ted and Michael, who were busy with their synchronized eating.

"I know that. Look, you're brighter than me…the way you planned that whole tack thing, and the lunchroom episode the other day. What is it with you? I can't figure you out."

He became animated, his eyes lighting up and his hands lunging forward.

"Don't you see? It's you and me, kid. We're the smart ones. We're the exceptions!"

He looked around the room and then turned back to me.

"So where is she? Where is that dog you were sitting next to?"

"Who? You mean Gwen?"

"You know her name? Yeh…Gwen. That's the one."

"I don't know. I don't know where she went. Why?"

He pulled his hands back and held them up.

"Just asking…just asking, kid. Maybe she was going to take a shower. She's the ugliest mutt in the school. Stay away from her. Do you hear me? Stay away. It's catching. Look, we've got serious business. We need to visit Clarence at home."

He thought Gwen was ugly? Apparently, he had never noticed her Sandra Dee face behind the stringy hair. *But forget Gwen,* I thought. *Why should we visit Clarence?* I had to deal with that.

"I'm not visiting Clarence."

"We have to."

I couldn't believe he was telling me what to do. He was even worse than my mother.

"Why?"

"Why do you think?"

"I have no idea."

Here was my opportunity to tell him I wanted out…that I wouldn't be a party to the kind of thing he'd done a few days before. But he jumped in just as I was getting ready to speak.

"Okay. Here's how it works. We have to remind everyone at school he's a retard while we make nice with him outside of school. It's part of a bigger plan."

I tried to stop the conversation with my hand like a policeman would traffic.

"I don't know what kind of bigger plan you're talking about, but I don't think you need me to be part of it."

That was it. Good. Now I was out. I'd made it clear. I could go on with my life, such as it was. Then suddenly, he stretched his hand out and grabbed mine in mid-air. He yanked it and pulled it under the table, beginning to squeeze harder and harder. I felt like if he continued, something would snap.

"Ted and Mike are even stronger than me. That's their gift. Not everyone needs to have brains. They should be in the Lower Zoo. But I need them, so I don't mind the clerical error."

He was still squeezing.

"Well? Capiche?"

"Okay, okay," I muttered in surrender.

"I know where Clarence lives. Meet me after school, bright boy. Front entrance. You won't need to take the bus home today."

He got up and walked away, just like that. My deserved torment had started in earnest.

# CHAPTER 6

I SPENT MUCH OF THE afternoon planning how I might escape from Robey after school. After some thought, I decided that the side or back doors were the obvious choices. Then I would avoid the bus and walk the two miles home. Every few minutes, I switched my focus from the plans to Mr. Schott. He was standing in front of the class teaching us how to diagram a sentence. I kind of enjoyed watching him put the modifying words on those little branches. He drew trees all over the blackboard with squeaky white chalk. He made it all sound so simple: The red rose was growing on the thorny stem.

As the roses and other nouns kept growing and the class neared its end, I noticed that Robey and the iron filings were keeping their eyes trained on me. I tried not to look at them, but it was like trying not to think of a certain number. Then the bell suddenly rang. I sprang up, grabbing my books from inside my desk and ran out of the room before anyone else had even started to leave. As I glanced back, I couldn't see them behind me. My plan was working. I headed for the side door and pushed the exit bar. The door swung out and I leapt out of the building…right into Ted. Like an angel of death, he had arrived before me. He grabbed my arm and pulled me along.

"Come on."

I didn't resist. It was useless. We half circled the building and arrived at the main entrance. Robey and Mike met us. Robey didn't bring up my aborted escape. I was beginning to notice that when he got what he wanted, nothing else was necessary.

"This way. We'll walk. He'll be there before us."

Clarence lived two miles away, just like me. But I knew it was a different direction, because he took a different bus. There was no conversation during the half hour it took to get there. They escorted me like a captured soldier. We walked through neighborhoods I'd never walked through, though I was sure I'd seen them from the car. The houses got bigger and the trees more plentiful. Finally, we walked up the sidewalk to a particularly spacious looking modern split level and arrived at what I suspected was Clarence's front door. The house was certainly bigger that mine, and newer. In a minute or so, his mother answered the door. Robey practically bowed as he introduced himself.

"Ma'am, my name is Robey. These are my friends. We've come to play with Clarence."

She apparently fancied plain, knee-length dresses over the flowered calf length ones of my mother, and her hair was down to her shoulders, rather than up like my mother's, pulled back with a head band. With her pointy black glasses, she looked like the receptionist at my doctor's office. But she wasn't as young or pretty. Apparently, she also wasn't as nice.

"I know who you are. And I know how you treated my son. This is one *refrigerator mother* who is freezing you out. Please leave now!"

*Refrigerator mother?* I had no idea what she was talking about. Robey spoke.

"Ma'am, I knew Clarence might be offended. We've come to apologize. It was my fault, and I just want to be his friend. You see, I have a dry sense of humor, and it sometimes gets a little out of hand."

He seemed completely believable, standing there as still as a tree waiting for her to answer. In fact he *was* believable because he probably believed what he was saying himself. Clarence's mother, almost speechless in the face of such humility, responded nonetheless.

"Well...I...I don't want to deprive Clarence of the opportunity to hear you apologize. I...I suppose I'll see if he wants to see you. Wait right here."

She closed the door. We waited outside for at least five minutes. I closed my eyes and leaned against the doorpost. Finally, the door opened.

"I'm sorry. He doesn't want to see you. I just can't convince him. When he makes up his mind, there's no changing him. But...I told him you apologized."

"What'd he say?" Robey asked without skipping a beat.

"Nothing. He said nothing."

Robey seemed genuinely surprised and expressed it with a simple "Hmm." I wasn't sure if it was because Clarence didn't come out or if it was because he said nothing.

"Okay. Well...thank you. You have a nice day, Ma'am. Tell him we'll see him tomorrow."

We turned and left. I was relieved we didn't see Clarence, and I was ready to go home. Robey pulled out a map complete with clear directions to my house, about a mile away.

"Stupid retard," he said when we got to the street. "Doesn't even understand we came to be nice. We won't be so nice tomorrow."

His change caught me by surprise. I really wanted to understand what was going on in Robey's mind. After all, this had something to do with me now, ever since Clarence looked at me with those fearful eyes in the lunchroom.

"Why not? And why were we nice today?"

There was no response. But somehow I suspected that it had something to do with that "do the crime, but do the time" mentality I'd observed earlier. Now was my chance to finally free myself. I realized it was now or never.

"Okay. Well, thanks for the map. I'm going home. Please just leave me out of this from now on."

He looked at me with some disappointment. But my plea didn't go unheard.

"Fine. Okay. It's a deal. But you gotta promise me you won't even get close enough to him to say boo. Capiche?"

"For once you and my mother agree. No problem," I said without explaining myself.

I was relieved that I'd extricated myself from Robey's clutches. As I headed home on foot, I held my textbooks and notebook at my side and walked fast. I could never keep the papers' ring holes from ripping, so the papers stuck out of the notebook, frayed and close to falling out. But I always kept an eye on them so I wouldn't lose any of them.

I came home in a reasonably good mood. I was free. Billy was fixing something for himself in the kitchen. I felt so good I decided to be nice to him. The old, brotherly affection welled up in my lightened heart.

"Well, how's it going?"

"What do you want?"

He was understandably defensive and turned his back on me as he took a jar of peanut butter and a plate of Ritz crackers to the yellow kitchen table.

"I don't know. I'm just trying to be nice."

"Okay."

He began dipping the crackers in the peanut butter one after the other. I could see I had his attention.

"Hey. I just want to ask, what did you mean when you said I was smart?"

"I guess I wanted you to know that you're smarter than all of them. That's all," he responded cautiously between munches.

I didn't know what he was talking about. That happened sometimes with Billy. When it did, I would at times actually go beyond twirling my curls and scratch my head in bewilderment.

"All of who?"

"Them."

He began to show some animation. *Here it comes,* I thought. *Thomas Edison.*

"Take Edison, for example. He didn't do well in school, but he changed the whole world."

I had heard this story many times before. Edison was Billy's hero. He even tried to build a phonograph like Edison's out of an oatmeal container and a few other items. He screamed his name as he turned a crank made from a math compass—"Billy Richman!"—but none of us could hear anything. Our father's response was "Keep going. Maybe someday you'll invent the phonograph." I stopped Billy mid-sentence.

"Thanks, Billy. Edison was really something. But I'm no Edison."

Billy spent another few minutes talking about how I *was* like Edison. For instance, Edison was never appreciated by his teachers. He ended up having to learn at home from his mother. He learned differently from others. But he read all the books in his town library when he wasn't much older than me.

After a few more legends about the master, he said, "I think you and I could add up to an Edison between us. You'd be the leader. You'll always be my big brother...my hero...after Edison."

I didn't expect him to say that. I looked away so he couldn't see my eyes.

The next morning I actually looked forward to school. I counted my blessings as I sat on the bus. My teachers were probably the most entertaining in the school, the homework was always minimal, and Robey wouldn't bother me again. I didn't even lean my head against the window. Instead, I sat up and looked straight ahead with an all-business persona.

I entered the school building in the same way. If Robert Rogers passed me, I didn't know it...or at least I didn't want him to know I knew it. I quickened my pace until I approached the classroom. I had almost crossed the threshold when out of the corner of my eye I saw Robey and his two henchmen continually shoving Clarence as he walked forward.

"You didn't accept my apology at your house. You made me stand outside your door. You're in big trouble, retard."

Clarence rocked back and forth and to and fro as he walked briskly and then broke into a clumsy loping run. A whistle blew as he cornered the hall and disappeared.

"No running!"

Robey and the iron filings coolly strode past me and into the room. He caught my eye. I looked away as fast as I could. I was in no mood for conversation with Robey Romero.

# CHAPTER 7

FALL'S CHILLY WINDS BEGAN TO blow through that first part of the school year. Turning and falling leaves that had been so much the theme of elementary school plays were just something to walk through and kick out of the way as I entered the school and 8H, the Upper Zoo. As the air got colder, the lockers filled with the jackets of the day—black and brown, navy and blue, and pink.

One day at a time I stayed out of trouble, like a lone convict who minds his own business. My grades were average, but no worse. It was easy to do okay without trying in the Upper Zoo.

Robey turned out to be a somewhat conscientious student. Mr. Garber and Mr. Schott seemed pleased with his level of participation. Gwen, on the other hand, never had her homework ready. And she never participated in class. At lunch, she sat on the end of the table, usually in her light brown dress, and said nothing to anyone. Her stringy hair never changed. And even though I couldn't see her beautiful face, I was sure that hadn't changed either.

When Halloween dropped us all off on November's doorstep, I realized that it had been almost a month since anything had occurred between Robey and Clarence. In fact, everything had settled into a routine that was quiet and perhaps even a bit boring. I longed for the kind of diversion that had taken place the year before in the month of May. That's when we had watched Walter Cronkite on a small portable black and white TV explaining the flight path of astronaut L. Gordon Cooper.

From flight control, Chris Kraft had told us, "T minus fifteen seconds and counting...T minus ten seconds and holding." Then there had been a commercial break while soap and deodorant ads ran that seemed so out of place in the classroom. They brought with them a strange sensation of embarrassment, as if my personal hygiene habits were being publicly exposed.

Then without warning, the routine was violently disrupted as November neared its end. Mr. Schott didn't bring us the news directly, and neither did a small TV. Instead, a disembodied female clerical voice from somewhere in the bowels of the front office told us through the cloth-covered speaker above the classroom door, "Sadly, President Kennedy has been shot in Dallas and has died. School will be released at this time."

An untimely bell rang. Mr. Schott whispered with a sadness I hadn't heard in his voice before, "Well, I guess that's it. May God help us. You are excused." As Robey slouched down in his seat, I thought I detected a tear in his eye...but then again maybe not. And then there were the girls. They were huddled with each other quietly weeping... except Gwen. She just quickly walked out. No one said a word to her or tried to stop her...not even Mr. Schott.

During the bus ride home, I didn't have to avert my eyes from Robert Rogers. No one's eyes were making contact with anyone else's. No one was speaking to anyone else. Even the girls weren't huddling during that ride. Everyone was looking either down or out the window. I chose my usual place to lean against.

As I entered the house, I could hear the television. Mom and Billy were on the couch in front of it, huddled like the girls in class. They acknowledged my entrance with a brief common expression of obvious grief before turning their eyes back to the TV. I had never seen my mother cry before, and I didn't exactly see her cry on this occasion. But I saw the redness in her eyes, the Kleenex protruding from her tightened right fist, and heard her deep sighs. She *had* been crying. I could see that Billy had been crying too, though he had dried his eyes so there was only a faint trace of it left.

Why wasn't I crying? Didn't I care about the fate of the president? To be sure, I felt sad like everyone else. But I wasn't crying. Even Robey had been crying...well, probably. I, however, actually felt a vague and guilty relief, as if a vacation from life had been declared. Whatever anyone at school expected from me...the teachers at the blackboard asking questions, the students around me throughout the day...and especially Robey...they couldn't expect it now.

Of course, the little break for stopping and mourning was short-lived. Life had to go on. Even though Oswald was killed on Sunday and the president's funeral followed the next day, we were back in school by Tuesday. The tinker toy science explanations and spellbinding storytelling continued, as did the light homework...and Robey Romero's hard-to-ignore presence.

The Christmas vacation was a welcome break. I was without a friend my age, so Billy and I finally spent some time together. He had gotten all As in the fall semester. I...well at least I passed with average grades. But this was our winter vacation. We didn't have to talk about school. We didn't have to. But we did.

We were building model airplanes. The room was filled with the smell of model airplane dope, an odor approximating the intoxicating juice of fermented pears. It clung to our clothes and the brushes we used to apply it. We spread it like maple syrup onto the thin tissue that was stretched tightly over our World War I wings. Model airplane cement covered our fingers like calluses. Our desks were cluttered with pins, wax paper, and strips and scraps of balsa wood.

And there was time to talk. Billy started the conversation.

"You're good at so many things. Look at your wing. It's straight. Look at mine. It's warped. Yours'll fly. Mine won't."

He picked up his wing and checked it with one eye open and one eye closed. I wasn't quite sure what to say. But I had learned a few things in my model building past.

"You've got to be patient and let things dry. If you wait, they'll turn out right in the end."

Finally, I was teaching Billy. Things were in order. But he put the wing down and continued.

"That's what I feel about you."

"What are you talking about?"

"It's like Edison. He turned out okay."

I rolled my eyes. Why did it always have to end up with Edison?

"Will you stop with Edison?"

"Okay," he said in a simple syllable of forced resignation. I nodded in affirmation.

"Thank you."

As he forgot the models and turned to focus completely on me, his voice took on a mysterious tone.

"You know when you get a feeling?"

At that moment I didn't want to hear about any feeling. I just wanted to build rubber band-powered airplanes and fly them in the crisp December air. But I played along.

"No, I don't."

"I mean, when you know when you know?"

"No."

He came close and almost brushed my shirt with the model airplane dope. I pulled back to get out of the way.

"Well, I just know that you're going to be fine. You're gifted."

That was too much. What was Billy doing? Was he treating me like a little kid who needed comforting? I thought *I* was the teacher.

"You mean like the gifted class, Billy? I'm in the Upper Zoo. So don't try and make me feel good and feel sorry for me. Just stop it and pick up your crooked wing."

He didn't skip a beat, except to press on his glasses with his free hand.

"No. I don't mean the gifted class. I mean gifted with something classes can't give you. I see it. You're my brother. I know it.

"You're scaring me. Just build your model."

He pressed the point, waving the brush in my face like a wand.

"And I'm gifted with telling you. Don't listen to *them.*"

"Listen to who? What are you talking about?"

"Don't listen to the zoo keepers. They don't know what they're saying."

I looked down at my wing for an instant to check and make sure it was drying properly and then looked back up at him, not knowing what to say. But now he wasn't looking at me. He was painting his wing again, probably too early while it was still wet with the prior coat. He was moving the brush with obvious pleasure. I knew he loved building airplanes with me. He didn't seem to care how they turned out. It was as if he knew they were all destined to crash anyway.

The rest of the winter vacation passed just that way. We flew our airplanes on the last day, winding the rubber bands and letting them go. Mine flew. Billy's didn't. And then vacation was over.

I entered the school in January like an animal that is being returned to its cage. And I wasn't looking forward to it. I didn't know what to expect. Would Robey want to be my strange and dangerous friend of earlier fall? Or would he ignore me? Would Gwen want to talk to me and then run away again? Whatever lay ahead, there was something entrapping about the Upper Zoo, something of that elevator caught between floors. Even though there were high points like Mr. Schott's reading, I was not looking forward to going back.

The only classroom that remained the same as last month, last year, and the year before that was not in junior high school at all. It was the Hebrew school at our conservative synagogue every Tuesday and Thursday afternoon. My birthday, along with the bar and bat mitzvah schedule, fell in such a way that my bar mitzvah would not take place until sometime in the fall of ninth grade at the end of my thirteenth year. And specific study for that would be crowded into the fall period. So I wasn't studying my portion in eighth grade. Instead we studied some Hebrew, Bible and Talmudic stories, and a smattering of Jewish history.

As loose as the Upper Zoo felt compared to the normal classes, Hebrew school was even looser. Middle-aged Mrs. Moliver tried to keep order, and a core in the center of the room followed her. But the sides and back of the room were beyond her reach. Behavior not tolerated in public school occurred in those extreme areas. Spitballs were the rebellious act of choice among the boys. Talking and passing notes sufficed for the girls.

I, however, avoided those behaviors. I actually listened to Mrs. Moliver. With her short, brown, pageboy hair, black secretary-style glasses, pleated dresses, and orthopedic shoes, she sometimes seemed more like a Jewish mother than my mother. I loved hearing the story of Abraham, who posed as one of his father's idols, "killing" the other, and then challenged him about the invisible God. Though she told us the story wasn't in the Bible, it seemed to fit right in to what I knew of Bible stories. I could see Abraham straightening his father out. He did what I wished I could do, if only my father was home long enough to do it. For me, it would consist of letting him know I didn't like him being away from home so much. I was ready to smash that idol, if I only knew where he was on any given evening.

Mrs. Moliver told us many things I took home with me. She said that anyone who called a Jewish woman a Jewess didn't like Jews. I could see that. It was sort of like calling a woman a thing instead of a person...like calling a female dog a bitch. She told us that many

Christians hated Jews throughout history. I could see that too. A few kids in the neighborhood had called me names like "kike" and "Christ killer," and I knew about what happened during World War II. She also said some Christians were nice. I could see that too. There were some very nice Christians in the movies. I particularly liked Father Flanagan of Boys Town. I watched that once on the Early Show.

Hebrew School was constant and reliable. It was like a warm glowing candle, especially in the winter when night began to fall before the bus took us home. I could feel the glow of the room amidst the darkness of night outside the classroom windows.

I didn't mind attending Hebrew school, like some kids did. I kind of looked forward to going back to it after the winter break. I loved the chocolate milk and cookie snack they provided before class And Mrs. Moliver always greeted us with "Shalom aleychem," which means peace to you. I felt safe when she said that.

One time Mrs. Moliver told us Jesus was a good man, but just a man. I thought, *What else would he be?* She didn't say much more about it. I liked Christmas shopping, and Christmas carols, and I knew Jesus was called the Son of God in the songs. I wasn't totally sure what that meant, or what other things like the virgin birth meant. But he left me with a good feeling too, even if there *were* mean Christians who hated Jews.

I knew Jesus couldn't be Jewish, because I'd seen pictures of him with straight stringy hair and a porcelain-looking face, on his knees looking up at the sky. And he certainly didn't look Jewish there. I knew Ben Hur was Jewish, even if it *was* Charlton Heston. But Jesus? I doubted that. However, Mrs. Moliver said he was, or had been, or something like that. And if Mrs. Moliver said it, I was sure it was true.

The only things that bothered me about Hebrew School were the odd little color drawings in the "History of the Jewish People" book. With their black coats, yarmulkes and curly side-locks, these strange figures looked like ghosts from a nether world. They also looked like my Great Uncle Moishe on my mother's side. His wife, Zelda, seemed like she was always bent over when she said the strange words "Kine Herra" to me in a strange-sounding tongue with a strange scent of onions on her breath. But it was Uncle Moishe I saw on seemingly every page of the book. I was sure that no such figure would appear in Robert Roger's Jewish history book. He attended the Reform synagogue. His family used to have a different name, but my mother told me his grandparents changed it. They wanted to be normal Americans. Men didn't wear yarmulkes in his synagogue, and I knew he couldn't have any Great Uncle Moishes and Great Aunt Zeldas in his family.

Somehow, I was convinced that Robert's synagogue was connected to his honor roll status. He kept up with his homework like the synagogue kept up with the times. They weren't ancient and strange like my great aunt and uncle. They weren't stuck between floors, like I was. They were fully American Jews, and their whole extended family must have been too, unlike ours.

I tried not to look at the pictures, especially while I was in the Upper Zoo. Instead I would close my eyes and listen to Mrs. Moliver. Her soothing voice would wash over me. Sometimes I would even doze. But that was when it was late in the afternoon and I was tired. Fortunately, no one ever noticed.

# CHAPTER 8

A SECOND DISRUPTION INVADED THE Upper Zoo on Monday, February 10. While Mr. Garber was teaching us about sound waves, he noticed that we were particularly unsettled and quickly diagnosed the reason. He knew what most of us had witnessed the night before. He explained that he would "perform an experiment to give us our fix" so we would calm down.

"I will now show you Edison's practical application of sound waves resulting from the vibrations of a needle."

*If only Billy were here,* I thought. *He'd go crazy.*

He picked up a grey metal institutional-looking box from the floor and placed it on his desk. He took the cord and plugged it into the wall behind the desk. Then, without saying a further word, he picked up a shiny new black 45 RPM vinyl disk off his desk blotter. I could see the swirling orange and yellow graphic design on the label as he held it between his fingers. He leaned over the box and placed the disk on a moving turntable.

As befitting a science teacher, he turned the black volume knob up before putting the tone arm on the record. Static noise came out of the metal speaker grid. A slight audio rumble gave way to claps and rhythmic guitars and then, "Oh yeh, I'll tell you something. I think you'll understand…I wanna hold your hand…." We responded in our seats to the rhythmic stimulus with twitching hands and tapping feet.

At first, I felt a bit of the same embarrassment I did the year before while watching the soap commercial. But it quickly vanished as we continued to respond together to what we were hearing. I gave in to the beat and sharp harmonies along with everyone else. When the two minutes and twenty-six seconds were over, Mr. Garber said crisply, "Terrible!" and returned to teaching. He never mentioned that almost three minutes of Beatlemania again.

It was during that same week in February that Robey went crazy. He had been somewhat peaceful for a few months. But then that Wednesday we were all marched single file into the auditorium for special mid-term awards. Mr. Kirkpatrick, our energetic, silver-haired, Irish principal, had a redder face than usual. He stood on the stage with the spotlight shining right on it. Bursting with obvious pride, he declared that it was a day to honor his successful students. Thankfully, the ensuing proceedings went by quickly…no speeches, just a vigorous handshake and piece of tan paper with a seal on it. After a few words like "You're a great American," each one left the stage.

I eventually realized that there were two students honored in each class. One class after another was represented. Each time two students would go up at once. One would wait while the other was honored. I watched their faces. After Mr. Kirkpatrick shook hands with them, they looked out at the audience, holding their papers like Roman conquerors flaunting their wreaths. I found a strange desire rising in me to go up and tear each certificate to pieces right in front of red-faced Mr. Kirkpatrick.

When he got to the eighth grade classes, he called Robert Rogers first, along with another student from my old seventh grade class. Robert seemed to take forever to get to the front of the stage. I just wanted to get out of there and go to lunch, which seemed a long way off. Finally, Mr. Kirkpatrick got to 8H. But he didn't call up 8H. He called up 8H *and* 8G as if we were one class. He said it in one breath.

"Next is 8HG. We have two students. They're both trying the best they can, ladies and gentlemen. And so…for outstanding effort…"

I just knew those were code words for "We mark the stupid ones on a curve."

"First…Robey Romero. Come on up here Robey, my boy. Give him a hand."

I couldn't tell whether the applause was the feel-sorry-for kind, but I could distinctly hear the jeering mixed with it. The word *retard* bounced around the auditorium like a silly beach ball floating from one side of the room to the other and from the front to the back.

Robey's face looked almost as red as Mr. Kirkpatrick's as he received the vigorous handshake and the few words. He was clearly trying to withdraw his hand, but Mr. Kirkpatrick wouldn't let go.

"As an Irishman to an Italian I say, 'Well done, pizano.' Stay here, boy. No, no. Stay here. Right here. That's it. The other boy is Clarence Carlson. Give him a little time. He's a little…slow on his feet, if you know what I mean. Here he comes. Come on, son. You can make it."

Snickers abounded as Clarence, rocking and swaying, slowly approached and awkwardly climbed up to the stage. Robey tried again to leave, not wanting to share the same air as Clarence. Mr. Kirkpatrick, grabbing his sleeve, spoke to him as one would a dog.

"Stay, boy. Stay, Mr. Romero. That's it. Good job, Clarence. You tried your best. What more could we ask?"

Mr. Kirkpatrick shook Clarence's clumsy hand like a stiff pump handle. Clarence looked as uncomfortable as Robey. When the principal put his hand on both of them and said, "These boys deserve a special award for effort," Robey's face seemed to betray that all of his hard work had come crashing down in futility and shame. His teeth were clenched like he was ready to utter a really foul curse word. Clarence swayed back like he was ducking a punch when Mr. Kirkpatrick touched him. And the whole school was watching all of it.

"You're off, boys. And you're *all* off back to your classes early. Maybe next time, others will be up here. Remember, it's what you do with what you've got, as these boys prove."

Robey raced out of the auditorium quickly, with Ted and Michael pushing through the crowd of kids to support him. I could see angry determination in his eyes.

That determination remained through Mr. Schott's class. No one else seemed to care that we'd been lumped in with 8G. I didn't. Gwen remained in her own world behind the veil. The fat kid (I learned his name was Marcus) dozed on and off in his post-lunch fat and sugar haze. And Mr. Schott continued his teaching as if nothing had happened. He explained nouns and verbs as if the world we knew still existed. For most of us it did…but not for Robey.

I felt like now I understood him just a little. He had actually applied himself in class. He had taken the noble path, the path of the warrior who pays the price and accepts all consequences. But all of this had been futile. He glanced at me with a disgusted, angry look, as if I had done something wrong to him. But I knew I hadn't. Then he looked down at his certificate. I was sure he wanted to tear it up like I wanted to, but for other reasons. Robey was like a lone gunman, a solitary man. When the bell rang, he came up and stood over me before I could even get up.

"You said you'd stay away from him. You stay away."

I played dumb.

"From who?"

"You know who. No retard shares an award with me. No retard!"

Then he bolted out of the room.

I walked the mile or so home that day. It gave me some time to think. I was so focused on Robey's response to the award ceremony that I hadn't given myself a chance to examine my own feelings. But I was quickly distracted. Gwen was walking across the street just ahead.

She didn't see me, so I could observe her for some time. As she walked, her head was bowed so far down that I didn't know how she navigated without going off course and smashing into a pole. She hadn't said anything to me since the day I sat next to her at lunch. Her words from that day often came back to me, "I like that you're sitting here. Will you sit next to me at lunch tomorrow?"

That never ended up happening. She ran away, and that was that. Still, she had been kind. She had asked about me being sick the day before.

All of a sudden, while I was remembering, she stopped and turned around. My thoughts quickly dissolved. She had seen me. Maybe she had eyes not only on the top of her head but behind too. It seemed she was looking right at me. But I couldn't exactly tell with all that stringy hair.

"This is where I live."

Was she talking to me? I figured she must be.

"Okay."

She stood in front of the highest grass I'd ever seen in a yard. Her light green, threadbare winter jacket blended in with it. And behind it was her house. Rotten wood and chipped, faded dark green paint was interrupted by barely hanging, beat up black shutters and dull, dirty windows. It was a little house, an old house…a very old house. We stood alone on the quiet street. No one else was around.

"I look for you every day."

"You do?" I asked, surprised.

"I look right at you and you walk away."

"I didn't notice you looking at me."

It must have been the hair obscuring her eyes. But I didn't say that.

"Why won't you sit next to me at lunch?"

"I didn't think you wanted me to."

She whispered in that gentle voice again.

"I do."

"Why did you run away from me a few months ago?"

Her voice got louder, and disapproving.

"I don't know what you're talking about."

"But…"

She interrupted me.

"This is my house."

"You told me. Umm…it's a nice house"

"No it isn't. You're lying."

I didn't expect her to challenge me so directly.

"No…I'm…"

I could just make out one of the school buses and hear the lumbering engine in the distance. I knew it would be a while until it got close to us, but I didn't want to get caught by other kids while I was talking to her. Still, I wanted to find out more about her.

"Well…forget it. Do you have any brothers or sisters?"

Her voice now took on an urgent tone.

"Could you please go?"

"What?"

"Please go. Walk!"

I began to protest.

"But…"

She stood there resolute.

"Please! Go!"

I thought about using a few weapons from the standard young peoples' arsenal like "It's a free sidewalk," or "Make me," but of course that would have been ridiculous.

"Okay. I'm going."

I walked on, passing her. After a half minute, I looked back. She was gone.

# CHAPTER 9

I WAS FINISHED TRYING TO figure out Gwen. As far as I was concerned, she could stay behind that curtain of tangled hair.

In fact, there were a number of things I figured I was finished with. And topping the list was Clarence. This was not based on Robey's advice, or even my mother's. I just couldn't take another weird person. If that's the only kind of kids there were in the Upper and Lower Zoo, I decided I'd rather have *no* friends. I wouldn't bother anyone and no one would bother me. I was stuck in that elevator between floors, and I was waiting for it to start and let me off on the next floor…or even to send me back to the last one. Meanwhile, I'd go it alone, like Robey… but not as angry.

These thoughts were going through my mind as I continued to walk home from school. Only I wasn't walking home from school. I had taken a wrong turn in a neighborhood I knew blindfolded. My feet were carrying me somewhere else almost apart from my will, as if I was floating inches above the street. I walked past the row of shops a half a mile from my house and then drifted farther, like a feather in a gentle breeze. The neighborhood changed, the houses got bigger and farther apart. Trees multiplied and grew in size. One strange, foreign street joined another. I had no idea where I was and, oddly, I didn't care. Then finally, a familiar street came into my view, and then another. Somehow I knew this would happen. And I knew that I had walked here before, though I wasn't paying much attention then. As if transported by an invisible force, I found myself standing in front of Clarence's house, on the same sidewalk where Robey had taken me several months before.

Hesitantly, I walked up the path to the house. The only memory I had of the place returned. I could see the annoyance on Clarence's mother's face behind the same door I now faced; hear the strange logic Robey expressed about the "act of kindness" in visiting Clarence; see the two iron filings, Ted and Michael, standing idly by. I could choose to walk away and head back home…or I could knock on the door…or I could stand there and do nothing, though I couldn't do that forever.

After one to two minutes, I decided to leave. This had been an exercise in wandering, and it was over. It was time to go home before darkness fell on the unfamiliar streets. Already the late winter sun had dropped between the large trees up the street and it was getting lower every second. Surely that was a good enough reason to leave. I turned around and faced the street. Suddenly I also faced Clarence, whose familiar rocking motions got closer and closer.

"Jonathan. Jonathan Richman…Richman."

An odd sensation of exposure went through me. He knew my name. I'd never shared it with him. He said it like he was picking me out of a police lineup, like he recognized me from some sort of long list. I responded as naturally as I could, hiding the surprise.

"Yes, that's me."

"Right. That's…that's…Jonathan…you. That's you."

He paused for what seemed like two minutes, except for the rocking. His grey winter coat seemed in a perpetual state of falling off. It was unzipped and open even in the cold weather, as if he didn't want to wear it but had to. He had a red sock hat over his Moe haircut. He reached up and pulled it off even though we were still outside the door. Then he beckoned me with a broad wave.

"Come in. Come in."

"But I was just…"

He turned around and banged on the door.

"MOM! MOM!" he more croaked than cried at the door.

"MOM!"

Mrs. Carlson opened the door. He rocked quickly past me and walked in. She put her hand up to stop me.

"Yes? What do you want?"

I realized that she saw me as Robey's friend, and even though he had apologized she still didn't trust me. I thought about just leaving. After all, I didn't really want *anything*. I didn't even know what I was doing there. But then an unexpected desire to defend my reputation rose within me. I wasn't Robey, and I didn't want to be lumped together with him. What had I ever done to Clarence? I was innocent! I put my hand out to shake hers.

"I'm Jonathan Richman. I just thought I'd come over to see Clarence."

She let me hold my hand out while hers stayed at her side. Clarence was still rocking, turning his head this way and that like he was in some other universe. If anything was my cue to leave, this strange sight was…me holding my hand out to nothingness, while Mrs. Carlson stood motionless and Clarence acted like my great uncle. But then the oblivious Clarence spoke in a flat, loud, emotionless voice.

"Have you come…have you come to…to be my friend?"

I tried to connect with his darting eyes the best I could.

"Yes…I mean, I don't know. Well…yes…I guess. I…"

I felt like I was starting to talk like him. A twinge of fear went through me as I stumbled over his question. Robey would kill me, or at least severely injure me, if he found out.

"There are cookies," he said tersely and without embellishment.

"Oh. There are? Oh well then…"

I hesitated, though my blood sugar was after-school low and I was hungry.

"Chocolate…chocolate…chocolate…chip…chip," he said tempt-ingly. "They're good…good."

He got behind me and rocked me fully into the house with his rather chubby frame. I was inside now. He closed the door behind me.

"Mom…we want…cookies…my friend…"

She hesitated a few seconds. Then she simply said, "You know where they are. Show Jonathan."

That was it. I was now welcome at the Carlson household. I followed Clarence as he loped into the kitchen. There on the tan Formica counter was a big red ceramic plate of large, soft, round Tollhouse cookies.

"Take five, ten, fifteen, fourteen…more. She makes them…my mother…lots. She…do you want to see the…the…the…refrigerator? There's a lot of them…twenty…thirty…forty…"

"It's okay."

"Well, these…these…are warm. Milk or juice?"

Milk and cookies seemed just right in Clarence's house. It was warm and homey with a thick, light brown rug in the living room and two big, light yellow fabric sofas with clear plastic slipcovers. The slipcovers made the rug more comfortable to sit on. But in the kitchen, the white painted chairs with little pillows to sit on were also comfortable.

"Umm…milk."

He was still rocking as he opened the refrigerator and poured the milk into a glass. Some spilled on the floor, but he paid no attention.

"Drink. Eat. Sit…sit…sit…here…here…here.

He shuffled to the table.

"Okay."

He sat with me and rocked back and forth, but didn't eat anything. I had grabbed two cookies. I felt strangely out of place sitting next to him as he rocked. My mother's admonition came back to me. What was I doing here sitting next to this retard? I moved away slightly as if whatever it was he had was catching. Finally, I spoke. I had just one question.

"Hey, how did you know my name?"

"Jonathan Richman, January 8."

I was startled. That was my birthday. I tried to be as stoic as possible in my response.

"What's with the date?"

"1950…a Sunday."

That did it.

"Hey! What is this?"

"Sunday. January 8, 1950…January 8…was a Sunday."

I became openly defensive. Something was not right about this whole thing.

"Hey, who told you? And how do you know it was a Sunday? Maybe it was a Tuesday or a Friday."

"No. Call…call…call…the phone…your mother. She'll…she'll… she'll tell you. It was a Sunday…a Sunday."

He cracked the first smile I had seen, a sort of gotcha smile. But it disappeared as soon as it came, like an infant's smile that could be gas.

"Your birthday…your birthday…was January 8. A Sunday…ask…"

"Look…"

"I saw the date…on a paper…on a paper…at…at…school. Not the day…not the day."

He was not only a retard. He was some sort of spy. But a spy for whom?

I tried to look directly at his darting eyes as I interrogated him.

"What paper? And what were you doing looking at it?"

"I didn't look at it. I didn't. It just…my eyes…my eyes…they just passed by it…passed…on the teacher's desk…the first day. I know…I know all of them…all the names and…all the…all the birthdays in eight G and H."

I stood up and threw my hands in the air.

"All right. Just stop!"

He didn't pay any attention to my protestations, but just continued as if I was still seated.

"My father says it's my mom...he said some big doctor named, named Bettel, Bettle...heim...Bettelheim...he says she's...she's a refrigerator mother, like a refrigerator...cold, really cold. He wrote a book...*Love...Love is Not...Not...Enough*...a...a book...about it. He's famous...and he...my father...my father read it...he says like this...he says...well he yells..."

His voice changed, deepened.

"'That's why Clarence is like that. You're a refrigerator mother—cold.' That's what he says...he says...refrigerator mother...my father says that...just like that...like that."

He loped over to the refrigerator and opened it. "Like this." Then he slammed the door shut so hard that the refrigerator shook.

"So I'm a retard...because...because I can...I can remember things, little things, lots...lots of things. I can't help it. I just...I... I can't...I can't...stop it."

I had no idea what Clarence meant by refrigerator mother or why he slammed the refrigerator door. I figured he was just completely crazy. And I couldn't understand how he knew all of those dates and days. But I also marked that up to craziness, and Lower Zoo stupidity. So I could do nothing but agree with him when he said he was a retard. And I just wanted to leave.

"Well...I guess you *are* a retard if you can do that. So it's okay that you looked at the sheet. I mean...it's a retarded thing to do. So... thanks for the cookies. I gotta go."

"Okay. Okay. Okay. Can we say The Lord's Prayer? Then you go. Okay? Okay?

"I don't think I know that one, Clarence. So I think I'll just..."

He interrupted me, insistent with his loud, flat voice.

"Okay. Okay. Okay...Psalm 23. Okay?"

I couldn't wait to get out of there. But Psalm 23 was short. I knew that. He would stumble through it and then I would go.

"Go ahead. You say it. Then I go."

"Okay. Okay."

He began. To my complete surprise his voice changed again, like when he was quoting his father. But this time it not only dropped down, but it got very steady and serious. His face changed too, like some kind of glowing light came on in it. He stopped rocking. He stopped stumbling through the words. His eyes stopped darting and looked straight at me, and, it seemed, through me.

"The Lord *is* my shepherd; I shall not want. He maketh me to lie down in green pastures: he leadeth me beside the still waters.

"He restoreth my soul: he leadeth me in the paths of righteousness for his name's sake.

"Yea, though I walk through the valley of the shadow of death, I will fear no evil: for thou art with me; thy rod and thy staff they comfort me.

"Thou preparest a table before me in the presence of mine enemies: thou anointest my head with oil; my cup runneth over.

"Surely goodness and mercy shall follow me all the days of my life: and I will dwell in the house of the Lord for ever."

He started, hesitantly at first, to rock to and fro again.

"You can go…you can go…now. You can go…but…come back."

"We'll see."

I wanted to leave now more than ever. Between the birthday, the refrigerator talk—whatever that was—and Psalm 23, I felt like I'd been at a freak show. Maybe this was the reason my mother told me I shouldn't be friends with Clarence. I said goodbye quickly and left without even saying goodbye to his mother. Then I started on the long walk home.

It wasn't until I was several blocks away and the trees became fewer that I began to go over the strangeness of it all…and the wonder. How did he know all those dates and all those days? How did he remember my birthday, let alone my name? And how could a retard from the Lower Zoo quote Psalm 23 by heart and quote it the way he did? No one in the Upper Zoo could do that and do it the way Clarence did… not even Robey.

Robey! If he ever found out...! But he wouldn't. He couldn't. Anyway, why did I even visit Clarence? I had no idea, but I was sure I would never visit him again.

# CHAPTER 10

NATURALLY, IT WAS LATE WHEN I got home. And just as naturally, there was Mom at the door as I entered.

"Where *were* you?"

I didn't feel like telling her, and I also didn't feel like just slinking off. Self-justification rose up within me, and seemingly out of nowhere came a victim's reply, the reply of an independent man of thirteen.

*"Dad's* late all the time! He never tells you where he is, and you never say *anything!* Where's *he?* That's what I want to know. He's *never* here!"

I left and slammed the door to my room, like Clarence slammed the refrigerator. I flopped down on the bed so hard that the 1957 Chevy jumped on the shelf. *All mothers were to blame for everything!* As if she heard my secret thought, I heard her threatening response.

"Don't you dare sass me, young man! Don't you dare!"

"Shut up, you old hag," I half whispered and half spoke out.

"What did you say? What did you say? Open up that door!"

I lay down on my bed.

"Open this door instantly! Where were you?"

I had to get her off my back.

"Please. I have a headache. I just want to rest. I was walking around. Okay?"

She took a long time to answer. When she did, she was quieter, and I could that her voice was quivering even through the door.

"All right then. All right."

I could hear her finally walk away and into the kitchen. In a little while I could hear some kind of quiet sobbing. Could I have caused that? Embarrassment and guilt began to descend on me. Then there was a knock on my door.

"Let me in."

It was Billy.

"Let me in."

Billy was the last person I wanted to talk to.

"Go away."

"Please! It's an emergency."

"Right. Okay. Is your room on fire?"

I let him in anyway.

"She's crying."

"I can hear. So? I didn't do anything."

I got up and got ready to show him the door.

"It's Dad."

"What's Dad?"

"He's cheating on her."

I turned and looked at him. His head was bowed down so far down that I thought his glasses would fall off. Then he sat down on the bed and I sat next to him, slapping him on the shoulder.

"Are you crazy? What's the matter with you? Dad wouldn't do anything like that. You don't know what you're talking about, Billy. Sometimes I think you're a retard like Clarence."

"Clarence isn't a retard, and I'm not crazy."

"You don't even know who Clarence is. So just shut up and go to your room!"

He looked at me and put his hand on my shoulder.

"I know who he is. His sister is in my class."

He doesn't have a sister. I've been to his house twice. So stop lying and leave."

He shook his head no, just like our mother did.

"You're wrong. He *does* have a sister. She stays with her grandparents so she won't be like Clarence."

I didn't believe him, but I was too tired to argue.

"Well okay, if you say so…since you know everything. But he's a retard…a strange retard. You don't know about *that.*"

"No. He's not retarded. He's what they call autistic."

Now he had taken that teacher's tone with me, and I would have none of it.

"You're making that up…that word doesn't even exist. You live in a fantasy. You're playing with too many toys. I'm glad I don't play with you any more. I don't know what's happened to you. You're strange, just like everyone else around here. Maybe you'll end up in the Lower Zoo."

"Jonathan?"

"You're a freak."

He stood up and quietly repeated himself like a parent with a defiant two-year-old.

"Jonathan?"

"Just stay away from me."

He started to tear up.

"Jonathan?"

I looked up at him as I sat there, ready to take a left swing at him. But then I noticed the tears in his eyes.

"What! What is it? What's the matter with you? Stop crying."

He got quieter and came close, standing over me. As he spoke, I withdrew my fist and began to twirl my curls between my fingers.

"I saw Dad with a lady. She had a sparkly necklace and blonde hair, like Marilyn Monroe, and a fur thing around her shoulders. They were in a red sports car in an alley near the drug store. She was at the wheel and they were kissing, like kissing a lot. I never saw him kiss Mom that way."

I just stared at him as I twirled. I couldn't just dismiss what he was saying.

"When?"

"Two days ago."

I pulled back.

"You're making it up."

"I'm not."

I sprang up, almost banging the top of my head against his chin in the process. My easy to access anger at Dad flared up.

"I'll kill him if that's true! I'll kill him!"

"You can't kill him. You can't do anything about it. And neither can I."

I couldn't believe I was having this ridiculous conversation with my little brother, and I wanted it to end. He had almost convinced me, but I snapped out of it.

"It wasn't him. It was someone else. You *always* do this. You tell me I'm like…like smarter than Robert Rogers when I'm in the stupid Upper Zoo. You tell me that Clarence isn't a retard and make up a crazy word that doesn't even exist for him. Now you tell me this. I should have seen it coming. You started acting strange after you read that kiddy Thomas Edison book with all the dumb pictures. So I guess you like to invent things, just like him. Only the things you invent don't work, Billy. So just cut it out and leave."

He pointed a finger gently my way.

"See…that was well said. You *are* smart, smarter than you know. You should be a writer."

I pointed at the door.

"*You* should be a liar. Go tell someone else your stories."

He pressed his finger to his glasses for emphasis.

"She was crying like that before you came home. I watched her from the stairs. It wasn't you. She was looking at that wedding picture of them. That's how I know she knows."

"All right. I'm going to listen to my Beach Boys record and go to bed now."

"Okay. Sorry I had to tell you."

I got up and put the 45 RPM record on my little silver and black suitcase record player, turning the volume up.

"'Round, round get around, I get around...," Mike Love sang.

Billy left the room and shut the door.

My father came home late that night, as he did almost every night. My door was open when he came in the house. I could hear him mumble as he took his pocket change out and put it in the little ashtray on the dining room cupboard. I heard the chink of the change and the mumbling, but I couldn't understand his words.

He didn't seem like the man Billy described. I couldn't even imagine him kissing my mother like that, with his balding head and little paunch belly, so I certainly couldn't imagine him in some red sports car kissing Marilyn Monroe.

His shadow passed by the open door of my room. He shut the door to the bedroom. I knew my mother was asleep. But I couldn't sleep. I tossed on my bed, and my mind kept tossing around the accusations Billy made about Dad. How could they possibly be anything more than Billy's inventions? The dial on my clock radio read two o'clock just before I finally drifted off to sleep. When I woke up at six, Dad was no longer on my mind. I had a new school day to deal with.

I almost dozed on the bus, leaning on my old friend the bus window. Another ten or fifteen minutes of sleep might help me get through a day I wasn't looking forward to. But I couldn't really sleep, with all those gear-shifting vibrations jiggling my brain.

When I finally entered the school, I passed by Clarence in the hall and totally ignored him. I could feel his eyes following me, but I was too tired to care. If I cared about anything, it was about keeping Robey from any hint that that I'd visited him. Just then, Robey suddenly appeared out of nowhere and draped himself over my slouched shoulder, as was his usual habit.

"Hey, Jonathan. Boy that Clarence is ugly…and dumb…dumb and ugly. Capiche?"

"I wouldn't know. I don't bother with him."

He leaned harder on my shoulder.

"You better not bother with him. Take it from me. *I* would know about Clarence. I had to smell his BO on the stage. He stank."

I had no comment.

"Have you ever been near him? He stinks like a toilet."

I *had* been near him, and I knew he didn't stink. But I didn't say anything to Robey. Just then, Gwen passed by. I tried not to pay attention, but I couldn't help noticing.

"Another ugly one. Capiche?"

This time, I extricated myself from his draping arm and looked right at him.

"No. She's actually pretty…very pretty."

"Yeh? Pretty? How would you know? Huh? How would you know?"

"I…I…I saw her face…behind all that hair. I could just see it. It's beautiful. It's a beautiful face."

I didn't know why, but something just told me I shouldn't have said that. Anger flashed on his face, and his teeth clenched. He picked me up by my shirt collar and slammed me against the wall, leaving my feet dangling off the floor. My heart skipped a beat and then sped up.

"What is it with you?" I gasped as I dangled there, my mouth drying out in an instant.

He backed off, dropping me so that my knees ached when my feet landed. He averted his eyes from me.

"It's nothing. Nothing. I'm a little upset today. Sorry, pal. It's time for class."

He walked away. At least he had apologized. But why did he do that? Maybe he just hadn't noticed what Gwen looked like, and I was acting smarter than him. After all, there wasn't anybody who could see much of her face. It was always hidden behind that curtain of hair.

I had already decided I wanted nothing to do with that odd, strange girl. So why couldn't I help looking at her as she passed us in the hall? One thing was for sure. I had to forget her, to get her totally out of my mind. The bell rang. Shaken, I entered the class as Mr. Garner began teaching.

I couldn't concentrate. I shouldn't have even been able to stay awake, but the ordeal with Robey totally woke me up. And I found myself starting to think about something even as I was trying not to think about it. The obsession grabbed me by the throat, making it hard to swallow.

I had to see Gwen's face, *really* see it. If it was rotten, I wanted to know it for myself. If it was truly magnificent, I had to view it in all its glory. I began to doodle the perfect oval face with my yellow, number 2 pencil on an empty notebook page, then I drew her distinctive hair as wiry, grey strings draping down over her eyes. I slouched in my chair, exhilarated at the thought of seeing the real Gwen.

"Richman!"

Adrenaline shot me straight up in my chair. Mr. Garner walked over to my seat and stood over me.

"What's that you're drawing?"

Gwen was just seats away. The drawing was too obvious…the oval face shape, the hair…especially the hair. I crumpled it the best I could with one hand.

"That is *not* what I asked. Get down to the principle's office. Now! Now!"

I stuffed the paper in my pocket as I walked slowly out of the room. The halls were empty, and I had time to kill. I inched my way toward the front offices. It was only 9 A.M., and already the day had been disastrous…a confrontation with Robey and a visit to the principle's office. But then there was Gwen. My prior vow to avoid her was rapidly evaporating.

Visiting the principle's office was a formality. Mr. Kirkpatrick always spent as little time as possible telling kids not to do it again, usually not even taking the time to find out exactly what *it* was. His red face never betrayed anger, just an Irish complexion issue of some sort. He brought me into his office from the outer office about five minutes after I arrived. It was obvious he wanted to get onto something else in his busy schedule.

"What did you do?"

"Uhh...I was doodling, and..."

"Fine. You're not to do it again. Here's a note. Get back to class. What class is it?"

"Umm...8H."

He betrayed a clear sign of pity in his eyes.

"Well...carry on, Mr....Mr. Richman. Just do your best. Do your best. That's what I always say. Do the best with what you have. That's what I always say. Well...get going, young man."

I had some time to think as I inched down the hall. And all I could think of was Gwen. Robey's attack was gone, as was any thought of Dad and Billy's hard to believe story. Gwen occupied one hundred percent of my imagination.

This kind of thinking was new to me. Last year I had spent a lot of time thinking of the balsa wood model airplane wing pinned down on my desk in my room, or about the matinee monster movie Billy and I planned to see over the weekend. But that was last year. This year I hadn't thought of anything much except predicaments, embarrassments, and strange events. Even music like the Beatles hadn't swept me up like it had others. The music was nice, but the year wasn't. So even the British invasion couldn't make the year a good one.

But now for the first time this year, I had something to live for. It wasn't an interest like Billy's Edison interest. But it *was* a curiosity I couldn't get out of my mind...even a mystery I had to solve. I *had* to see that face. I *had* to see what Gwen really looked like.

# CHAPTER 11

THE OBSESSION ONLY INTENSIFIED WHEN I walked out of the building after school. The Ides of March had arrived on the rays of the springtime sun, and that was only the day before. The warm breeze on my face and scent of the early spring flowers were still a surprise, and they only served to enhance my newfound feelings. I would definitely walk instead of taking the bus, and walk past that mysteriously dilapidated, yet now somehow quaint and charming, house.

I didn't have to walk very far. There, not twenty-five yards ahead of me, was Gwen. I could just make out that she was carrying her book bag in front of her, as girls generally did. I slowed down and continued at the same distance behind her. I had no plan, no idea of what I would do next, no idea of how I would get from here to there. This went on for some time. Finally, I threw caution to the gentle spring wind and let it carry me forward. I caught up to her a few blocks from her house.

No one seemed to be around. I ran the last few feet and arrived in front of her, dropping my books like a sack of worthless potatoes. The frayed papers that had been sticking out of my notebook scattered on the ground. I stooped and quickly scooped them up, stuffing them back in. I had blocked her path and she almost ran into me. I looked up.

"Gwen."

"What are you doing here?"

I could see that I had surprised her. She held her books against her tightly, like a protective shield. I tried to look up at her face through the veil of tangled locks, but it wasn't working. So I stood up and faced her. I struggled to smile.

"I…I seemed to have dropped my books. Oh well…they're kind of messy."

She tried to pass, but I walked backward, blocking her path as disarmingly as I could. She raised her voice.

"Sorry about your notebook. Can I pass?"

"Umm…no."

I continued to walk backward, blocking her view.

"What are you doing, Jonathan? Let me pass!"

I stopped and she almost ran into me. She grasped her book bag even tighter. I dropped my books again. This time they landed in a stack and didn't scatter. I stood face-to-face with her, except that I couldn't see her face. It was now or never. I slowly extended both hands toward her face. They seemed to take forever to reach the veil. She just stood there all that time, holding her books tightly against her chest. Then she said in no more than a whisper, perhaps even a whimper, "What are you doing? Stop."

I gently parted her hair on each side, and kept it apart between my thumbs and fingers. Then I very gingerly held her face in my hands and looked into her brilliant, electric blue eyes. She looked right at me without flinching and started to tremble. But she stayed right there just looking at me until tears began to fill them.

"And?" she whispered, not knowing what else to say.

"And I knew you were beautiful. I just knew it."

I carefully wiped her tears with my fingers. I had never touched a girl before, let alone wiped her tears. Her trembling increased.

"No."

"Yes. More beautiful than I ever could have imagined."

I had been holding her face for what seemed like an eternity.

"Please don't…"

"Please don't what?"

"Just please don't…"

I withdrew my hands. The veil fell back in place. She was still trembling.

"Thank you, Gwen," I said.

I grabbed my books off the ground and quickly walked away, while she just stood there trembling. I was a block and a half away when I looked back. She was walking again, clutching her books even more tightly.

I had seen Gwen's face up close. Now maybe I could get on with my life. I got to my house as the early spring sun rested on the roofs and trees surrounding me. It glowed through the back windows and through the front ones like rays of lemon yellow light through a crystal chandelier, landing on the green grass on the front lawn. As spring air filled my lungs, the feelings I had put to rest were still lingering. I walked into the house and into the kitchen. There was Mom. I immediately noticed her damp eyes, remembered Billy's words, and was just as quickly prompted to put on a naïve veneer.

"You ready for dinner?" she ventured as she wiped her face. She didn't even ask why I was late or where I'd been.

"I think so."

"I…I still have to cook it."

It was very unusual for her not to be at least cooking dinner by that time. She just stood there in her flowered dress and apron, appearing paralyzed by some force. Her hands were at her side and appeared useless. I could see that her right hand was holding a tissue. I didn't know what to say, but I wanted to make her feel better so I said the only thing I could think of.

"That's okay."

"It'll only be a few minutes."

I wasn't hungry anyway. I was too filled with spring fever.

"Okay. Where's Billy?"

"He's over a friend's house," she mechanically responded.

That was unusual too. Mom always insisted that Billy be home by dinner on school nights.

"Oh. Well...I'll be in my room."

I shut the door to my room and lay on the bed. A strange question entered my mind. *What would Robey tell his mother in a situation like this?* Then, *Who cares what Robey would do.* Still, I wondered, would he drape his arm over his mother and tell her he knew why she was crying? "Capiche?" he might say. And then everything would be all right. Would he talk to his father, man to man? Would he say, "Here's what I want you to do?" or maybe "Don't see that woman. I better not catch you talking to her. Mike and Ted'll take care of you if you do." That is, if the whole thing between Dad and that woman ever even happened.

The truth was, the thought that my father kissed a blonde lady in a fancy car was like the Kennedy killing four months or so earlier...a shocking and unimaginable event. I had always understood that he worked hard selling insurance to make ends meet for us, and that's why he couldn't be home more. At least that's what he always told us. If Billy was telling the truth, perhaps that was all a lie...if....

As I stared at the ceiling, I thought I heard a key unlock the front door. I wondered who it could possibly be. It was early for Dad to be home. But who else would have the key?

The mumbling and stray intelligible words were definitely Dad's. Then I heard Mom's soft almost whispered response.

Then, "Where? Billy's where?"

After that, more soft responding.

"Yeh. Dinner. Fine."

He went into the bathroom and shut the door. I got up and left my room.

"What's *he* doing home?"

Mom was scurrying around the kitchen, moving pots on the stove and stirring ingredients into them.

"I don't know. Set the dishes out."

I resisted.

"Why?"

"Because, dinner will be ready."

I tried to hold my ground.

"So?"

"So, we're having dinner together."

"What? How many?"

"Three, of course. Billy is eating over Drew's house."

Dad almost never ate with us. But he was going to that night. He walked out of the bathroom and sat at the dinner table as I put his plate in front of him. I cooperated, not wanting to add to my mother's obvious sorrow. He grabbed a piece of bread and motioned to me.

"Sit down. You make me nervous. How's school…you know, that class you're in?"

"Okay."

He hardly ever asked me about school. I knew he would sometimes tell Mom what he thought about my grades and, in the case of the Upper Zoo, why I ended up there. But he rarely spoke to me about it. He always seemed distracted, mumbling, looking at something else, talking to someone else. And I wasn't about to have a conversation with him now, knowing what I thought I knew.

Dinner was bizarre. I was trying to be more silent than usual out of protest. I just sat there twirling one set of curls after another while making a distinct point to keep my mouth closed and not ask for any food. Of course, the message wasn't getting through. Dad punctuated his eating with meaningless comments. By this time, Mom was sitting down with us.

"This is good. It's better than all those restaurant meals."

Was my Mom also in protest mode? Perhaps. She kept staring at him. And he kept up with the small talk.

"Well…this sure is good. Nothing like a home cooked meal. You're better than the guys I usually eat with."

More staring.

"Too bad Billy's missing this."

Finally after several of his comments, she spoke.

"What are you doing home?"

He put his fork down and stopped in mid-bite. He squinted his eyes and his countenance changed as he sought to defend himself.

"What do you mean? Something got canceled. I thought I'd come home for dinner. That's all. I have to leave again soon. *That's all.* I have to leave…in a few minutes."

"*Do* you?"

She was definitely getting angry. Her face reddened. He responded like an innocent victim being accused.

"What the hell's wrong with you? Yes, I *do.* I have to leave. Come on. If you have something to say, say it."

"Jonathan's here."

"I can see that."

I grabbed some chicken and started chewing, trying to be invisible. She continued.

"That's all. I can't say more with him here."

Finally I said, "Should I leave?"

"No. You eat," she said. Dad stood and put a hand on either side of his paunch.

"Come on. If you've got something to say, say it…with Jonathan here. I come home to *my* house. I eat with *my* family, in a house *I* pay for, food *I* pay for…"

"I've had enough!" Mom said, and walked away from the table. That left me sitting alone with Dad, which was clearly unacceptable. I started to get up and leave too.

"Where are you going?"

"Where are *you* going? That's what I want to know."

He banged his hand on the table as I left.

"What? It's none of your damn business. Don't you smart mouth me! You come back here! Come back!"

"Drop dead!"

That was the most disrespectful thing I'd ever said to my father. I slammed the door to my room and flopped down on the bed. I waited, expecting him to follow me to the door. But he didn't. I heard him get up and soon after that he slammed the front door. His car started up and he drove off. He was gone. And I was relieved.

# CHAPTER 12

THE NEXT DAY WAS IMPACTED by the revelations about Gwen's face, Dad's alleged affair, and Mom's tears, all mixed and stirred up with the spring sun.

Things at school seemed different somehow. Robey seemed less wise, but more angry. Mr. Garner seemed more tired and less exciting. But perhaps it was all me. His creative way of explaining numbers and equations had lost the novelty it had earlier in the year. All I could imagine as his teaching went on and on was Dad and some blonde, sitting in some red sports car in some alley. All I could picture was Gwen, just a few rows behind me, her beauty hidden behind a veil. All I could feel was her trembling face and warm tears. But I never looked back in her direction.

When we went to lunch, I saw Clarence sitting in his usual place, swaying to and fro, back and forth, side to side. There was something I wanted to ask him. But I knew I couldn't, not with Robey around. And I didn't want to visit Clarence again and endure the freak show. Nevertheless, I realized that there were some things only a freak could tell you. So I knew I had to see him at home again. And I needed to let him know I was coming. That would require a pen. So I turned to chubby Marcus as he was filling his mouth with French fries.

"Hey Marcus, do you have a pen?"

He spoke with his mouth full, as was his habit.

"I have a pencil…for the rest of your chips."

"Chips? You're already eating fries. What are you, a human vacuum cleaner? Fine. Here."

He grabbed the chips and started munching them along with the fries.

"Gimme the pencil."

"Oh yeh."

He tossed it at me. It hit the table and the tip broke. It was unusable on one side, and barely usable if I held the pencil the other way.

"Thanks for nothing."

I felt like grabbing the remaining chips, just to get back at him. But I didn't. I used a nearby napkin, and wrote quickly in block letters, CAN I COME OVER AFTER SCHOOL TOMORROW? JONATHAN.

The bell rang. I watched as Clarence staggered out with his class. He walked slowly through the door, out of the room and down the hall. Robey walked at about the same pace as Clarence and almost next to him, sauntering in his tapered pants and pointy shoes while Clarence limped in his too large khakis with cuffs. It seemed to me like Robey was trying to keep me from giving Clarence the napkin. But I knew that couldn't be.

I walked behind them until Clarence walked into his class. I could see him sit down and rock back and forth. His teacher, a thin pretty blonde lady in a ponytail and a frilly dress, was standing in the front. She began to teach, if indeed that's what they did in the Lower Zoo.

"Mary, did you have a good lunch?"

Mary was rocking in a different direction than Clarence.

"Yes, Ma'am."

"Let's look at the new *unruly* words for today."

She pointed to three words on the board, written in large letters.

"See how they break the rules? Say them with me. bread, head, read."

I looked through the open door. Some of the kids were swaying. Most were not. I realized I had a window of opportunity, and I walked in and up to the teacher.

"Can I help you?"

"I have a note for Clarence from his mother."

She quizzed me with her eyes.

"On a napkin?"

"Well…I guess she was…eating at the time…and…gave it to me. She called and…and I picked it up on the way to school. We're friends…that is, Clarence and me…very good friends…very good."

She looked at Clarence, who was smiling in assent and bobbing his head up and down.

"I see. Well, please give it to him and go to your class."

I stepped quickly over to Clarence and handed him the note, opening it in the process so he could see it. I looked at him, waiting for him to read the few block letters on it, but he wouldn't focus on it. His eyes were darting around as usual. I knew I couldn't stay any longer.

"Well, I'll go."

"Yes. That's a good idea," she said.

I took a last look at the Lower Zoo class on the way out. *There was a reason why they called it lower,* I thought. *They were all retards and freaks.* I had thought maybe Clarence knew how to say read and read…but maybe not.

My note-passing strategy resulted in a mild rebuke by Mr. Schott for being late to class. And then the class went by quickly. None of Mr. Schott's quiet lecturing penetrated even the outer regions of my brain, even though he was reading another story, and I was usually riveted during those times. But I was too distracted even for that. I just sat there twirling my curls and staring off into space. Fortunately, no questions were fielded my way before the bell rang. I was left with only one thing on my mind…my meeting with Clarence the next day.

When I finally came home after Hebrew School, there was Billy in the front yard, polishing his used three-speed bike with an old rag.

"What were you doing at Drew's last night?"

"Having dinner."

I didn't want to let him off the hook that easily.

"Yeh? Mom never lets you do that."

"She did last night."

"Yeh? Well, Dad was home…for dinner."

Billy shot back as he rubbed the handlebars with the rag.

"I'm glad I wasn't. I don't want to be around him. I don't like being around you anymore either."

"That's too bad. What are you doing out here?"

"I like the sun."

I looked around and laughed sarcastically.

"It's almost dark."

"The sun is right there."

He pointed to what was apparently west.

"Okay. Fine, Edison. Hey, what'd you call Clarence again?"

"I didn't call him anything. I don't call people names. That's what you and your friends like Robey do."

"Will you shut up? He's not my friend."

He rolled the bike into the garage. Then he came out and went in the front door. I went in after him before he had a chance to close it.

"Listen to me!"

He walked into the kitchen.

"Wait a minute!"

He opened the refrigerator.

"What's that word you called him…that disease or something? I need to know."

"What word?"

"I don't know. It starts with an A."

A light bulb went off in his spectacled eyes. He pressed his glasses like he was pushing a button to retrieve an answer.

"Oh. Autistic?"

"Yeh, that's it."

He turned and smirked. Then he turned back.

"I thought I made it up. That's what you told me."

"Did you?"

He pulled out a jar of peanut butter.

"Why would I make it up?"

It was time to apologize, so I could at least get more information out of him. He pulled a spoon out of the drawer under the sink and stuck it into the jar. I held his hand before he put the spoon to his mouth.

"Okay. Sorry. So what's the disease?"

He shut the refrigerator door and treated the spoon like a lollipop. With it sticking out of his mouth, he continued.

"It's not what they say it is. His mother isn't a refrigerator mother."

"What is that? He said something about that."

"You really want to know?"

I'd had enough humiliation from my kid brother. Now I just wanted the facts.

"Don't play around with me, Billy. What's autistic, and what's a refrigerator mother?"

"Okay. It isn't about the mother being cold to her baby, like some scientists say. That's what a refrigerator mother is supposed to be. The mother doesn't like her baby and he becomes autistic. But that's not right."

"How would *you* know?"

His hands became animated as he withdrew the spoon minus the peanut butter. I knew what was next. He waved the spoon at me as he recited *the name*.

"Because...Thomas Edison's mother loved him and taught him when the teachers at school couldn't...or wouldn't."

"Billy...why is everything about Edison? What's he got to do with Clarence?"

He became deadly serious.

"Jonathan, Edison was probably autistic…at least a little bit. I read that somewhere. Some people think that's how he could invent so many inventions."

"Edison was a genius, stupid."

"Yes, that's right."

I had him now.

"He wasn't a retard."

"No. And neither is Clarence."

"But he rocks back and forth."

Billy rolled his eyes, betraying the impatience that he felt, which was more humiliating than anything in the conversation so far.

"So? Does he also remember dates, and days, and lists, and…?"

"Yes. Yes he does. How do you know that?"

"I told you; I know his sister. She's in my class. She wouldn't end up like him, which is what they claim. He wouldn't hurt her by being around her. It's something in *him*, not in his mother or his sister or anyone else. He's special, like Edison. So…"

I interrupted him.

"And he's a retard. Robey says he's a retard."

He threw the spoon in the sink.

"Robey's a jerk. Maybe you've caught what *he* has. What *he* has is catching."

I knew how to end the conversation.

"Where's Mom."

"I think she's in her room. I guess we have to make our own dinner. I don't want to bother her."

The fact that this was the second time Mom skipped making dinner took me by surprise. I realized we might not have dinner if one of us didn't make it. I stepped up to the plate.

"I'll…I'll make us something."

I boiled some hot dogs that night. Mom complimented me when she came into the kitchen and saw what I was doing. She put her arm around me like I was the heavyweight champion of the world. I felt a little bit like the head of the home...a very confusing home, but still *our* home. Since I entered the Upper Zoo, Billy sometimes seemed older than me. But cooking that simple meal made me feel older. For the first time since I entered the Upper Zoo, I really felt like the older brother.

I went to sleep and woke up with one thing on my mind. I had given the note to Clarence. Now all that was left was a sign from him that I was welcome at his home that afternoon.

As I sat through Mr. Garner's creative explanation of simple pre-algebraic formulas—using stick figures—I made plans for signaling Clarence during lunch. It had to be clear enough to elicit a response and subtle enough not to get Robey's attention.

I held my books as the second hand on the clock ticked toward the twelve. If I arrived in the lunchroom early, I could get the confirmation before Robey even arrived. Three...two...one...

I raced out of the room as the bell sounded. I walked down the empty hall as quickly as I could while still not breaking the no running rule. My strides were wide and my pace quick. When I arrived in the lunchroom, Clarence wasn't there yet. I didn't expect him to be. But maybe he would arrive before Robey, Ted, or Michael.

I waited and waited. My whole class arrived. The whole Lower Zoo arrived. Robert Rogers arrived. Everyone arrived...except Clarence. Finally, I stepped up to the line last and waited until I received my portion of the old favorite, shepherd's pie.

Clarence never appeared. I didn't want to wait another day to ask him the question that was on my mind. I wondered if I could just show up after school. I spent the afternoon thinking about it, and finally came up with a plan.

As I sat at my desk I began to design a get-well card, which I kept well-hidden most of the time under the paper I used for class notes.

"Dear Clarence, I hope you feel better."

I drew a stick figure of a shepherd, courtesy Mr. Garner's morning art work, with a little cane in his hand, and several puffy little sheep around him...Psalm 23. For the second time, I was hoping a written message would get me where I wanted to go.

# CHAPTER 13

ON THE WAY TO CLARENCE'S house, I thought about my talk with Billy. It seemed like whatever the subject was, something about Edison always came up. Now Edison and Clarence were supposed to have the same strange illness. They were also both supposed to be some kind of geniuses. But Billy was only in fifth grade. How could he really know whether Clarence was just retarded or really smart?

As I kept walking, my imagination began get the best of me. I had to admit, there was something scary about Clarence. He was different, weird, strange—maybe even a religious fanatic. How did I know he wasn't going take a knife out of the kitchen drawer and stab me? Some kid in the newspaper did that to some other kid, and then chopped him up. They found him in the trash can out back. Would I be next?

I stopped in the middle of the street. The trees were getting bigger, as were the houses. Though I had walked most of the way, I thought maybe I should just go home. But I took a deep breath and stamped my right foot to bring myself back to reality. I spoke out loud to the houses and the trees.

"This is crazy. Anyway, what can he do to me with his mother there?"

I wouldn't stay long, but I *would* visit him this one time. I had something to ask him. I held my get well card in my right hand and continued on my journey.

When I finally got to the front door, it suddenly opened as if I was at a supermarket and the electric eye saw me. There was Mrs. Carlson waiting for me on the other side...with Clarence just behind her.

"Welcome, Jonathan. Clarence gave me the note."

"Yes, I did" Clarence intoned, sounding mechanical but proud. "I did."

"Yes, well...here. I have this...this sort of get well card. I hope he feels better. I hope you're feeling...umm, better, Clarence....I mean from your sickness...of...of today...when you were out."

Clarence's mother took the illustrated card from me and glanced at it.

"Clarence isn't sick. Why in the world did you think he was sick?"

"Well...he wasn't at school, so..."

She smiled kindly, putting me at ease.

"He has a special appointment once a month."

"Oh."

She was completely different from the last time I was there. Apparently I hit it off with Clarence, even though I couldn't wait to leave after he recited the Psalm 23 in a voice that wasn't his. She escorted me into the house with a sweeping gesture, like I was being announced at a ball.

"Come in. He's very happy to see you. Well, I'll leave you two alone. I baked a cake. It's on the kitchen table."

She seemed overjoyed at the thought of me sharing her cake with Clarence. I imagined he didn't have too many friends. I responded politely.

"Thank you."

I headed for the kitchen. The cake looked like the picture on one those Duncan Hines boxes. My mother's always turned out like a lunar landscape with icing barely filling the craters. This one was as moist and fluffy as the advertisers promised and as lemony as lemons could make it. The pieces were cut evenly, and there next to them was a knife. Clarence's mother started to leave.

"Well, I'll be upstairs. There's milk in the refrigerator."

There was that word—refrigerator. Clarence approached the cake.

"You…you want…some?"

His hand came closer and closer to the knife every time he rocked in that direction. He was a lot closer to it than I was. I could almost see him grab the knife and plunge it into my short sleeve shirt and through my heart. Instead, he grabbed a plate from the counter and offered it to me for my slice of cake.

"Please, sit down. Sit down here. I spill…I spill milk. You can get it. It's there. It's in there, and here are the…the cups."

He offered me one of those colored metal cups, the kind I remembered drinking from as a five-year-old when I ate peanut butter and jelly sandwiches with Billy. But I declined. I wanted to get down to business.

"No thanks."

I sat down with my piece of cake.

"So…you remember things…I mean things you read."

"I remember things…I read…yes…yes."

Was he just copying me? Did he understand? I'd know when I got to my question. It had to do with that sheet he saw at the beginning of the year.

"Right, like that page at school. Remember that sheet, Clarence?"

"Books…books."

What was that about? What was he saying?

"Books?"

"Pages of…all the pages…of books. Hardy Boys. Books."

"Hardy Boys?"

This was not going the right direction. And he was off and running, becoming more and more excited by the topic, his rocking increasing threefold like a horse in a rodeo.

"*The Secret of the Caves;* one hundred seventy five pages. One hundred seventy...seventy five."

"Really. That's nice, but..."

"Page one...'Don't kid me, fellows,' Chubby Chet Morton said, moving his metal detector about the Hardys' front lawn. 'You can find all kinds of swell things on the beaches with this gadget.'"

I had to stop him before he went further.

"That's okay."

"I...I know all of them. *The Mystery of Cabin Island.* Page one. 'What a reward!' Joe Hardy exclaimed. 'You mean we can stay at Cabin Island over the winter vacation?'"

"That's okay. Okay. I believe you. But...stop!"

Could he possibly know all these books by heart? That would be impossible. But that's not what I came to talk about.

"Mother says...she says it's a gift...a gift from...from Jesus."

I didn't know what to say, so I didn't say anything. I just sat there, took a deep breath and a bite of cake, and started twirling my curls with my left hand.

"She...she...says it's a miracle, not...not bad...a bad thing...like... like that Dr. Bettelheim says. She...she...he...makes her angry...very angry."

I still didn't know who Dr. Bettelheim was and I didn't care. But for some unknown reason I wanted to say something about miracles.

"I don't believe in miracles. When I was in second grade, my Hebrew school teacher told us that when the Red Sea parted it was really low tide. 'The miracle was the timing,' she said. But I don't even believe that."

Now it was Clarence who didn't know what to say.

"Besides, I don't believe in Jesus," I added.

Suddenly Clarence became defensive, something I hadn't seen in him before. He flailed his arms like flags in the wind.

"Well...well...why do you have to believe...to believe in...in Jesus for...for Him to...to do a miracle for me. It's...it's *my* miracle, *my* miracle...and *my* Jesus."

I couldn't argue with that, or at least I didn't want to.

"Okay. It's your miracle…if that's what it is."

"My mother says it is!" he demanded in a loud monotone.

I really wanted out of this conversation. I was arguing with an angry retard about his religion. Even if he wasn't one of those mean Christians, this wasn't what I had planned, and I wanted to end it. I would agree with his mother.

"Well, then I guess it *is* a miracle. I haven't started my bar mitzvah lessons yet. So what do I know?"

"You don't know…you don't know…Jesus. You don't know *Him*."

It was time to get to the point.

"I guess not. Listen Clarence…I have a question to ask."

"Well…but it is a miracle. Would you like another…another… piece of cake. I'm sorry…another piece?"

He started to calm down. The cake was great, but I was there for more important matters.

"That paper you saw on the first day of class…do you remember that paper?"

"What paper…what…?"

I tried to focus the conversation. I spoke slowly, like Mr. Schott.

"The one with the names, addresses, birthdays…in eighth grade.

"That paper…I do remember that paper. Yes I do remember it."

"Okay. The name is Gwen…"

I realized for the first time that I didn't know her last name. I never thought about it before. At first I didn't care. Then, when she started running away, it still didn't matter. Now for the first time it mattered, and I needed it to ask Clarence the next question. He couldn't possible know the answer. Still, I'd ask it. But he spoke first.

"Gwen Anderson. Gwen…Gwen Anderson…Anderson."

"Are…there any other Gwen's…in eighth grade, I mean?"

"No."

He shook his head back and forth. Clarence always seemed to know a lot more than I expected. So that unusually short answer, for

Clarence, anyway, and the nod settled it. Gwen Anderson was her name. Gwen Anderson. I liked it. Then before I could ask the question, he answered it.

"April 5, 1950, a Wednesday."

"That's Friday!"

He emphatically shook his head no again and rocked to and fro at the same time, like a clown punching bag.

"It's a Wednesday. You ask her mother. It's…it's a Wednesday…a Wednesday…a…"

I stopped him

"No, no! I don't mean that."

He insisted again.

"Wednesday, April 5, 1950."

"No. I mean that's *this* Friday. Her birthday is this Friday. And this is Wednesday. It could have been any time of the year, and it's this Friday! I can get her something. I can wish her a happy birthday. I almost missed it. Wow!"

Clarence got even more excited, so excited he could hardly get his words out.

"It's…it's…it's…a…miracle…a miracle. See…it's a miracle. Are we…are we friends now?"

I tapped his shoulder gently. That was the first time I ever touched him. He stiffened nervously.

"Yes, Clarence. We're friends."

For the first time, I realized that I genuinely liked Clarence. He was harmless, and not just that, he was actually a nice person. At that moment, I didn't so much mind his being strange. I impulsively reached out and gave him a quick hug. It wasn't a pleasant experience. He stiffened again like he didn't know what to do with it, and he continued to sway. But I was being genuine, and I wanted him to know that. After the quick hug, I took his hand and shook it like a pump handle. He seemed to handle that better.

"Do you…do you want to…to play with Legos? I have…I have Legos…a lot of them…lots…Legos.

Over the next few hours, I was introduced to those funny little plastic bricks for the first time. I found out that they were made in Denmark since 1949 and that the newest ones (of which he had a few samples) were made out of something called ABS plastic, which was better than the old plastic. I was amazed that Clarence, a part of the Lower Zoo, would know that kind of thing.

We made structures that looked like houses, cars, and airplanes. His looked better than mine, almost like he had gone to architectural school. The corners were neat and the color patterns were almost hypnotic, the reds and blues swirling around with the yellows and greens. And I had another piece of cake. His mother looked in on us a few times. She had a big smile on her face each time.

I began to feel like Clarence was another little brother, like playing with Billy when we were younger. And I actually enjoyed it. Besides, no one else was around…especially Robey.

I had a lot to think about on the way home. And it wasn't about Clarence. I had noticed daffodils on a yard near the school. I would pick a few of them after school Friday. They were near the curb, which would make it easy. I would buy a nice card Thursday, something at the drug store.

I had never done anything like this before. But the idea of knowing something about Gwen that she didn't know I knew—and surprising her with it—elicited a quiet warmth in my heart like the soothing spring breeze blowing around me. Certainly, I had given birthday cards to my mother, father, and brother. And of course I'd given gifts—baseballs, Colorform sets of the Flintstones and Jetsons, models—to friends and neighbors like Robert Rogers. But I'd never given a birthday card to a girl, let alone one who didn't expect it or didn't know that I knew when her birthday was. This was definitely a whole new experience, and I liked it.

The next few days crept along. When I saw Gwen at school, I gave her a very subtle wave. Of course I couldn't see her expression clearly, and she didn't gesture back. But I had Friday to look forward to, so I tried to be patient. Robey was somewhat quiet those few days and mostly stayed out of my way, except for one huge stinging back slap and an "April Fools, Richman!" on April 4. Did he wait a few days to shock me? Was he confused about what day it was? Did the celebration last the whole month, and could I expect another attack at any time? Who knew.

I ignored Clarence. I really liked him, but he was someone to spend time with and be nice to only when I visited him at his house. I told myself that at least I wasn't mean to him like Robey was. Besides, I only saw him at lunch, and it was easy to stay on the other side of the room. I knew he wouldn't come over to greet me. I had my side, and he had his.

That afternoon, I visited the drug store. It took me almost an hour to choose the birthday card. "Happy number 13 to a wonderful girl," a little cartoon teddy bear exclaimed on the front of the card. The inside said, "Here's a big bear hug...Happy Birthday." His arms were extended and there was a big smile on his little bear face. She had to like that.

I spent an hour that night deciding what to write on the inside next to the smiling bear. After several handwriting tests on scrap paper and various creative drafts, I finally came up with a repeat of Happy Birthday with Gwen at the end and Your friend Jonathan under that.

Finally, Friday arrived. For the first time that I could remember, I gave extra thought to what I would wear. It's not that I never cared.

But I never cared that much. I put on a white dress shirt and black pants. They were at least a little more tapered than my usual ones. Billy stepped out of his room just as I did mine.

"You headed for synagogue?"

"None of your business."

"A school play of some sort?"

I tried to ignore him, but I had to stop him. I pushed him against the wall with a slight shove of my arm.

"Leave me alone."

That didn't stop him.

"A girl?"

That was the last straw.

"Get off my back!"

I pushed him out of the way once again. He smiled tauntingly.

"Have a nice day."

I didn't want to be mean to him. But there was no time for regret. He was just the first minefield in getting out of the house. Mom was next, of course. I quickly ran down the steps and through the kitchen, grabbing a banana while her back was turned.

"Gotta go."

"Wait. You need to eat breakfast."

Before she could see, I was out the door and down the street. I had escaped interrogation. Now all I had to contend with was a few stares. But there were very few. And a response from Gwen before class started made it all worthwhile. Her head turned exactly my direction as if to say, "You look nice today."

What a breakthrough! I wanted to tell her, "I dressed this way for you," but of course I didn't say anything. My heart sped up in my chest. This was the first day in a long time that I was looking forward to. It flew by on the wings of romantic anticipation.

The bell rang. School was over. As we poured out through the heavy front doors, the sun spilled onto our faces, except for Gwen. Hers was still hidden from the light by twisted strands of hair. I followed her from a distance. The buses pulled out and passed me. I knew some of them would catch up to me as they dropped kids off. But for now I was almost alone with Gwen, except for a few kids trudging to their various homes, books in hand and back packs in tow. I kept my distance, quickly grabbing a few daffodils from the front yard of that house.

As we approached the street before Gwen's house, I sped up, reaching her at the street corner. She was wearing a thin, grey jacket that was well-worn. But it was a glamorous mink coat to me. I tried to steady my breathing and hoped she couldn't hear my heart, which was beating rapidly from a combination of fast walking, extreme nervousness, and excited expectation. Suddenly, she turned to me.

"Well? What do you want?"

That was not a good beginning. I could see I startled her.

"Umm…"

She could see the flowers and the card. There was no turning back.

"Umm, Gwen? Happy birthday."

I reached out my hand and gave her the flowers first and the card next. She stood awkwardly, holding both of them.

"How did you know it was my birthday?" she asked suspiciously.

I didn't have a ready answer other than the truth, so that's what I told her.

"Clarence Carlson from the Lower Zoo told me. He knows everyone's birthday. It's part of his being retarded…sort of."

She backed up like I was pulling the wool over her eyes, which were of course already covered.

"Why should he know it, especially if he's retarded?"

I would have asked the same question before I met Clarence. I had to say something to her. Of course, I didn't know the answer either. I only knew what I saw at Clarence's house.

"Well…it's a long story. He knows what *day* everyone was born on, too. I don't know. You were born on a Wednesday. He remembers things, crazy things, especially when he sees them on a piece of paper, or…"

I paused. I had to get the focus off Clarence.

"Look, I just wanted to surprise you and wish you a happy birthday. Okay?"

"That's...that's..."

I braced myself.

"So nice of you. But...what do you want me to give *you?* What do you want from *me?*"

"I don't know. Like, thank you, maybe?

From what I could tell, she was looking right at me.

"Well then...thank you. It's the nicest thing anyone's ever done for me. Really, the nicest thing. Thank you. May I open the card?"

"Sure."

This was going a bit better. She opened the card and read the simple salutation like it was Shakespeare.

"Happy Birthday...your friend, Jonathan. Look at that little teddy bear. He's *so* cute."

I could almost see tears forming in her eyes. Then suddenly she turned to leave.

"I've got to go. Thanks again. That was very nice. I've got to go now."

I watched her walk away. I had to stop her. What could I say?

"Wait. No, don't leave. Please...here, let's sit on the curb over there. Please don't just leave again...please."

She was surprised at my plea, and this time she complied. Without saying a word, she chose a spot near the corner where the curb was a bit higher and sat down.

"I can't stay long, maybe five minutes."

I sat down. I knew I had only a short time to ask her anything I wanted.

"Why do you wear your hair like that?"

"Don't you like it?"

"No. No, I don't. It hides your beautiful face."

I began to blush, and she began to laugh. I'd never heard her laugh before, and it made my heart jump. It was a high laugh, a giggly laugh, a wonderful laugh. And it was a total surprise.

"You're funny."

She playfully bumped shoulders with me. I liked her teasing me. But she hadn't answered my question.

"Why do you wear it like that?"

She cupped her hand over her mouth and whispered.

"It's a secret."

"A secret? But everyone can see your secret."

She became serious, insistent, no longer whispering.

"No they can't! It's not the hair. No one knows, not my mother, no one."

"Well…you can tell me. I promise I won't tell."

She shook her head insistently.

"You will."

"I won't."

She repeated herself.

"You will."

"I won't. I won't tell anyone. I promise."

For the first time, she seemed to almost plead.

"You'll hate me. I don't want you to hate me."

All at once, like a storm coming in without notice, she began to weep and shiver just like the day I saw her face for the first and only time.

"I won't hate you. I promise."

"I don't believe you," she whined.

"I promise."

She whispered again, cupping her hands over her mouth like before.

"And you won't tell anyone…ever…never?"

I got close to her ear and whispered back.

"I promise."

"You'd be the only one I ever told. I'm never telling anyone else, ever."

"I promise. I swear."

I couldn't believe Gwen was about to tell me something she'd never even told her mother. I was glad I gave her the card and the flowers. I was glad we were talking. I felt grown up, like a man on a mission.

Then she pulled back her hair all the way and turned her head to the side. I had forgotten just how pretty she was. Even her ears were perfect.

"See that?"

"Your face? Now I do. I couldn't before."

"No, silly. Do you see that mark?"

I had to look carefully, but I did see a little reddish spot on her neck just behind her ear.

"Yeh. It's nothing. You can hardly see it. You hide your face about that?"

She became impatient.

"It's part of the secret. Guess the rest."

I didn't have a clue, but I guessed anyway.

"A bug bit you?"

"No. That's not it."

I didn't want to play twenty questions.

"I don't know. I can't guess. You look fine. You should change your hair. That's all I know."

She got really close to my ear and whispered like there was a big crowd around us.

"Someone touches me."

I whispered back in her ear again.

"Well, that's better than hitting. Just ask my brother Billy. He doesn't scream when I touch him, only when I give him a good whack…which hasn't been for a while. But I did kind of push him this morning. We don't hardly even hang out anymore, which I feel bad about."

She stood up and I followed. Then she looked straight in my direction.

"You don't understand."

"Understand what?"

"That's okay. You're a very nice boy. I like you. I have to go now."

I had to stop her. I wanted to spend more time with her. I pleaded back, putting my hands together and begging.

"Don't go. Please. Help me understand. Please. I'll listen."

"No."

"Why?"

She buried her face in her hands.

"You'd hate me," came her muffled response.

"I won't hate you."

She looked up and responded soberly.

"You'd tell."

"I won't tell."

"Promise?"

We were there again. I just nodded this time.

"Okay. My stepfather…"

She got close to my ear and whispered again.

"He touches me. I don't like it. I don't want him to. I hate it."

I had no example to summon up, no one I knew. But all at once I understood that a man was doing something to her that he shouldn't be doing. I was almost speechless.

"Oh."

I just stood there.

"You hate me now. I can see it."

"I don't hate you. Why should I hate you? I would never hate you…never."

Though it wasn't by any means hatred, a thought did flash through my mind that, if I would have spoken it in full sentences, might have sounded something like this:

"It's because she's in the Upper Zoo. The girls in Robert Rogers' class don't have this happen, grown men touching them and doing things to them, whatever they are. They're just girls with pink phones and pink book bags and crushes on boys like Robert Rogers. I wish I

wasn't in the Upper Zoo. I wish I didn't know Gwen, and Clarence…
and Robey. I hate the Upper Zoo. I hate school. And I hate…"

All that lasted about a millisecond. And then I was sad for her, I
was worried about her, and I felt a warm feeling about her deep in my
heart…and I wanted to protect her.

"Does he…does he hurt you in some way? I mean, is he hurting
you at all?"

"Yes."

She looked down and bowed her head again.

"Yes. Yes, he is. He hurts me, Jonathan. He hurts me. That's the
secret."

She started to cry again uncontrollably. I felt a dull pain in the pit
of my stomach. Then she grabbed my hand with both of her hands
and squeezed it hard while she shivered again. She made no attempt
to wipe her tears, which were soaking the hair covering her eyes.

I had a lot of questions like, "Why don't you tell your mother?" and
"Can't you just run away from him?" But all I could say was, "I would
never hurt you…ever. I'll keep your secret. I wish I could beat him up.
But…I won't tell. I promise."

"Promise?"

"Promise."

The bus turned the corner, and headed our way. She dropped my
hand.

"I've got to go. I've got to go now."

"Wait!"

She got up, grabbed her books with the flowers and card, and
quickly ran away without once looking back. I looked at the bus as it
passed, headed for its corner stop, and saw Robey's face staring at me
out of the back window. I grabbed my books and started the long walk
home.

# CHAPTER 14

I KNEW I HAD TO keep Gwen's secret. When I got home, I passed by Mom and Billy in the kitchen and headed right for the refrigerator to put something substantial in my mouth so I wouldn't have to talk to anyone about anything. Mom turned toward me just as I was stuffing myself with half of a medium size banana.

"I've told you over and over, don't take such a big bite. You'll choke yourself to death."

Then she cocked her head to the side like a curious pet and looked at me quizzically.

"Why are you wearing that dress shirt and those dress pants?"

"Hmm…hmm. Hmm…hmm."

After my mumbled response, I immediately fled to my room…but not quickly enough to miss Billy saying to her, "I asked him the same thing this morning."

Just outside my room, I tossed the peel in a not very appropriate living room trash can. I shut my bedroom door behind me with my other hand. Finally I was alone.

"I told you not to throw fruit in the living room trash can!" sounded in the distance, muted by the door. I didn't respond.

Now I could process the afternoon. Why was I the only one to hear Gwen's secret? Why me? Why did she say she only had a few more minutes? And how did she get that mark? Did he hit her or burn her? No, it didn't look like a burn. What in the world was it?

I was sure of one thing. Whatever he was doing, he was hurting her. And I couldn't get it out of my mind. Maybe he was hurting her now. Maybe she had to leave me on the street because he wanted to hurt her some more and if she didn't let him, worse things would happen. I imagined that he put her in a cage, like Pinocchio, so he could hurt her whenever he wanted. Did he pinch her somewhere or scratch her? Just where did he touch her? I didn't know hardly anything about girls, but I did know a few places where it would be wrong if he did. And I couldn't rescue her. I couldn't tell anybody. That was my promise, and I was bound to keep it.

I did have pleasant thoughts of her saying, "That's the nicest thing anyone's ever done for me," and "Look at that little teddy bear. He's so cute." They repeated over and over in my mind. And I could see her tears soaking her straggly hair. For short seconds I had those other feelings about the whole thing being part of what I hated about the Upper Zoo. But then the new feelings crowded out the old and increased until they were stronger.

I went to bed early that night. It had been a big day, as exciting as it had been. And I was tired.

On Monday morning I didn't have to hide from Mom or avoid Billy. My clothes were unremarkable. There was nothing to discuss. Fortunately, they never asked about the clothes I wore Friday. But I noticed that Mom looked very sad. I could see it in her eyes. They were red like they were when President Kennedy died. She tried to keep her back turned to me, but she had to get milk out of the refrigerator and cereal from the cupboard. She tended to look away. But I could see the sadness not only in her eyes, but also in the turned down corners of her mouth.

Billy was unusually quiet, especially since he was eating his cereal and not even reading the box. Instead his eyes were focused on the frosted flakes. But then he looked up at Mom, and made an unusual request.

"Mom, can I get you anything?"

She responded in a monotone. "No, Billy. Just get ready for school."

He stood up.

"Are you okay?"

She shut the refrigerator and walked over to him.

"No, I'm not Billy. But I will be. Don't worry about me. I just don't feel so well. You get ready for school."

That was the most unusual thing said so far on this unusual morning. Normally Mom put on the best face she could for our sakes, even if things weren't going well. Her response prompted an even more unusual response from Billy, especially since he knew that skipping school was reserved for those high fevers and nothing else.

"I'll stay with you today, Mom. I can miss one day of school. I'll help you."

"No Billy." Then she said, "Come here."

He drew close to her and she gave him such a long, huge hug that I thought he would miss the bus, and I would too just watching them. Of course, I knew that he knew what he had told me about Dad…at least what he *believed* he knew. But she didn't know he knew…if there was anything to know. At least I didn't think she did. And I was sure she didn't know what I knew…or possibly knew.

I just stood there and stared at them. And suddenly without warning the deepest widest darkest sadness I had ever known swept through me from somewhere deep in the bottom of my stomach. I couldn't tell quite why it came just then. But now *I* was sad. I was profoundly sad, and tears started to form. I had to leave before I started crying, or others might notice later. And that's just what I did…even before their hug ended.

Suddenly, I was out on the sidewalk walking toward the bus stop, feeling like I was in a depressing movie about a sad family. I couldn't hear the spring sounds, the birds, or the breeze. I couldn't even hear the bus as it came down the street and the screen door as Billy ran out of the house…just thick silence.

When I got to school, I was still sad. My head, which had been leaning in its usual place during the bus ride, was cast down as I walked through the hallways, so at first I passed by Gwen without noticing her. But an odd, strange, sweet sense gently invaded the sadness, like the scent of roses I might pass by in a garden. That's when I lifted up my head for the first time and noticed what everyone else was now observing…the loveliest face in the school in radiant, full bloom.

It was indeed Gwen. She had the cutest haircut I'd ever seen in my thirteen short years. It wasn't so much in bangs as it was combed over. The curls were somehow tamed, perfectly framing her smiling face and playfully dancing over her ears. It rested on her shoulders in a regal flourish. She actually *did* look like a brunette Sandra Dee, only prettier…and glowing.

In fact, I thought she might be the most beautiful girl I'd ever seen…ever in my whole life. Her old, faded brownie dress without the award patches just made her face look that much lovelier. I couldn't stop staring. Now it was she who blushed. And her nose wrinkled as her eyes connected with mine.

"What?" She said it with a sprite little laugh, not like she had the day before when she saw me on the street. I was speechless.

"You're…you're…"

I just couldn't say it. There were too many other kids around. It would be too embarrassing to state the obvious, even though I encouraged her with the word just a few days before.

Then the bell rang and we were in our seats. Mr. Garner began the day's lesson. He was calling on kids in front of me and behind me. But I found I couldn't turn around. I couldn't look at Gwen. And I couldn't risk her looking back. I just sat there wondering if her new haircut had anything to do with me.

I looked to my side and noticed that others were looking back, especially a few of the boys. Marcus in particular was giggling and gaining the attention of the boy in the next seat. He started pointing back to where Gwen sat, mouthing "Wow!" I hated him more than ever. His sloppy, fat appetite repulsed me. His gawking at Gwen sickened me. The secret of her beauty that only I had known was on display for even someone as disgusting as Marcus to see. I wanted to go over and punch him in the face.

Suddenly, it felt as if a ray of heat was focused on the back of my neck from behind me but from the other side of the room. Someone was staring at me. And it wasn't Gwen. It was someone else. I could sense it, like I sensed the sweet presence of something like roses before class. Only this was a different sense, a troubling sense. Who or what was it?

I ventured a quick glance since I knew Gwen was on my other side. There was Robey, piercing me with his threatening eyes, angrier than ever, ready to pounce. What had I done *this* time?

I couldn't concentrate during the rest of the class. Molecules and math equations were jumbled into an incomprehensible tangle of words and concepts. Mr. Garner was in rare theatrical Upper Zoo form, but it didn't matter. I didn't get any of it. When the bell rang, I headed quickly for the lunchroom. But Robey, Michael, and Ted caught up with me in the hallway before I could turn the first corner.

"Come here!"

Robey grabbed me with his long arms and handed me over to the iron filings, who dragged me out of a side door and into the spring sunlight.

"Now…what were you doing with Gwen yesterday?"

"Nothing…I…?"

"Liar!"

He had never really hit me or punched me, just slapped me on my back jokingly, or squeezed my hand hard to make a point. This was different. He hit me hard in the stomach, and I was too surprised to tighten the muscles. I went down as Michael and Ted started kicking the same area. My heart was racing wildly. Could this be happening to me? I had an overwhelming feeling that I needed to throw up. The pain was intense. I couldn't breathe. Suddenly Robey gave the command.

"Stop! All right. Enough."

He called them off like obedient dogs. They gave another quick kick or two.

"Enough! Jerks. Stop!"

I looked up as he stood over me.

"Okay. You don't talk to...no...even look at...Gwen Anderson. Capiche?"

I was getting my breath back and the pain was slowly subsiding. But my heart was still racing. I got one word out.

"Why?"

"It doesn't matter *why*. I warned you about Clarence. And see what happened in that assembly with Kirkpatrick? I'm warning you again. You stay away from the ugly slut."

"Sl...sl...slut?"

The word cut me. But he went right on.

"You heard me."

"It's a free country Robey. You can't..."

"Is it? Then feel free to get a worse beating next time. You stay away! Any other person is fine, but not those two. It's like that story about Adam and the tree. You stay away from those two and I won't bother you. You're smart enough to do that, right Richman? Now go eat lunch...if you can keep it down. Pick him up!"

Michael and Ted pulled me to my feet and pushed me through the door and back inside. I walked slowly to the lunchroom, but I felt too nauseous to eat or even to think. Deep fear mixed with sudden fury coursed through my veins. I entered the lunchroom and sat in my usual place, shaken but fuming. How dare Robey treat me that way! But no one seemed to notice. Out of the corner of my eye I could see Gwen. She was sitting next to a few girls, more engaged in conversation than I'd seen her before. I looked away.

When the final bell rang, I didn't think such a horrible day could possibly get worse.

I didn't want to go home. I wanted ice cream. I rarely resorted to food for comfort. But the warm spring breeze and fragrant blossoming trees stimulated nostalgic feelings about ice cream cones on warm summer afternoons, and now that the nausea had subsided, I was ready for a total escape from the oppression of Robey's violent intrusion.

How could I have ever craved his attention and valued his friendship? He was everything I didn't like about the Upper Zoo... just one in a group of caged animals with whom I was trapped. Some animals were nicer than others. Some were prettier. But all of them belonged in one zoo or the other. And I was on that elevator stuck between grades eight and nine, thrown in with the filthy animals.

Or maybe I wasn't just thrown in with them. Maybe I was *one of them*, just another animal stuck in the cages of the Upper Zoo, on display for everyone else in the school to see.

I didn't want to think about it anymore. So I thought instead about whether I was going to get the butter pecan or the vanilla fudge. When I decided on butter pecan, I then meditated on which cone I would choose. Would it be cake or sugar? Furthermore, since I had a quarter in my pocket, I had the luxury—and I was in the mood for luxury—of getting the twenty-cent cone with sprinkles...or jimmies, as we called them. Would it be chocolate jimmies or multicolored? Finally, I decided on a sugar cone with chocolate jimmies. Even in appearance they went well with butter pecan...very classy.

The drug store was among several shops in a small strip about a mile from both the school and my house and near center-of-town buildings like the library and police station. I entered as the bells over the door jingled. Behind the fountain stood Randy, as if he was waiting for me to come along. Randy was always there. He was middle-aged, maybe 55, balding, with a friendly face and thin mustache, and he loved kids. He knew everyone in the neighborhood and always made good on the certificates for free ice cream cones we received when we were sick or on our birthdays. But this day I had to spend my own money.

"What'll it be, Jonathan, the butter pecan or the vanilla fudge? Cake or sugar cone?"

"Butter pecan in a sugar cone, Randy…and chocolate jimmies."

"The big time, eh Jonathan? Okay."

He scooped an extra big dip from the large round cardboard container behind the glass display and then dipped that carefully in a bucket of jimmies behind the counter. Then he wrapped the cone in a napkin and exchanged it for the quarter, giving me a nickel back from the register. I pocketed it and thanked him. As I left the store, the bells above the door jingled again.

On the sidewalk, I proudly eyed my as yet uneaten and slowly melting cone. This was not a time to think of Robey, Gwen, Clarence, or anyone. This was a time to…

As I stepped across the alley a half a block from the drug store, I saw out of the corner of my eye what looked like a red sports car, a Thunderbird convertible to be exact, with the top down. I quickly ran to the other side of the alley. Suddenly, I felt the cone become very light in my hand. I looked down to see my uneaten scoop of ice cream, complete with jimmies on top, already gathering dirt and with ants headed toward it. The knowledge that I wasted the ice cream and the experience of tasting it, along with twenty cents, made me want to rage at the world. But I soon forgot about the ice cream.

I peaked into the alley from behind the building wall and saw Dad sitting not fifteen feet away from me in the passenger seat of the red sports car, with someone who looked at least half the age of Mom. What's worse, she bore a close resemblance to the magnificent Tuesday Weld from TV's Dobie Gillis of a few years earlier, and on whom, like Sandra Dee, I secretly had a crush.

My father hadn't seen me. I just stood there frozen like my now deceased ice cream cone as he gave her a quick kiss on the mouth and then left the car. I saw that he was headed my way and slinked back, then ran down the street with my heart pounding furiously. When I looked back, I saw that he had gone the other way, the direction of the drug store. He still hadn't seen me. I wouldn't have known what to do if he had.

On the way home, and without the numbing comfort of the ice cream cone, various emotions rose up in me...all of them angry ones. Now I was convinced this was the worst day in my life.

# CHAPTER 15

CAGED WAS THE PERFECT TERM for it. And there seemed to be no escape. The Upper Zoo was only the beginning. As I lay on my bed that night, I listed in my mind all of the areas I was trapped.

There was the Upper Zoo itself. The animals surrounded me, and the bars held me captive. Every day I faced the shame, the disgrace, and the lunacy of these defective creatures.

In particular, there was Robey. He was the rabid tiger, or maybe lion, and I was defenseless. His two friends were like weasels serving their master. And I was his prey. I never knew when he would pounce.

There was Gwen. I couldn't tell her secret to anyone. And I couldn't speak to her or see her, or the lion would pounce on me.

There was Clarence. I couldn't see him either. I knew the consequences if I tried to. But even apart from Robey, I wondered whether Mom was right. Perhaps we shouldn't be friends.

Finally, there was Dad. I couldn't tell Mom what I knew. And now I saw his…I shuddered as I let the term into my consciousness… girlfriend. I hated him. But I couldn't tell him why. And he was never home long enough for me to talk to even if I could.

I could feel the stress in the pit of my stomach. In the past, it was about things like not having my homework done. But this was different. This was more confusing. And it kept me up most of the night.

The next day at school was torturous. Three hours of sleep gave me the equivalent of a drunken stupor, and I quickly developed a sleep-as-you-sit technique. I drifted in and out of consciousness before lunch and even more after lunch, when my blood sugar rose. And no one noticed that I was holding my head up with the palm of my right hand. I felt the agony of quiet twilight sleep right in the middle of class.

It was somewhere between my sleeping and waking state that I decided to visit Clarence that afternoon. There is a recklessness in the unconscious that the clear mind suppresses.

As I roamed silently toward the larger trees and houses after school, the warm air and breeze awakened my senses to the reckless danger. But my mind was settled, and so I proceeded. I figured Robey was probably in another part of town headed home on the bus, but even if he wasn't it didn't matter. All caution was cast to the spring breeze. And suddenly the stone walkway to Clarence's house lay before me.

The cookies were even better than before. They were warm, having just been baked. The welcome was just as warm. Clarence's mother was very glad to see me. She received me like a valiant fighter for the resistance, and I was whisked without delay to the dining room, where Clarence seemed like he had been waiting since my last visit.

The Legos were strewn over the rug, and I was invited to partake in the constructive ceremony like a privileged visitor to the headquarters of an unpopular ruler. Between us, we built two jets, a fort, and several houses in various shapes. I worked on mine, and he worked on his. He pressed one Lego onto another with his stubby fingers…never looking up, content to say nothing, designing masterpieces of color and shape.

But I wasn't content. There were several areas in which I was bound to remain silent, especially concerning Gwen. But there was one area I felt strangely compelled to bring up.

"So…"

He finally spoke, still not looking up.

"More cookies? They're good…the cookies…really good."

"Yes. The cookies are good."

"Very good. They're *very* good. *Very.*"

I was bound to agree.

"Yes. Very."

"Not just very. *Very* very."

He was taken with his own humor and giggled in his own strange way. His laughter was rhythmic like a robot, like his consistent rocking. I was bound to agree again.

"Yes, they are. Clarence?"

"Do you…do you…do you like my jet?"

He held his cluster of Legos up proudly and rocked back and forth, which created an unusual flying pattern.

"Yes. Yes I do. Clarence?"

Clarence wasn't one to respond with a word like what. He just kept playing.

"Clarence?"

Nothing again. I just started right in.

"Do you like your father?"

His answer was uncharacteristically short.

"No. But…I…I…love him though…love him."

I didn't pay attention to the last part.

"Why? I mean, why don't you like him?"

"He's…he's…mean."

"Why's he mean?"

He still didn't look up, and he didn't answer. So I expressed myself.

"Well, I don't like my father either."

He continued to add one Lego to another. I continued.

"He has another woman. I saw him kiss her in the alley next to the drug store, where Randy is…in a fancy sports car."

"I…I…like Randy. I…I like the ice cream cones…the cones…ice cream…he…remembers birthdays…like me…like I do…like me…like I remember them."

I knew that Randy just had to reach into a file and check the birthdays for the day. He didn't really remember them like Clarence did. As I expected, he didn't respond to my comment about my father. So I decided to give up going further with my questions.

"I like Randy too. Nice man, good ice cream."

Then after what seemed like hours or days, but was only a minute or two…

"That…that…that's mean of him…kissing that woman…not nice to your mother…not nice…not…"

"No…or to me, either."

"No…no…or to…you…to you."

He had heard me. We seemed to finally be connecting. Then he finally ventured, "My father…he hit me…he hit me, and it made big red things…big red…marks…big red marks. It hurt."

I remembered that strange mark on Gwen's neck, whatever it was. How many fathers did things like that?

"I'm sorry."

He rocked and worked without looking up. That made his next words even more surprising.

"You hurt too. I know. I know because…because…my…my father has…a girlfriend."

He paused, and then spoke again.

"He even married her. He…he married his girlfriend…married… her."

Then he said with all the emotion his flat expression could summon up, "Fathers…sad fathers…sad."

Inside, I agreed—Clarence's father, Gwen's stepfather, *my* father.

"Fathers!" I repeated after him. "I hate them."

He swung his head wildly in a sign of disapproving disagreement. "No. No!"

His short answer surprised me. I didn't know what to say. Then still without looking up, one hand let go of the Lego jet he was holding and pointed up.

"He...He isn't bad...*The* Father. He isn't."

I knew he was talking about another one of his gods. *The last time it was Jesus. Now it was this Father. Next it would be the Holy Ghost,* I thought. I knew about that from marriage ceremonies I'd seen on TV shows.

"He...He...is...love."

"I guess he is. Look..."

"You don't...you don't know...that's okay. Do you want another cookie?"

"No, thanks."

Then he stopped rocking and looked up at the ceiling.

"Charity suffereth long, *and* is kind; charity envieth not; charity vaunteth not itself, is not puffed up, doth not behave itself unseemly, seeketh not her own, is not easily provoked, thinketh no evil; rejoiceth not in iniquity, but rejoiceth in the truth; beareth all things, believeth all things, hopeth all things, endureth all things."

There was that voice again, the Psalm 23 voice. It was like another person, like an announcer inside him or something. Who knew where in the Bible that came from, if it *was* from there? Wherever it came from, I didn't understand why he said charity. I thought charity was doing something for someone you felt sorry for because they were like Clarence.

Maybe I was the person the speech was about. After all, my mother said Clarence was somebody to feel sorry for. Only I didn't feel sorry for him this day. I felt something I'd felt the last time I was there, only more so. I felt friendship.

"He wasn't kind...and...and...he was mean. But..."

He started rocking again and pointed in the air, making little circles with his fingers in the process.

"...He isn't. Remember that. Remember that, remember...

"Okay, I will," I said to change the subject.

"Tell your father...tell him...tell him...He isn't...*He* isn't like that. If I could tell my father...if I could tell him...I would. My mother says I can't. Oh well. Another cookie?"

I left Clarence's house with a napkin full of five warm chocolate chip cookies in my hand. If I lost the ice cream cone, at least I had these to comfort me in my distress. By the time I got home, the cookies had disappeared and the napkin was stuffed in my pocket.

Billy was sitting in the kitchen eating his own cookies, which weren't as good as the ones I'd been eating, being Oreos. Still, I grabbed one off his plate as I gave him a directive.

"Come into my room. I want to talk to you."

"What'd I do now?"

I gestured and walked out of the kitchen without looking back.

"Just bring your Oreos with you and come into my room."

"All right. I'm coming."

I went upstairs and waited for him in my room. Cautiously, he entered.

"Close the door and sit down."

He sat down on my bed. I sat on my desk.

"Yeh?"

"Don't get crumbs on my bed. I saw them...together."

I could tell he knew what I was talking about. But he didn't let on.

"I'm not. I've got a napkin. Who?"

"You know who. Them."

"Oh."

He sighed as I continued.

"He kissed her in that car...that sports car. He kissed Marilyn Monroe."

"Where?"

"Who cares where? In the alley next to the drug store."

With one hand he pressed his glasses to his nose nervously while he downed a half an Oreo with the other. He responded with his mouth full.

"I see."

"What we should do?"

After swallowing, he gave his usual word of wisdom. Immediately, I wondered why I even said anything.

"Nothing."

"Nothing? How can you say nothing? I *saw* them. He *kissed* her!"

"Mom has to do something. We can't."

I didn't know where he got that idea. Maybe it was in that Thomas Edison book. And even though I'd never admit it, I knew he was right. But I had words of wisdom myself.

"Look…maybe it's time we tell Mom we know."

"I told her already."

"What?"

I was shocked. I couldn't believe Billy already talked to her about Dad. Now I knew I would have to tell her I actually saw him with Tuesday Weld. I wasn't looking forward to that. Billy, cookies all gone, got up and headed for the door.

"Okay. Can I leave now?"

"No, Billy."

"Why not?"

I blocked his path.

"I want to ask you something else."

"Yeh? What is it?" he asked flatly.

I could tell he was still aloof because I hadn't been treating him the way I used to. He was hurt, and it made me feel badly. But things weren't the way they used to be. Everything changed when I entered the Upper Zoo. I knew we couldn't be friends like before. He was in regular school and I was in the Upper Zoo. That made all the difference. Still, I had something I wanted to ask him.

"You said Clarence was artistic."

"I said *autistic,* not artistic."

"Whatever. So what does that mean?"

I hated to ask him anything else, but he obviously knew more than I did on the subject. Still, he admitted with a shrug that he didn't know everything.

"I'm not a doctor. I'm not sure."

That made me feel good. But of course, he didn't stop there.

"But I read a few things when I saw that word used somewhere about Edison."

"Forget Edison."

"Well...I think it means that you can't talk and listen and be like a normal person. Everything seems different if you're autistic."

Anyone who knew Clarence knew that. I shook my head disapprovingly like my mother would.

"That doesn't explain anything, stupid! Thanks a lot."

"I told you, I'm not a doctor! I don't know where it comes from, and I don't think they do either. I know it makes people act a little strange, and some of them know things other people don't."

That caught my attention.

"Like knowing right away what day a certain date was on?"

"Yeh, like that...and like playing piano the first time you sit down, and memorizing a whole page when you just look at it...stuff like that. Some people call those people idiot savants or something."

"I understand the idiot part. But what's a savant?"

He shrugged again.

"I don't know. I think it's a French word or something."

"Right. That shows what *you* know. What he does is *not* being an idiot."

I don't know why I felt I had to come to Clarence's defense, but Billy simply agreed and defended him along with me.

"No, probably not. He's not an idiot. They just call it that."

"Okay. Thanks. Well, you can go now."

He reached up and tapped my shoulder.

"Jonathan?"

"What?"

"I think Clarence is pretty sensitive. I mean he...well, it may not seem like it, but I think he feels things. You know what I mean?"

I quickly stared him down, making my short response sound as offended as I could.

"No!"

"I mean...you shouldn't hurt him...I mean, his feelings."

Now I was really angry. I got in his face.

"Why would I hurt him? I don't hurt people! I don't do that! You think I don't know that?"

"I'm just saying..."

"Just leave me alone."

I knew I was hurting Billy's feelings, but what he said really bothered me. Typically, he continued rubbing it in.

"If you're going to be his friend...be his friend. He probably doesn't have any other friends."

"I told you, get out...and take your crumby napkin with you!"

I picked it up off the bed and threw it at him.

"You're mean, Jonathan."

"I *am not!* Just get out."

He left without a further word and shut the door after him.

# CHAPTER 16

THE LAST MONTH OF THE school year always breaks down. The teachers act like the surrendering army of a conquered nation. The rules and restrictions dissipate, and the stream of regular homework thins to a trickle.

If that was true in regular class, it was even more the case in the Upper Zoo. The breaks were longer. The special sixteen-millimeter films, outings, and breaks increased.

Along with the loosening of the regular regimen came the loose, short sleeve cotton shirts, khaki pants, and short haircuts of the 8H boys, and the loose, light, short sleeve blouses and pageboy and Jackie Kennedy hairdos of the 8H girls. This was true of Robey, and the iron filings, and the girl with the imperfect nose who sat on the tack...and even Marcus.

Gwen was no exception, though she was indeed exceptional. She was part of the Upper Zoo, yet she was now in a class by herself. And the closer we came to the end of the year, the more exceptional she became. She seemed to be in full bloom in the springtime, like the daffodils I gave her, and I had a hard time taking my eyes off of her. But I trained myself to do just that. Robey was never far away.

So when something was different and troubling about her during the afternoon class, I didn't notice it at first anymore than I had noticed her new haircut earlier. In fact, it was Mr. Schott who called it to my attention.

"Miss Anderson. Miss Anderson!" he said sternly and slowly.

There was silence. I hesitated to look back.

"Miss Anderson, please take that off," he said in his deliberate whisper.

I had to look back now, even though I knew the eyes of the whole class were already trained on her. I turned my head toward her as subtly as I could, scanning past Robey as I did. Finally, I saw what Mr. Schott was talking about.

"Miss Gwen Anderson, you are not to wear that to class. Please take it off now or go to the principal's office."

Gwen slowly stood up, a dark brown silk scarf covering almost all of her hair and half of her face. I noticed that she had a deep pain in her eyes that I could only compare to Mom's. She walked toward the door as if she were a trapped kitten looking for a way out of a lion's cage.

"I didn't say you could go. Come back here! Where are you going?"

Without turning around to acknowledge Mr. Schott's words, she opened the door and walked out of the classroom. Mr. Schott sighed with frustration.

"Just wait heeerrre," he said, stretching the here.

He followed her out and shut the door. As soon as he left, kids started talking. A few got up and chased each other around the room just because they could. Others sat in their seats and chatted with those seated near to them—that is, all except Robey. He just sat up and stared at the door. The decibel level in the room increased second by second until the Upper Zoo was filled with laughter, shouting, grunts, and various other noises. Robey turned his focus back to the room and stood up authoritatively.

"Shut up! Now!"

The room instantly quieted down at his command. Everyone just froze.

"They're coming back, and no one says a word. *No one!*"

Just as Robey predicted, the door swung open and Mr. Schott came in. Immediately, he began teaching again as he walked from the door to the blackboard.

"Open your books to page 78. Someone read the poem."

Even before someone could volunteer, in came Gwen...without her scarf. I could clearly see the red mark on her cheek. It looked different from the red mark on her neck, redder and a bit raised. She tossed her hair around defiantly and sat in her seat. I could hear whispers in every part of the room.

"Page 78...Richman. Read!"

I opened the book. It fell within a few pages of 78, and I quickly found the page. I had to divert attention from Gwen. I read loud and clear, demanding attention so she wouldn't be embarrassed.

"Whenever Richard Cory went down town,
We people on the pavement looked at him:"

I hesitated for a split second, and then continued.

"He was a gentleman from sole to crown,
Clean-favored and imperial...ly, imperially...slim.
"But still he fluttered pulses when he said,
'Good Morning!'...and he glittered when he walked."

I began to experience the same feeling I had when Mr. Schott read. The words were taking on a rhythmic and descriptive life of their own.

"And he was rich, yes, richer than a king,
And admirably schooled in every grace:
In fine—we thought that he was everything
To make us wish that we were in his place."

I paused again briefly without looking up.

"So on we worked and waited for the light,
And went without the meat and cursed the bread,
And Richard Cory, one calm summer night,
Went home and put a bullet…in his head."

The shock of the last line surprised me more then anyone else. I held and then let go of my final breath. There was silence for maybe five long seconds. Then a slight, short, nasal chuckle broke the mood.

"Mr. Romero…stand up!"

Robey stood hesitatingly. I noticed he was slouching more like a common rebellious teenager. He had never slouched quite like that before.

"Is there something funny about that poem?" Mr. Schott whispered slowly and intensely.

"I don't know…no."

"No sir! I thought Mr. Richman did an admirable job reading it. Don't you?"

I had never been complimented in the Upper Zoo. He had thrown a banana in my cage, and it tasted good.

"I guess so."

"Then what's so funny?"

"Well…"

After the "well," Robey managed to stand straight up and turn the discussion around in a few well-thought out paragraphs. He talked about the jolt the poet intended in the last line, and the social commentary that was hidden in the irony of it. He talked about the nervous state the poet left his hearers with. This was the reason for his nervous chuckle earlier. As I listened, I was convinced that if his comments were part of a paper, he would have gotten an A.

"Very impressive, Mr. Romero. You have saved yourself a trip to the principal's office."

Instantly, Robey rose in my estimation. He wasn't only powerful, intimidating, and dangerous. He was sensitive, maybe more sensitive than Billy said Clarence was. It turned out he *did* have a soul, and that of an artist. *And…we had collaborated.* Two artists had joined forces, and both received high marks. Maybe Robey would view me differently now and treat me with more respect.

This day was going better than most. I almost forgot that bruise on Gwen's face. But that too was somewhat redeemed. After class, I watched as Robey approached her and looked at it. Their eyes clearly connected for a brief moment. That was something I'd never seen before. He seemed almost concerned. She smiled slightly, shyly, as if to say, "Oh well." He walked away, leaving her standing and watching him. I didn't know quite what to make of it. Did I detect real compassion? Was he capable of the real thing? I had only seen him fake it with Clarence's mother. I'd never seen the real thing.

I spent the rest of that day almost completely in my imagination. This happened only rarely, but when it did it occurred with such obsession that little else mattered. Usually it increased until nighttime while I was lying in my bed. Then it ended when I drifted to sleep. In the morning, it was usually gone.

In my imagination, I was always a hero. And the one I was saving was usually a little child in danger or sometimes a girl I knew, though once or twice it ended up being my little brother. But that was when I was younger. Once it was even Mom.

Of course, this day it began with Gwen. She was walking near her house. She seemed unconcerned and unaware of any danger. As the story unfolded, I was watching her from behind a tree. A need, or maybe a desire, to protect her arose in my heart. I had to do something about her situation. In my daydream, I wasn't concerned about keeping our secret. I was only concerned about saving her.

Suddenly, a shadowy man appeared. I played out his appearance and her response to it many ways. He came from behind and startled her. He came out of the house and walked up to her. He watched her from behind a wall. I spied on him as he eyed her threateningly. I tried each scenario over and over. Finally, I settled for the one where he came out of the house.

Here was my chance. I couldn't let him go into the house with her. I had to stop him. I could see that her face was paralyzed with extreme fear. I knew what he would do with her, even though I really sort of didn't. But this wasn't real, so I figured I knew all about it.

I remained in the daydream's trance all afternoon and into the evening. But my family didn't notice. I hid it by pretending I was watching afternoon cartoons that I'd seen a number of times before... Bugs Bunny, Popeye, Tom and Jerry, Huckleberry Hound. I'd never been too interested in them before, and I had no interest in them now. I lay down on the rug in front of the TV staring blankly at the cat chase the mouse. But that just provided cover, as did time spent in my room supposedly doing my homework. Over and over, the shadowy man came out of the house. By the evening, after a quick liver and mashed potato dinner with Mom and Billy, he had grabbed Gwen and was trying to pull her, force her into the house. I caught up with them just outside the front door and pulled him off of her.

Suddenly the scene in my mind's eye changed to the inside of a yellow bus as it was passing by. Robey was on that bus. He saw us out of the window and yelled to the driver, "Stop! Stop the bus!" The bus driver hesitated but Robey insisted, putting up quite an argument. He ran to the front of the bus as it was still rolling and demanded that the driver stop. Then he lurched forward as the bus screeched to a halt and the door opened, running out and toward us.

I was on the ground with the shadowy man on top of me, trying to strangle me. With great effort, I forced him off of me and onto the ground. I could see Gwen, frightened but grateful. She was half inside the doorway, her new hairdo gently tussled over her face. Finally, Robey arrived in time to help me finish the job. We worked creatively together like we had with the poem in Mr. Schott's class. We alternatively punched the shadowy man until he limped away.

"Don't ever come back!"

First I had me saying that, then Robey. I liked Robey saying it better. Robey turned to me, hands outstretched in a congratulatory gesture.

"She's yours. You can talk to her whenever you want. You've earned it."

Gwen approached me with grateful tears in her Sandra Dee eyes.

"Thank you, Jonathan. Thank you so much."

I reached out to her and took her hand.

"He'll never bother you again."

# CHAPTER 17

BY MORNING AND FOLLOWING A good night's sleep, my dream wore off. I didn't even want to repeat any of the scenarios. I'd had enough of my imagination. It was Saturday…a very good time to re-engage the real world. And the best way for a boy of thirteen to engage the real world is on a bike.

My used, chipped, black enamel Schwinn had taken me many miles through winding suburban roads, and today it took me toward the strip of shops where the drug store was. Hand breaks were new to me when my mother bought the bike at a yard sale a few years earlier. But they were second nature now; I only had to remember not to apply both when I was going downhill too fast. Everyone learns that lesson at least once, hopefully not with a result similar to Ben Hur's close call in the chariot race. And of course, unlike Ben's case, with a bike there'd be nothing standing to climb back unto.

The roads were rather flat in that part of town, and I was gently pedaling, coasting toward the drug store for no particular reason. I certainly wasn't ready for another ice cream cone disaster, so I didn't plan to go inside. I just wanted to cruise for its own sake. I felt like the king of the highway as the offices, residential homes, and an occasional storefront drifted by.

Then, out of the very corner of my eye I viewed up on the left the unmistakable appearance of *the* red sports car...the Thunderbird. I never thought much about different kinds of cars, not withstanding the robin's egg blue '57 Chevy model on my bureau. But I knew instantly that this was *her* car, the one I'd seen in the alley. It had to be. And it was parked in front of the dentist's office. I figured she must be in there seeing the dentist.

I passed the office before the thought came to me to go in and see if she really was there. Then I realized that Dad might be in there with her. That made one part of me want to forget it altogether and another part of me want to go in and confront him right then and there in front of her. That part caused me to go back and toss my bike down unceremoniously on the side yard of the office just out of sight of the street. Without giving myself enough time for a second thought, I went up the front steps and into the office. The bell rang as I entered.

There she was, sitting between two other patients, with Dad nowhere in sight. It turned out I was relieved about that. I could fly under the radar. She didn't know who I was, and I knew at least something about her. I noticed she was in pain, which gave me some pleasure. Every once in a while she put her hand up to her cheek. *Good,* I thought. *That's a small fraction of the pain Mom is in because of you.*

I noticed how pretty and young she looked. She had a flawless face, like Gwen's, and what people call a perfect figure. I tried not to look anywhere near her legs, which stood out in her sheer stockings and a rather short, tight black dress. I couldn't figure out what she saw in my father, with his graying and balding hair and kangaroo-like paunch, but it wasn't hard to imagine what he saw in her. I was halfway thinking of approaching her and asking her that very question when a woman in white came from behind the counter and approached me with a clipboard.

"Is this your first time here?"

I didn't know what to do but nod.

"Well, please put your name down here and fill this out. Bring it up and give it to me when you're finished. What time's your appointment?"

"Well, I…I think…it's…"

"11:30?"

"Umm…I think so."

"Well, you're a bit late. I'll let the doctor know you're here when you finish."

She walked away. I sat and stared at the form for several seconds without marking it at all. But I also stared at *her*, sitting there with her Tuesday Weld face and Marilyn Monroe legs. I despised her, and I didn't care if she knew it…not that my hatred registered at all with her. She did look back at me once…rather blankly. Then she walked up to the receptionist and spoke a few short words.

"Will it be long?"

I knew I had to leave. Finally, I considered an exit strategy. I approached the woman in white.

"Oh, I must be in the wrong office."

"There isn't any other dentist's office near here."

"Oh, then it must be in some other part of town."

I endured stares as I returned the board and quickly walked out of the office into the sunlight. The bell on the door called further attention to my exit. But I was just glad to put this ridiculous situation behind me…far behind me. Before I grabbed my bike and rode away, I had to get one look inside the car. After all, it was a convertible, and the glove compartment might hold some secrets worth looking into. I actually ventured to reach out and open it. But it was locked, and a police cruiser was headed down the street. So I quickly grabbed my bike and left for home.

I put my bike in the garage and walked into the house. Immediately, I saw Mom as if she was another woman, and not the mother I knew. She was in the kitchen cleaning up. I figured it was possible she was about the same age as the woman I just saw in the dentist's office. But she looked much older, and much sadder. I saw the lines in her face, the circles under her eyes, the stained apron around her waist, and the worn, brown women's orthopedic shoes on her feet.

Dad's girlfriend was like a movie star. Mom looked like a maid. Her brown hair was bleached to hide the grey, but it showed through anyway. It was sprayed into place and looked like a wig. I had always thought of my mother as youthful, beautiful. But all that was changing. Her back faced me as she stood at the sink in the early afternoon spring light of the kitchen window. She could sense that I was there and spoke without turning around.

"I looked at your last report card a few weeks ago. You're still not applying yourself, according to Mr. Schott."

I hadn't been "applying myself" since second grade, according to every teacher since then. And several times during each year my mother had this little talk with me. This was one of those times.

"You'll have to buckle down next year, whether you're in a special class or not."

*There was another classic phrase... "buckle down."* My response surprised even me. I raised my voice.

"Why will I have to buckle down? I don't see any reason to."

She finally put the dish she was drying down and turned around.

"Jonathan! How can you say that? An education is the most important thing you can have. In today's world, you can't do anything without it. You've got to stop daydreaming and start studying, like your brother does."

I'd heard this speech many times before. But I had a very different speech, though an unprepared one.

"So I can be like *him?*"

"You don't have to be like Billy to do well..."

"I'm not talking about Billy."

She knew who I meant. Still, she pretended not to.

"Well, who are you talking about?"

"You know who."

She paused and leaned against the sink, focusing her eyes on mine for emphasis. I knew what was coming. I'd heard this defense argument many times.

"Your father supports this family, puts a roof over your head, works day and night…"

I rudely cut her off.

"Yeh, yeh, yeh. I know. Day and…*night*…especially night."

"Don't you sass me, young man!"

"I'll be in my room," I said like a business executive leaving a meeting. Actually, I didn't go up to my room. I went up to Billy's and knocked.

"Hey, you in there?"

"Yeh."

I entered.

"I saw her again."

"Who?"

"Oh come on…first Mom about Dad, now you. Who do you think, genius?

He sat up in his desk.

"Where?"

"At a dentist's office."

At this point he got up, a somber look descending from his eyes to his mouth.

"What in the world were you doing at a dentist's office?"

"Getting my teeth cleaned…not really. Who cares? What's the difference? I was there."

"Okay. So?"

I had thought about what I was going to say, and I delivered it with confidence.

"I think we should spy on them…on Dad and her."

"Why?"

"Because…when we accuse Dad to his face, I want the facts. I want her name. I want to know who she is."

Billy started to invoke Saint Edison, which was the last thing I wanted to hear.

"Okay. Well, Edison used a horn to amplify his bad ear. We could gather sound with something like that."

I rolled my eyes and put my hand to my forehead.

"Oh my goodness! Will you *please* stop that nonsense?"

"Well, he recorded sound, right? We could record them somehow."

I realized that this discussion was giving Billy immense pleasure. We could play spy and talk about Thomas Edison at the same time. But I was ready for it to end. Then, suddenly Billy came up with a brilliant idea.

"We need a listening device. That's all we need. Why don't we throw one of our walkie-talkies in the back seat of his car, and one of us ride behind him on our bikes? If he goes to see her, maybe one of them will say something."

"But they're always in *her* car."

"I know that. But maybe he'll say something in *his* car."

I tried to think of the downside before we went any further.

"We'd have to be like a hundred yards or less behind him to hear him. That's pretty close."

"So?"

"Who'll push the talk button down?

He had apparently already thought of that.

"We'll tape it down. That way it'll always stay on."

"If you and your dead friend Tom are wrong, this'll be a big waste of time. And I'll never let you forget it."

He wasn't listening. He was thinking.

"This is the end of the school year when things get loose. We've got plenty of time on our hands. We can plan it carefully."

He had a point. I was starting to get into this now.

"Okay. I'll ride the bike. I'm faster than you."

"That's fine with me. Edison always had his assistants do the manual labor."

"Will you shut up about Edison? Listen, you plant the walkie-talkie in the car. I'll follow him when he leaves the house…if he even comes home tonight."

"You want to do it that soon? I'm game. He's got to come home sometime."

"Don't remind me."

He didn't remind me again later that day, and Dad didn't come home that night until we were both asleep. In fact, it took almost a week to put our plan into effect. And by that time, I was having second thoughts. It seemed like a waste of time to even try it. But Billy was still enjoying the planning, and I played along. I figured it met some kind of childish need in his life. But if we didn't try it or we did and it failed, it was back to the proverbial drawing board.

Finally, Dad came home one night just after dinner, grumbling and mumbling like he usually did. Mom at least made like she was glad to see him and wanted to fix him something. But Billy and I could hear him say he picked up something earlier and that he would have to go out again soon. This was our chance.

Within a half hour he was in his frayed, taupe trench coat and almost out the door. I had to make a quick excuse about picking something up somewhere. Almost all the stores would be closed in the next fifteen minutes or so, so I said I was in a real rush. That part was true. And Mom seemed to think it was reasonable. She didn't say anything in response except, "Be careful." Fifteen minutes earlier, Billy had snuck into the garage and put the walkie-talkie under the front seat near the back passenger compartment. He handed me the other one like we were part of a World War II movie.

"Good luck, old chum."

"Get over it, Billy. This isn't D-day. Does it work?"

I could tell it was coming…Edison again.

"Edison always tested his inventions. Yes it works…at about a hundred feet."

"What? I thought the instructions said a hundred yards."

"Well, they're made in Japan. What do you want? Okay, maybe two hundred feet. You'll find out."

"Oh brother. I don't know. Maybe this isn't such a great idea."

I left through the back door anyway, picked up my bike, stuffed the walkie-talkie in my side pocket, and waited for my father to pull out of the driveway.

Finally, as he put the car in reverse and pulled away, I pulled out and followed under the cover of dusk. Following him was more difficult than I imagined, and I was glad he didn't choose any main roads where he could open up and go faster. Twice I came near to being hit by a car going the other way as I weaved my way forward, trying to follow his black Ford Falcon. And once a horn honked at me from behind. But this didn't seem to distract Dad's attention from what was before him. He was clearly concentrating on his goal.

Then at an intersection near the drug store, he pulled the car into a small parking lot. I should have suspected he would meet her in that area of town. There she was, waiting for him on the sidewalk. I stopped the bike and dropped it quickly as I nervously removed the walkie-talkie from my pocket. I put it to my ear just in time to hear, "What the hell is that noise in the back seat...hey Margaret... don't you look nice tonight, Baby?" Baby? They began to walk to some location where I knew the Thunderbird must be concealed. But I'd gotten what I came for. Her name was Margaret. I got on my bike and pedaled home as quickly as I could.

When I got home I couldn't wait to report the news to Billy. After letting Mom know that the store had closed before I got there, I burst into his room without knocking. He stared at me, surprised and impatient.

"Well?

"Margaret. Her name's Margaret!"

"Margaret. I hate that name."

Then he let out a giddy laugh and jumped up and down several times until his glasses flew off. He caught them deftly with his right hand.

"We did it. We did it!"

Then, for some reason I couldn't quite figure out, I confided in him about Gwen and her secret. Maybe I just wanted to talk about another father, or stepfather, who did rotten things. But whatever the reason, I did it. I broke Gwen's promise. Billy's response was quick and sure.

"You have to tell someone."

"I told her I wouldn't tell anyone."

"You told *me*."

I had to think fast. He was right. But I couldn't leave it at that.

"You're not *anyone*. You're my little brother. And you better not tell *anyone*! Here's your walkie-talkie. You can get the other one later. Of course, the battery'll be dead."

I threw it at him. It bounced off his arm and landed on the floor. But he didn't seem to care. He retrieved it and held it up with great pride, like a prize trophy. He must have felt like I did with Robey when I read Richard Corey...like we were partners who had joined forces.

"Who cares about a stupid dead battery? It's a small price to pay for such a successful mission. If we only had her last name..."

I stopped the conversation.

"That's enough for one night. I'm going to bed."

# CHAPTER 18

THE TRADITIONAL FIVE-DAY COUNT TO the end of the school year arrived with nothing but questions. Would I find myself in the ninth grade Zoo the next year? I hadn't even wanted to ask the question. If I could just get out of the present cage, then freedom over the summer would be its own reward. At least I wouldn't have to go to summer school, and I could put this bizarre year behind me for June, July, and August. Summer vacation always feels like it will go on forever—until, of course, it doesn't.

The first thing I noticed when I walked into the classroom that last week was Gwen's face. The mark was almost gone, which I was very glad to see. And her auburn hair seemed like a glowing halo, shining and vibrant, celebrating her life. Anybody who failed to see that the formerly sad and shamefully hidden child was one beautiful young girl would need the help of extreme lenses. But my reverie was quickly broken by a familiar back slap.

"Hey, Jonathan."

Robey's slap was unmistakable, as was his voice. I was extremely irritated by the shock, but as usual he didn't give me time to respond.

"Richman, you need to spend some time with your old friend Robey Romero…I mean, we need to celebrate the last week in this rotten Zoo. That's why I'm treating *you* to some ice cream served by none other than Randy…just you and me…no Michael or Ted. Capiche?"

"I…I don't know."

He insisted in his towering overshadowing way. It was obvious he hadn't noticed that I'd been staring at Gwen. That was a relief anyway. He continued to insist.

"Meet me there after school. Let's be friends. We're so much alike, you and I. The only smart kids in a very dumb class."

"Well…"

"I'll see you there."

He walked away and took his seat, exuding his usual confidence as the class began. Almost immediately, his words began to have their usual effect of unsettling me and flattering me at the same time. This continued all morning, during lunch, and into the afternoon class. *Were we really alike?* I saw something attractive in his explanation of Richard Cory, in the sincere look he gave Gwen after class, in his quick, clever way of thinking. The old desire to be best friends with this enigma of a boy…the vision of the dual heroes we played in my daydream…these things came back. The beating I took at his hands seemed like an exception that occurred in the distant past and would never occur again. I would meet him for ice cream. We would sit at the drug store counter. We would talk. That couldn't hurt.

I left for the drug store right after school. He arrived a bit later than I did. He walked right up and sat on the fountain stool next to me.

"Randy, two double dip sundaes with double chocolate chip ice cream and hot fudge. Does that work for you, Jonathan?"

On other days it may not have, but on that day I wanted to have what Robey was having. After being served by Randy, who had a particularly full counter that day, I began to eat the slowly melting sundae while Robey spoke in kind gentle tones.

"You're a Jew, Richman. I could tell by the name. Just kidding… *Richman*, get it?"

He caught me mid-spoon. But I tried not to respond. He continued.

"You're one of the good Jews. Somehow, Jonathan, I don't think if you were there two thousand years ago you would have killed Christ. You're a good one. Capiche?"

I was about to say something, but the fudge sauce was not quite ready to cooperate.

"Now the ones with beards and big noses, they're a different story. They're always griping about those six million Jews. That was almost twenty years ago. Jesus Christ, what are they crying about? Plenty of other people are dead."

I knew he was using that name as a swear word. I'd never heard Robey swear before. But that paled next to the nerve he struck when he mentioned beards and noses. Did he know about my Great Uncle Moishe and Aunt Zelda and their strange dress? How could Robey possibly know that? Who could have told him?

"I like you, Jonathan. You're a good man...and I need a good man to be friends with. I want one of my friends to be a Jew...a *good* Jew. You know what?" he declared, slapping the counter. "I want you to meet my father sometime. He doesn't like Michael or Ted. They're too stupid. They belong in the Upper Zoo. You and I don't, Jonathan. My father likes smart people. I think he'll like you 'cause you're a *good* Jew, one of the *good* ones. I think it'll be okay."

Somehow, I knew he meant his father would like me *even though* I was a Jew. Part of me wanted to just leave. But like the overwhelming richness of the ice cream sundae, something about Robey was appealing in spite of everything. And weren't there bad Christians too, like Mrs. Moliver said? Maybe there were bad Jews also. Perhaps Robey was making sense. He leaned over me, almost touching my ice cream with his chin.

"You want to meet my father?"

I nodded mid-bite.

"Good. I'll eat now."

He almost inhaled the half melted sundae in a few spoons full.

"See you later, Jonathan. You're a good friend. I've had a good time. I'll pay."

He *did* pay, putting a dollar bill in Randy's hand, and then walked out. Randy called after him.

"Thank you, Robey. Say hi to the folks. That was nice of him, wasn't it, Jonathan?"

I was almost out of breath from the prior conversation.

"Yes. Umm...yes. That was a good sundae."

"Only the best for my young friends...catch you later."

I staggered out of the drug store like it was a bar and walked down the sidewalk, standing in front of the empty alley. It had all happened so fast, I didn't know quite what to think about it. Was he complimenting me or making fun of me? It seemed as if he didn't like most Jews very much. But he liked *me*. At least it seemed like he did. He wanted to be friends, anyway. *But that's a crazy way to be friends,* I thought.

As I stood outside the drug store, my mental rationalizations began to disintegrate. Somewhere inside me I knew that Robey's father didn't like *any* Jews. And Robey probably didn't either. I wondered, in fact, whether Robey was in fact one of the bad Christians.

I looked toward the alley. Of course, the red T-Bird wasn't there. But a few tears still formed as I stared down the empty alley; tears for Mom, for Billy, even for me...but not for Dad.

That night, those feelings still hadn't subsided. I watched my father as he walked from one room to another, unengaged, mumbling, lost perhaps in the thought of his beautiful girlfriend Margaret, passing regular old Mom in the hallway. She stopped him.

"Stay home tonight."

His answer shocked me.

"Maybe I will. Yes, there's nothing I can't put off to tomorrow, as they say."

She held his arm in her hand.

"Let's take the boys out to eat."

"I don't know…"

"Come on. Let's celebrate the end of the school year with them."

Surprisingly, Dad agreed. We hadn't been out as a family for perhaps two years. He always said it was a "royal waste of money," as he put it. And since Mom knew something was going on, I certainly didn't expect her to be motivated to go out with him. But some slight wind of hope must have blown her way that day, because she suggested it and was glad when he said yes. She actually smiled, which had become rare for her.

She took off her apron, which revealed her full flowered dress underneath. I walked out. I knew I had to talk to Billy about this latest development. I climbed up to the second floor, knocked on his door, and walked in.

"Believe it or not, we're all going out to dinner, including Dad. It was Mom's idea."

"Great. I'm hungry."

I closed my eyes and tightened my fists at my side in utter frustration.

"I can't believe you're thinking about food at a time like this!"

"I generally do that around dinnertime" he smugly responded.

I loosened my fists, but then began to nervously twirl my curls between the fingers of my left hand.

"I don't want to sit at the same table with him."

"If Mom wants to go, we should go…for her."

"Fine. Maybe we should invite Margaret."

He didn't think that was funny.

"Hey, let's forget Margaret for one night. This is for Mom."

"With *him* there?"

"Yes. Let's act as if there *is* no Margaret…like things are like they used to be…when Dad was busy, but not too busy…and Mom was happy, and laughed a lot…and you were nicer to me…before you were in the Upper Zoo."

I sneered at him.

"You idiot. Stop dreaming. Anyway, he was never not too busy."

He just stood there, obviously not knowing what to say next. I knew the ball was in my court. I relented with a long sigh.

"Okay. We'll do this for Mom's sake."

After fifteen long minutes of meaningless comments by Dad while the car all but circled the town, we ended up at a cheap local family restaurant that we hadn't been to in several years. I may have been in fifth grade the last time we darkened the door. It had become run down and unpleasant. The waitresses were rude, and it seemed half the forks were bent. The lettuce was rusty, and the Cokes were flat. But Dad acted as if we were at the Waldorf. He was gregarious and talked constantly about how great the food was.

Mom toasted our school years with iced tea. She said nothing about my last report card. And Dad, who hardly ever confronted me to my face about school anyway, said nothing about the Upper Zoo. A dozen times I wanted to turn to him and say, "Tell us about Margaret, Dad." But of course, I didn't. And I raised my flat Coke with the rest of my family out of respect for Mom. The fact was, I loved Mom and wanted to protect her. I wouldn't have said it quite like that, but those were my feelings. So I went with Billy's advice…for Mom's sake.

Dad actually came home and went right to bed in my parent's bedroom that night. That wasn't something I saw often. But he said he was tired and that was that. I went to bed early too. But I stayed awake thinking about Robey and the ice cream sundae discussion. Somehow, I felt like an unwilling accomplice to a bloody crime.

# CHAPTER 19

THE LAST DAY OF SCHOOL finally arrived. I had no access to the other classrooms, so didn't know exactly what was going on in them. But the noise emanating from our room must have been audible on the other side of the school. I hadn't experienced that kind of mayhem since somewhere in my elementary years, and probably not even then.

Everyone was in the altered chemical state of a sugar fix. And Mr. Garner made no effort to restrain the behavior, as he would have earlier in the year. He totally gave up on the class. They were on top of desks, chasing each other around the room, screaming at one another. I felt like I regressed five years…no, ten. As zoo noises swirled all around me, I could only imagine what Robert Rogers must be experiencing on that same day. It was probably quiet and orderly in his classroom. Could he hear our class as it echoed through the halls and into other classrooms? I'd long since tried to forget what he thought about me since we were separated into our individual fates. But I couldn't help it as I watched the chaos. This was too much.

Of course Robey was above the fray, holding court with the iron filings and a few others around him. The fudge sundae summit still rattled around deep inside me. I realized that I liked him, feared him, and was repulsed by him all at the same time. And I was repulsed at myself for liking him even a little. It seemed like he *made* me like him, which caused me to fear him even more.

I turned to see Gwen sitting and carefully peeling a cup cake. She was above the fray too, in her own way. By this time she had attracted a few girls who wished they were as pretty as she was. But though she laughed and joked with them, it always seemed like the laughter could turn to tears any moment. I had been steering clear of her lately, not only because of Robey's warning, but because I didn't know what to do with my feelings. I admired her from a distance, and I was glad she didn't have any marks on her face, except sometimes one of those funny ones on her neck. But there was no mark even there that last day.

At lunch Clarence boldly came up to me while I was sitting on the other side of the room, catching me off guard, which surprised and unsettled me.

"Last day, Jonathan…last day…and then…will you come over? Come over…today…tomorrow…we could play Legos…ABS plastic Legos…the new Legos…ABS."

I turned red with embarrassment. He was talking about baby toys right in front of everyone. Even Robey could see it. I spoke quietly through my teeth, like a ventriloquist.

"I'm aware that it's the last day, Clarence."

"I know…but…will you come over?"

Something in me just snapped. I spoke out for everyone to hear, staying seated as he rocked rapidly in my direction.

"You're a freak, Clarence…and…and…I can't be around freaks right now, so…"

He just stood there rocking, his eyes darting this way and that. Others may have thought he didn't understand what I was saying, but I knew he did.

"Leave me alone, Clarence. Go away!"

"But…"

"Go away! Now!"

He loped away without looking back. Suddenly, I felt about the most rotten I ever had up until then. I sat there for at least a minute, closing my eyes in an effort to disappear. Then with everyone watching, I went up to get my lunch and passed by him as he sat with the 8G class. I said as quickly and subtly as I could, "Look, maybe I'll see you next week. I'll call you."

His head faced his tomato soup as he spoke. It was obvious I had hurt him.

"My number...my...my...phone number..."

"I'll find it," I whispered as subtly as I could from several feet away.

Robey caught my glance. He was staring at me. But I shook that off and headed for the lunch line.

The next day, I thought I'd feel free from the Upper Zoo. But surprisingly, I didn't. It was as if the cage had opened only to reveal a wider cage. And it felt like there would be no escaping it through the summer, if not through ninth grade.

But I knew Billy wasn't in the cage. And suddenly, I experienced a deep longing to be close friends with him again. When I asked him to hang out with me the next day, he immediately ran to the phone on the living room end table and called one of his school friends to cancel a planned time with him.

"I'm sorry, Andy. I have to do something with my brother," he declared proudly. When he got off the phone he approached me excitedly. He was hopping up and down with his arms going the opposite direction like he was trying to fly.

"What do you want to do, Jonathan? What do you want to do?"

Frankly, I didn't care what we did. I just wanted normalcy. After some deliberation, we ended up going to the movies the next day and seeing a ridiculous Jules Verne movie with some kind of black and white cartoonish look. It was extremely boring, but I was resigned to sitting next to Billy as he explained how Edison thought of each invention that came onscreen before Verne did. This was as close to feeling free from the cage as I was likely to get, and I settled for it.

The next day, since we had no model aircraft in flyable condition, we took an old Frisbee out of a drawer and tossed it around a park near our house. Billy had improved in Frisbee tossing since the year before, and I almost felt like I could hang out with him again and be friends, tossing Frisbees and going to the movies. I didn't need or want anyone else. For Billy's part, he came alive when we were together. He'd been waiting for this focused attention all year. The short time we spent during Christmas vacation had just whetted his appetite. I imagined that none of his peers were able to take much of Edison. And I considered lectures on the subject a small price to pay to be able to have nothing to do with Robey, Clarence, Robert Rogers, and everyone else…including Gwen.

It was after the Frisbee toss and matching ice cream cones with jimmies served by Randy at the drug store counter that my little summer vacation cocoon had a hole punched in it.

Billy and I walked out of the store, cones in hand, and were just crossing the alley. I had looked down that alley so many times before to see no red T-Bird convertible…but not this time. Leaning into each other on those bright red leather seats were Dad and Margaret. If we were startled to see him, he was even more startled to see us. And we both knew he did. We could feel the shock and see the alarm in his eyes. But he quickly turned away in an effort to ignore us.

On our way home, Billy and I didn't say much to each other. We had now seen together the same thing each of us had seen separately. Somehow, the shared experience seemed to double the pain and shame of our discovery. There was nothing to say, no words to express our distress.

That evening, the silence ended. Dad walked through the door at about 7:30. I had been avoiding Mom. I didn't want to see her eyes. Moreover, I didn't want her to see *my* eyes and even get a hint that I had seen *them* together. And most of all, I didn't want to look at Mom and compare her to the glamorous Margaret. That would make the pain even more acute.

But there was no way to avoid *him*. He would not let us do that. He entered my room without knocking. Billy was with him, his eyes tense behind the horn-rimmed glasses. Dad had apparently entered his room before entering mine.

"I was with a business associate today. That's who you boys saw me with. You looked like you were enjoying your ice cream cones. Randy really piles it on high. You gotta say that for him."

Billy wanted to agree and get out of the room. I knew he considered further discussion pointless. He was already facing the door as he spoke.

"Yeh, Dad. They were good. I gotta go. I got something in my room to do."

I, on the other hand, wasn't in the mood for letting things go. My anger had had no outlet...until now. It let loose like a bursting balloon, like a cannon being shot, like a bomb being dropped.

"Are you kidding? You *liar!*"

Dad clearly didn't expect that. He shot back.

"Who are you calling a liar?"

I came within inches from his face and screamed.

"Liar! Liar! Liar!"

I knew Mom could hear us, and suddenly I didn't care. Dad pointed his finger directly in my face as he continued the volley.

"Don't you dare call your father a liar! Don't you *dare!* You little... you...you...!"

Now he let completely loose as well, which was just as unusual for him.

"You little brat...stupid little brat! I'll beat you to a pulp, you spoiled little piece of..."

His finger got dangerously close to my eyes, and I instinctively grabbed it with my right hand and tried with all my strength to bend it backward. He howled in pain.

"No," Billy cried softly. For a few seconds it looked like we were arm wrestling. And then the rest of our bodies got involved, as he grabbed my other hand and we struggled with each other. I was feeling fury I didn't know existed.

"You don't hit your father!" he shouted.

"You cheated on Mom. You kissed her…that…that…"

I couldn't think of another word, except the one Robey had used about Gwen.

"Slut! We know her name. Margaret. We know that about her… liar! Cheat! *Scum!*"

He pulled his hands free and started punching me as hard as he could. But I punched back, pummeling his chest. He punched me in the face, not considering any consequences. We were in a full-fledged fistfight.

"You don't know anything! She's…she's…"

He was out of breath.

"She's a friend. That's all…you ungrateful little piece of…!"

"Mom knows there's someone! She knows something!" I screamed in his face.

He ended up scratching my face with one of his fingernails. I could tell he drew blood by how it stung. We pulled back. He acted like a wounded animal, breathless and with his tail between his legs.

"Your mother and I…we…she doesn't need to know…we're just friends…it was a friendly kiss. Don't say anything more to your mother. Don't…"

He began to catch his breath. He looked at me and then at Billy.

"Look…I'll talk to your mother. It's just a misunderstanding."

I didn't argue back. I was still shocked by my own rage. Guilt began to set in. My conscience was nagging me about hitting my own father. I had always been innately repulsed by that kind of behavior. He tried to comb back his unkempt few hairs with his hands, and regained as much composure as he could.

"I'm sorry about the scratch. I'm leaving."

"Yeh, go," I spoke in a whisper like Mr. Schott's.

I was pretty sure where he was going, but I was too exhausted and emotionally drained to challenge him. He left the room and then the house, shutting the front door behind him. Billy and I looked at each other for the first time since he walked into my room. I knew my shame and guilt showed. I tried to hide it the best I could.

"What's your problem? You just stood there, talking about ice cream, didn't you? You and your stupid Edison."

"At least I didn't…"

I wouldn't let him finish.

"I'm hungry. Get out my way."

Of course I wasn't hungry. I left Billy in my bedroom and went down to the kitchen. I was headed for the cookie jar, but met Mom instead. She instinctively reached out and touched the dripping scratch on my cheek.

"We should put something on that scratch."

She left and came back in a minute or so with Bactine. In my shame and emotional exhaustion, I suddenly craved some old-fashioned mothering. And Mom obliged me as any good mother would. But she was too troubled to just leave things at that basic mothering level. As she applied the liquid from the squeeze bottle, she admonished me.

"You should never talk back to your father. You know that."

"I know. I know."

"I don't know how this started, but you should never *ever* hit your father. You know that too. He's you father. He means well."

I was in no mood for arguing. I just sat there receiving first aid and agreed with her.

"I know."

"You should apologize to him."

I had no intention of apologizing, in spite of my guilt. So I made a halfhearted attempt at agreeing.

"You're right. I…I'll think about it."

She continued to dab the minor wound. I couldn't let her know how much it stung, as I would have when I was younger.

"And you should spend time with friends your own age. Billy should have his own friends. It's good that you spend time together, but only to a point," she said as she dabbed.

I was surprised she threw that in, and it bothered me more than her previous comments about Dad. I knew she felt the need to comment on my friends. She'd done that with Robey and Clarence, and those were not the first cases. There was a boy the year before that she had warned me about without ever having met him. It seemed his name, which was Bruno, bothered her. Apparently, she pictured him as a big, tough Italian kid. Actually, he was a small shy boy. But I never tried to correct her impression. I just dropped the subject…and the friend.

But that was last year. And this was my brother. I knew she thought he would hold me back because of our age difference. She said as much. But she was wrong. Billy made a great friend when I wanted him to be a friend. And he was good for me…when I let him be good for me. I had avoided him all year long. And now, after a year in the Upper Zoo, he was safe…and comfortable, and…okay, not my age. So if she didn't want me to hang out with Billy, who *did* she want me to hang out with? I knew who she *didn't* want me with. She didn't want me to hang out with Clarence. And it occurred to me that if she didn't want me to spend time with my brother or Clarence, then I would spend time with both.

"Mom, I'll hang out with whoever I want."

She screwed the cap back on the Bactine. The scent of the antiseptic spray brought back memories of scraped knees and little boy tears, and made me even more resolute. When she pressed her point, I jumped in.

"I'm just saying…"

"I know. I heard you."

There was no more discussion. It occurred to me as I walked away that she must have known we were arguing with Dad about Margaret.

But she didn't seem to want to talk about it. And that was fine with me. I just wanted a couple of cookies and then bed. But before I turned in, I took the phone book from the closet in the kitchen and looked up Clarence Carlson's number. There it was, with his street address. I summoned my courage and dialed the phone in the living room. His mother answered the phone. When I asked if I could visit the next day, she was hesitant at first.

"Well…I…I don't know. I…well, I don't see why not. Let me ask Clarence."

After a minute or so she came back to the phone. I could detect a hint of excitement in her voice.

"Yes…yes, okay. Just come any time. He'll be here."

As I lay in bed, I looked forward to the first visit with Clarence since the school year ended. I felt a freedom to spend time with him in addition to my brother, despite my mother's concerns. If they both held me back, so be it. It was summer vacation, and it was time to lay back and relax.

Somehow, I felt a freedom from Robey, too. My time with Clarence was now less his business than ever. The next day would be great. I fell asleep comforting myself with that thought in the face of what had been a very painful evening.

# CHAPTER 20

It took more time than I expected for Clarence to warm up to me again. It turned out he remembered my hurtful words as well as he remembered the days of birthdates. After the chocolate chip cookies were served, he asked, "Why…why…were you…you mean that… Tuesday at school?"

"I don't know. Can we forget that?"

"I remember. I remember, you said 'You're a freak, Clarence… and…and…I can't be around freaks right now,' and…and…'Leave me alone, Clarence. Go away! Go away!' I remember…remember…I remember."

Of course he *did* remember. He remembered every word, every inflection…every pause. He even did a passable impression of me, though I wouldn't admit it.

"All right. I'm sorry, Clarence. I said I wanted to see you. Don't you remember that?"

"I remember. I remember you…you said that. I remember. But you also said 'You're a freak, Clarence…and…and…I can't be around freaks right now, and 'Go away'…so…okay…okay…okay…okay. You're…you're sorry."

"Thank you, Clarence. Okay? Listen, I want to tell you some things."

I had already decided to break my word to Gwen again and tell Clarence about her stepfather. So I told him about her secret, and the marks on her face and neck. And I told him what Billy said. And then I asked him what he thought I should do, which was very unusual for me. I don't even know why I did it. He rocked as I talked. Then he sat silently for a full minute or more. Finally, he broke the silence.

"Another cookie?"

He got up and went into the kitchen. I don't know what I'd been expecting or why I opened up to him about Gwen. He didn't say a word in response to even let me know he had heard me. And I didn't ask him if he had. But for some reason, it felt good just to share about it out loud with someone who I was somewhat sure wouldn't tell others. So I shared about something else when he returned with the cookies.

"Can I tell you something else?'

Clarence rocked to and fro in his way. I took that to be a yes. So I bounced more off him, even if he *was* strange—some might even say mysterious.

"Robey treated me to an ice cream sundae at the drug store. And he told me I was one of the good Jews. He said most were bad, but those Jews had big noses and beards. He said I was an exception. I probably wouldn't have killed Christ, whatever that's supposed to mean. I mean, why would I ever do anything to Jesus Christ? I don't have anything against him. Maybe you can tell me. You're one of those good Christians, aren't you? Anyway, I didn't know what to think. I mean he bought me an ice cream sundae, right? Sometimes he scares me, and sometimes he's really nice to me. I've never met anyone like him. I don't think he likes you very much. In fact, I know he doesn't."

Clarence looked at me in a way he never had. There was none of the usual darting around of his eyes. Maybe I shouldn't have mentioned the fact that Robey didn't like him. Maybe this was his way of acting angry. Those eyes were now piercing mine as he spoke the next words in that voice I'd heard only a few times before.

"And I will bless them that bless thee, and curse him that curseth thee: and in thee shall all families of the earth be blessed."

I had no idea what he was talking about, but I figured he might be quoting the Bible again.

"What's that mean, Clarence? I don't know what you're talking about?"

His voice reverted to normal.

"He doesn't love you. He doesn't…he doesn't even…he doesn't even like you. He…he hates you. He hates the Jews. He hates me. Stay away. Stay away. Stay…stay…"

"Okay. Okay."

"Stay away…away, far away."

He was beginning to get on my nerves.

"Okay. Okay. I heard you. I'll stay away."

"Stay away from 105 Green Tree Street. Stay away. Stay away."

"Okay. But…Clarence, you're really confusing me today. First you don't want to talk about Gwen. You don't say anything when I tell you things nobody knows but my little brother Billy. Then you talk about cursing and…and I don't know what all and from where. And then… you tell me Robey hates me. Fine. Maybe he does. And then all of a sudden, you go back and mention Gwen's address, because you saw it on that stupid sheet. You didn't even answer my question about her, and you're telling me her address…and to stay away. You're scaring me, Clarence. You know what? Maybe I should go now."

I got up to leave.

"No. Stay. More cookies? Please? What about Legos? Let's play Legos. I'll get the Legos. ABS…ABS. We'll build a big house…not 105 Green Tree Street…another house…this house…your house."

"Why do you keep mentioning Gwen Anderson's house? I get it. You know it. So?"

"Yes, yes…Gwen Anderson. And… and…Robey…Robey Romero. Gwen and Robey."

Why did he mention them together? From what I could see, they wanted nothing to do with each other...or at least Robey wanted nothing to do with Gwen. And I was pretty sure it was mutual. Listening to Clarence, I felt like I was listening to a record that skipped all over the place and made no sense. I figured that's what autism was. But to me it was just gibberish. Still, I questioned him about it, useless as it seemed to do it.

"What are you talking about? You're not making sense."

"Robey...Robey...105 Green Tree Street."

"Yeh, well you're wrong. You're finally wrong, Clarence. I guess sometimes you don't know what you're talking about."

"No...no, not...not wrong."

There was an insistence in his voice beyond his usual speech pattern.

"Yes you are," I responded in kind.

"No. Not wrong."

He rocked and waved his arms like a child having a temper tantrum.

"Yes."

"No."

"Yes."

He wouldn't let go.

"No. No. No! No!"

We could have gone on like that forever. But we didn't. I dropped it, and we ended up building a house, a big colorful house of Legos. After that, I went home. The day hadn't turned out as I had expected the night before. Billy met me in the kitchen. He was having an afternoon bowl of Frosted Flakes, which was his sometime habit. I couldn't wait to tell him Clarence had flipped his lid.

"I think Clarence thinks this kid Robey lives where this girl Gwen lives, or something like that. He keeps mentioning her address with his name. I told him he's wrong, but like the idiot he is he insists.

What an idiot! Now I know why they call his kind that. Idiot! I'm finished with him."

"What do you mean *this kid* Robey and *this girl* Gwen? I know who Robey and Gwen are."

"Fine. That wasn't my point."

This wasn't about Billy, but he was making it about him. I wished he would just read the stupid cereal box and not pay attention to me so I could get on with my day, whatever that meant during a lazy summer vacation.

"Okay. Whatever. Forget it. All I know is he's an idiot. He doesn't know anything."

I was on my way out of the room.

"He's right. If he said it, he's right."

I turned.

"Yeh? How do *you* know?"

"It's like Edison. He was always right."

"You're an idiot too, and so is Edison. They can't both live there in that same run down old house."

Billy had the final word. He turned from his cereal bowl and asked the ultimate question.

"Can't they?"

I left the room and tried to forget the whole day. I didn't know why I had to be so upset about a stupid mistake anyway. I lay down on my bed and listened to the radio. The song "My Guy" played. It was catchy and I tried to use it to blank out everything else but the loping rhythm and melody and Mary Wells' voice. But it didn't work. Billy's words "can't they" came back to me, and I jumped up off my bed.

I walked out of the house and grabbed my bike. I rode it through the neighborhood and over to Gwen's house, just to see if Robey might show up, as crazy a notion as that was. It didn't do any good. During the summer, there was no school bus for Robey to get off of. And he was nowhere in sight. The house looked dark inside and all the shades were drawn. Of course, it always looked like that. And though I would have loved to see Gwen, with her perfect face and newly radiant hair, I didn't have the courage to knock on the door. I just stood there and felt useless.

Finally, I rode away and through the small town area. On the outskirts I saw Margaret again as I coasted on the bike. She was getting into another fancy car with a man who was not my father. It wasn't a sports car. It was big and shiny and black, and he was in the driver's seat. It looked like they were arguing about something. I liked seeing her with another man. Maybe she would leave Dad. At the very least, maybe she would reject and hurt him. And I wanted her to hurt him. They drove away and out of sight.

I walked my bike all the way home. It seemed like I could think more clearly when I walked than when I rode. Who was this man? And what was Margaret doing with him?

As my journey home continued, I found a desire rising in me to talk to Mom. I had been very close to her when I was very small, before Billy was born; always clinging to her as a toddler, holding onto her long, pleated flower dresses, even longer than the flower dresses she wore now, falling asleep in her arms on nights I was frightened, feeling her reliable breathing and her consistent heartbeat.

Maybe that's the way it is for most children, but the impression remained very deep in my heart and infrequently it surfaced. After Billy was born, I shared her affections with him, as all first children do. Still, there were always close times of connection over the years. But there hadn't been even one since I entered the Upper Zoo. I knew Billy had those times, but I didn't. And I craved a time of connection now. I wanted her to know what I was going through. I wanted to hide nothing from her. I wanted to tell her everything.

But I had to be selective. I decided by the time I got to the front door what I would talk to her about. It wouldn't be about Gwen, or her stepfather, or Robey, or Clarence. She knew a little bit about at least Robey and Clarence, and I had no reason to tell her more. I was already aware of what her opinions were there.

She was in the living room ironing. I got my courage up and told her I wanted to talk to her. She looked up from gliding the iron over one of Dad's white dress shirts. My heart was beating fast, because I knew how straightforward I would have to be. She didn't want to stop ironing, but I insisted. We went over and sat on the couch. Billy was out. Dad, of course, was nowhere in sight. This was the perfect time.

"Yes Jonathan, honey? What is it?"

My heart was beating faster. I hoped she wouldn't notice. I just blurted it out.

"I…Dad…Dad has another woman. I saw her."

She looked away, startled. I didn't have the heart to tell her how pretty Margaret was, or that I knew her name. But I had told her enough. She began to cry, which somehow I knew she would. I dreaded that. The tears fell steadily down her cheeks.

"I know. I know."

She hugged me with one of those motherly hugs that is totally self-denying and all about her child. But I knew those tears came from her own pain. Then she let go and sat back.

"I'm sorry you have to go through this, Jonathan. Your father… is…he's not happy. And…I want you to be happy. I want you to learn from this."

I was surprised she moved into the lecture mode so quickly. But I let her do it. I figured she needed it. She tried to dry her still-tearing eyes with her hand and sat up on the sofa, looking at me.

"You will make a great husband. You'll be faithful. You won't be like your father. You won't hurt the one…"

She started to cry again, which tore me up inside and made me angry at the same time.

"Why Mom? Why did he do it, when you're so…when you love him? Don't you?"

She answered quickly, I thought maybe a little too quickly.

"Sure. Of course I do. This woman's probably just some poor-side-of-town, not too bright, plain-looking girl that's a bit desperate…and he just went for the trap…because he's…he's not happy with *himself*. That's why it's important to be happy with *yourself*. Remember that."

She was struggling to convince herself as she tried to convince me. But I knew Margaret wasn't poor from the T-Bird. And of course, she was anything but plain. Still, I wanted Mom to hold onto the picture she described. She continued trying to comfort me and yet lecture me at the same time.

"He takes care of our family. Deep inside he loves you and Billy. He'd never knowingly do anything to hurt you. You know, you shouldn't have had that fight with him the other night. He's still your father, no matter what."

I decided that lecturing was okay at that moment if it made her feel better. But I wasn't satisfied with just letting her lecture me to comfort herself. I had to let her know that I both loved her and blamed him. I put my hand on her arm and spoke as sincerely as I knew how.

"You are the best mother and wife in the whole wide world, Mom. And Dad's just totally crazy and wrong. She doesn't hold a candle to you, Mom. She's…"

I began to cry too. I wanted to stop the tears, but I couldn't. Between the heaves of weeping, I shared from the deepest place in my teenage son's heart.

"You're beautiful…the most beautiful woman in the world. I'm going to marry someone just like you…just like you. I…I…love you, Mom."

She reached over and squeezed me harder, and a fountain was released from somewhere inside of her. Her salty tears and runny nose ended up all over my shirt. She convulsed as she wept for maybe three minutes or more. I felt her heartbeat like the old days, but faster. Finally she let me go and tried the best she could to compose herself. I ran and got some Kleenex, handing her one after another like a dutiful servant. Then she sat still for a long time.

"Mom…I think I'll go now. Is that okay?"

"Yes, of course. You go," she sighed.

As I left, she said, "Thank you," which made me tear up again. I realized she probably needed another grown up to talk to about Dad, and maybe she had even talked to one or two. But that day I was there. I was there for her. And it made me feel not just like her little boy, but also a little more grown up than I felt the day before.

The next day, I rode my bike up toward Gwen's house again. There was no reason for me to go there. But I still couldn't get Billy's words out of my mind. And anyway, I thought just possibly she might come out of her house. I hadn't seen her in the last few weeks, and I missed just looking at her. But as it turned out, I didn't see her. Instead, Robey appeared around the corner, riding his slick, new, ruby red ten-speed bike. I pulled back and hid behind a tree, watching as he got closer and closer. He slowed down as he approached 105 Green Tree Street. Could it be?

Sure enough, Robey rode up the driveway and got off the bike. He pulled up the creaky cracked old garage door and walked the bike in, closing the door and disappearing behind it. I realized that there must be an entrance to the house inside the garage, and he wasn't coming back...at least not anytime soon.

I had so much to think about on my way home. But I didn't get much of a chance. As I was coasting past a car dealership three or four bocks from the drug store I saw what had to be *the two cars*, Margaret's and the strange man's, parked next to each other just outside the front door. I knew I had to go in, just as I had gone into the dentist's office.

As I entered, I immediately saw the man who was with Margaret just the day before. He was leaning on a desk in small a cubicle toward the back. I was startled by a voice coming from the opposite side of the showroom.

"Hey, boy. Can I help you?"

A salesman approached me. He was fat and bald, and looked at me suspiciously. I figured it was because I was a kid coming in alone.

"Umm…I'm just looking."

It felt very uncomfortable being in the same position I had been in the dentist's office.

"Yeh? Maybe you should come back in five years…and bring your parents."

I had to get a closer look at the man in the back.

"Well…they…they're looking at a car. And I wanted to just look…"

In a split second, he handed me a card.

"Here. Give them this. What kind of a car do they want?"

"I don't know. Maybe a station wagon."

"Well, check that one out over there. You tell them about that. That's a brand-new 1964 Chevy wagon. You can't beat it for economy and quality. Go ahead. You can check it out. Just don't go in it, if you know what I mean. Your parents can do that later when they come in."

He pointed to the card in my hand.

"Just give them this and tell them you saw the best station wagon on the road. It's fully loaded and very reasonable. You tell them that. Here. Let me have their phone number. I'll tell them about it too."

He gave me a pad of paper and a pen. I hesitated. I could have given him a phony number, but I gave him our real number. I wanted to be as authentic as I could be. Of course, they weren't looking for a car. And I might be exposed in the end. But I might not be. At any rate, I wasn't thinking clearly. I just wanted to get a better look at Margaret's friend.

After he walked away, I drifted past the station wagon and toward the back. There he was, arguing with another salesman about some sale or other. He was tall and thin, and had a thick head of curly black hair streaked with gray. And there on his desk was a picture of none other than Margaret, looking typically like a movie star…like Tuesday Weld. I had seen all I came in to see, and I walked out as quickly as I could.

Back home, I confessed to Billy about Robey entering Gwen's house.

"Well, I won't say I told you so. But maybe you owe an apology to Clarence."

"Maybe. I'll think about it," I said smugly.

I probably owed an apology to Billy as well for the way I had treated him during the eighth grade Upper Zoo year. But that was nowhere in my mind. I was just trying to figure out what was really going on at 105 Green Tree Street. How could Robey live in that house? He spent the whole year in the Upper Zoo, and never said one word about living in the same house as Gwen. It didn't make any sense. Still, at least a few things did seem to be true. Robey was at least using Gwen's address for something, as Clarence had told me, and at the very least he sometimes visited the house.

Of course, I had discovered something else that day as well, something at the car dealership. But I saw no reason to share that with Billy yet.

# CHAPTER 21

I SPENT THE REST OF the day trying to figure out how to get to the bottom of what was going on. I kept thinking, *What in the world is going on inside that house. Did Robey sleep there? Did Gwen have a room, or was she lying to me and was her house actually elsewhere?* I realized that I'd seen Robey enter through the garage, but I'd never actually seen Gwen enter the house…except in my imagination. But Clarence had mentioned her name too, and Billy said he was never wrong.

After much consideration, I decided that I had to get inside that house. I was tired of guessing, of probing from afar. But how would I get inside?

If I had been thinking more practically, I might have settled for something short of what is arguably trespassing—perhaps a chance meeting with Gwen along with a couple of well-placed questions, or maybe a stakeout near her house waiting for something suspicious. But it was a particularly hot summer, there was plenty of time to plan something dangerous, and I was too impatient to be satisfied with anything less than a full explanation of the double address mystery.

I knew that if I didn't act within the next twenty-four hours, I never would. So I spent the rest of the afternoon on my bed, with the still, summer air stagnating outside my open window, going through all of the steps. By evening, I knew I would act. Dad was still out, and by 9:30 Mom and Billy had turned in. It was an easy thing to quietly leave the house, gently closing and locking the door. The hard part lay ahead.

I almost turned around at least five times during the dimly lit journey. The noises were more frightening than the shadows. Crickets, owls, screeching tires, and an occasional disembodied voice from an open window had their effect. By the time I arrived at 105 Green Tree Street, I almost turned around a sixth time.

The house looked more sinister at night, with its lopsided shutters and crooked gutters. There were a few lights glowing from deep inside. And there was a dark upstairs room with a wide-open window facing the street. That was my only hope. Part of me couldn't believe I would or could do such a thing, and part of me had already made up my mind to do it, even though I knew anything could be behind that window. It might be a bedroom, though it didn't look like it. It was too much in the middle of the second floor. But it might face the hallway, exposing anyone who climbed through it to whomever would be walking between rooms. And I also knew that Robey might be somewhere behind that window. He could have a gun, though I doubted it. In spite of all of these questions, if I could just get up to that window and listen for voices I might learn something.

My heart was going crazy. It warned me that this was complete foolishness. But I ignored the warning. I stood at the curb, trying to compose myself. I could clearly see the route to the window. A tree, which looked fairly easy to climb, would transport me to the eave in front of it. For the first time ever, I stepped onto the front yard of Gwen's house—if it *was* her house—and in the process onto private property. Instantly, I remembered seeing her at the curb of the same house when she had a curtain of straggly hair covering her face. How much did her talk with me have to do with her change in appearance? Could I have had that much impact on her? That question, along with the mystery of Robey's address, drove me forward, and I drew near that tree, finally standing right under the low-hanging branches.

I'd come that far. Now I took the bold step that seemed so unbelievable just hours earlier. I grabbed the branch and started climbing. It was almost as easy as I thought it would be. One branch led to another and the lower limbs got farther and farther away. Before I knew it, I was staring directly at a screen covering the window I'd chosen. As quietly as I could, I stepped onto the eave. I grabbed the window frame and immediately looked down through the dark night to the concrete walkway adjacent to the house. I hadn't meant to, but it happened naturally. I wasn't a big fan of heights, and I resolved not to do it again.

Now I was finally up against the screen. I listened as hard as I could. But there was nothing...just dead, still, summer air and the crickets. This was not the quick success of the walkie-talkie adventure just a few weeks earlier. As I looked carefully, I could see an open door on the other side of the room through distant light from inside the house. So it *was* some sort of room and not just a hallway. Now I knew that I had come too far to go home with nothing to show for my all my risky work. Like a soldier on a dangerous mission, I had to press on and complete what I had started.

I noticed that the screen was the pull-up kind. I decided that if it were in any way locked, I would just leave. But if it lifted, well... that would be my cue. I gingerly pulled it up from the bottom. It rose smoothly and quickly, exposing the room inside. Immediately, I knew what I had to do next.

As gently as I could, I crawled through the window and stood upright in the small dark room. In the light of what was obviously the hallway, I could just make out some boxes, a few old chairs, and a desk and chair in the left corner. I saw the outline of what appeared to be a closet to my right with that door also partially open. I slowly turned around and pulled the screen down. Then I headed for the door ahead of me that led to the rest of the house.

My heart was pounding in my ears now. I very carefully approached the open door and looked into the upstairs hallway. No one was there. It looked almost as rundown as the outside of the house. The words *really old* came to mind. There was a dirty, stained, and ragged old rug on the floor. I could see down the hallway to the left what appeared to be a bathroom at the end of the hall.

Then suddenly, the man I saw with Margaret and in the car dealership came out of a room in the opposite direction and walked down the hall. I recognized him instantly, having seen him twice. He passed within inches of me. I could see that he had on an old, faded, grey tee shirt and blue jeans in place of the fancy suit he wore at the dealership. I froze like a statue in the doorway and stopped breathing. Then I slowly pulled back into the room.

"Robey, get the hell out here! Margaret wants you to take out the trash. Capiche?"

From down the hall I heard a familiar voice shout, "I'm busy!" So Robey *did* live here, and the man at the dealership was his father! Could it actually be that Margaret also lived here?

"Get out here, you moron! Now...or I'll beat your stupid head in!"

After a pause, Robey responded.

"Okay, Dad. Just cool it!"

Maybe Gwen lived somewhere else, but Margaret and Robey definitely lived here in this house. He was, in fact, now in the hallway just feet from me. I pulled farther back into the room and tried to control my breathing, but it was becoming more and more difficult. I was sweating so much my eyes were burning.

"Get stupid Gwenny to do it. I'm not her slave."

The man began to rage at Robey. Gwenny? Was she here too?

"I'll break every bone in your body, Robey! Get the hell over here!"

I saw him grab Robey and practically push him down the stairs. As he turned around, I was sure he saw me. I slinked back even more and held my breath again. He hadn't. Another voice sounded, a woman's voice. I knew from the few words at the dentist's office that it was Margaret.

"Gwen honey, can you come down here?"

"I'm…I'm in bed, Mom."

"Oh, okay."

*Mom!* It couldn't be! Margaret was Gwen's mother? I saw Robey climb two steps at a time to the top of the stairs. His father gave his back a loud slap.

"Well, good boy!"

I knew it was time for me to leave. I had heard and seen enough for one night. And I knew I could still get caught. Very carefully, I tiptoed to the window and pulled the screen up. Suddenly the door swung open, and I froze. Someone came in and started looking through a box. He was just a few feet from me, and fuming.

"Damn! Damn!"

It was Robey's father…and apparently Gwen's stepfather. I very slowly walked toward the closet as he rummaged. Just as I entered it and gently closed the door, the room light came on…and he bellowed in a loud voice.

"Where the hell is that shoe horn? She hides it, that dumb, blonde idiot. Where is it! Oh, forget it."

The light clicked off, the door to the room closed, and I shot out the window and almost off the roof. I caught my balance on the edge, and gently pulled the screen down. From that angle, I could see another room with the window down and a night-light inside. Through sheer pink curtains, I thought I could just make out Gwen lying in bed with a pillow wrapped around her head. I knew that if anyone found me where I was now, I would be accused of more than breaking and entering. It was definitely time to go.

I grabbed a branch and quickly climbed down the tree, glad to greet one branch after another on the way down. As soon as I touched the ground, I was at the curb in a split second and headed for home.

If I was happy not to have gotten caught, the relief didn't last long. A headache developed and got stronger with each quick step. The sounds of night no longer frightened me. I was too busy thinking about the convoluted connections between Gwen, Robey, his father, her mother, and my father. And that only made the headache worse. By the time I slipped back into my house, I just wanted to take two aspirin, which I had never taken apart from Mom dispensing them. But I did that night. And then I just wanted to go to sleep. Though I suspected my dreams would be about all the complicated relationships, I went right to bed.

The next morning I didn't remember the dreams, but the headache was replaced by stark anger. I was angry with Robey for threatening me about speaking to Gwen. I was angry with his father for whatever it was he was doing to Gwen. And I wondered how much Robey knew about it—which made me even angrier with *him*. I was angry with Margaret for hurting Mom and cheating with Dad. And of course, I was angry with Dad...*very* angry.

But I couldn't quite figure out Gwen. On the one hand, I felt sorry for her. She had a mean stepfather, and worse. And she had a mother who had at least one boyfriend besides her husband. But I also had other feelings. First of all, that boyfriend was *my* father. And second, how did I know she wasn't just like her mother, or wouldn't be someday? Everything around me felt like the Upper Zoo, and everyone around me seemed like a caged animal. This wasn't the proper world of Robert Rogers. This was the strange world of Robey and Clarence, of Margaret, and dads like Robey's and mine...and of Gwen. It was the world of retards and sickos and crazy people. And it was my world, even in the summer.

Dad came home late that evening. It took a while to get to sleep, so I heard him. I guessed Margaret made some sort of excuse with Robey's dad so she could go out, just as Dad did with Mom. Was it shopping, or visiting her sister, or some other excuse? I saw Dad through my partially open bedroom door. He seemed much older than

Robey's father, especially when he shuffled. Robey's father sauntered, at least in the car showroom. Dad fumbled around, especially when he was looking for something. Robey's father was a man of action even when he was looking for a shoehorn. He spoke boldly, though he did shout sometimes. Dad mumbled as he shuffled. I wondered again what Margaret saw in him.

As I continued to hear him wander from the bathroom to the kitchen, my hatred settled into a silent rage. Like the famous painting of the silent scream, I ached inside, but was shouting nothing. Who could I shout to…and to whom could I tell the secrets I had discovered the night before last? Not Billy. He might share it with Mom, and I wanted to shield her from the whole horrible thing. The first time I saw her crying, it shook me terribly. And I didn't want to see that even one more time.

Then right in the middle of despising my father, I decided that there was one and only one person I wanted to speak to about all of this. I would do it the next day. That was settled.

# CHAPTER 22

THE NEXT MORNING, I WASN'T so sure about my decision. It involved a risk similar to the one I took just a few nights before. Half of me wanted to be finished with risks. But the other half longed for things I couldn't have without them. And the longing won out. I had to see Gwen. I had to ask her about Margaret, and Robey, and his father, and the whole rotten mess.

That evening after nightfall, I once again snuck out of the house and headed down the road to 105 Green Tree Street. This time, I wouldn't climb the tree or enter the house. I just needed to get Gwen's attention. Of course that meant I might get someone else's attention at the same time. I had to carefully avoid that. The moon was slightly brighter than a few nights before, and that would help me...but it could also give me away.

I arrived at the destination about 10 P.M. I knew which window was hers from the last time I was there. And I also knew that her bed was behind that window and to the right. I'd seen several old movies where the boy tossed pebbles at the girl's window. So I planned to use that approach. But I needed something more accurate, more effective. And I had it. The summer before, Billy and I had practiced a few times a week with a genuine Wham-O Frisbee flying disc. I worked at accuracy until I could hit a can off a fence at fifty feet…maybe half the time. The other half, the angle of attack would take it in an unpredictable direction.

But I had sharpened my skills with Billy this year at the beginning of the summer break. I felt like I was at the top of my game. Still, I knew that a miss could result in a hit on some other window. That would spell total disaster. I stood next to the climbing tree and looked up. The house was dark, but the window reflected the moonlight.

With the familiar pounding of my heart, I wound up and spun the Frisbee at an upward angle toward Gwen's window. It bounced off the crooked shutter next to the window I had climbed into. That was nowhere near good enough.

Like a man possessed I kept at it, despite the risks. I hit her shutter and the wall next to her shutter. Finally, I scored several bulls' eyes of her window. The rubber disc slammed against the glass. I hoped it wouldn't break. Fortunately, it didn't. But she didn't come to the window either.

After more than twenty tries, I was just thankful that no one else had woken up. I'd had enough. I turned to quickly cross the yard to the street when I heard a window slide up, followed by a thin whisper.

"Hey."

I turned on my heel.

"What are you doing here? What are you doing in my yard?"

Gwen was leaning out the window, the moon accenting the shadow of her face in a silver outline. Even in the dark I could tell she was upset.

I whispered, "Please…please come down. I need to talk to you. Please…"

"Are you completely crazy? It's eleven o'clock."

Actually, it was 10:10.

"I know," I said anyway. "Please…"

She disappeared into the black. I waited for what felt like several minutes and was about to leave again. I felt so foolish. How would

I face her later after showing up like this after 10 at night and then begging?

Then suddenly, yet slowly, the front door opened. There she was, her pajamas covered by a silk robe. It looked red, but it was hard to tell in the moonlight. She stood in the doorway like an exotic queen who just left her chamber, her royal feet clad with big fluffy pink bedroom slippers.

"Now what is it, Jonathan? What in the world are you doing here?"

She did not look happy to see me. But at least she showed up at the door.

"I *have* to talk to you. Can we go somewhere?"

She responded by whispering as loudly as she knew how.

"Are you out of your mind? I was almost asleep. Come back tomorrow."

My begging continued. I had come this far, and I wasn't going to leave. I whispered back just as loudly.

"I can't. Please?"

Just as she tried to close the door, I stuck my foot in it like a brush salesman. I was desperate and this was my last chance.

"Wait! Just for a few minutes. Please…I have some secrets to tell you. You told me your secret. Well, now I have some. Remember when you wanted to sit with me at the beginning of the year, and then you ran away? Well, *please* don't run away now."

She stared at me like I had three heads.

"No…I don't remember. I never did that. What are you talking about?"

"What are *you* talking about? You did. You walked away."

"No, I didn't. You must be insane."

I dropped the point, but not the conversation.

"Okay. Just please don't run *now*. I need to talk to you."

She sighed with resignation.

"All right. Let's go to that park across the street. *I can't believe this.*"

She wrapped her red silk robe tightly around her and tightened its silk belt, although it was as warm outside as it was inside. Then she gently closed the door and quickly walked ten steps in front of me toward the street.

"Come on. Hurry up! I don't have all night."

The park was small enough to be a large back yard. I had passed it many times in the daytime without giving it a thought. In the middle was an old set of swings. She went over and sat on one. I took the one next to it. The moon threw a silver shroud on her face that obscured it like her hair had the day I first met her. She turned toward me.

"Okay, Jonathan. What do you want…and it had better be good."

"Well…are you sitting down?"

"What's it look like I'm doing, Jonathan? Standing on my head?"

"Right…that's just a saying."

Then I let my guard down.

"Why aren't you being nice to me? I mean, you told me secrets, we were friends…"

That seemed to soften her up a bit, though perhaps she was just trying to speed things up.

"Okay…I'm ready…I'm sitting…what is it?"

"Okay."

I tried to compose myself. Then I started.

"Umm…I've met your mom. I mean I've seen her."

"So?"

"And I've met your stepdad. I mean I've seen him."

She seemed equally unimpressed.

"So? Do you want an award?"

Now came the hard part. I took a deep breath. Then told her about Robey and me, and about Clarence. I told her how Robey treated Clarence, and how he didn't want me to ever talk to him or her either. I went on from there to tell her about seeing Robey's father and her mother in his car, and about how I knew he worked at a car dealership.

"Is that what you got me out here to tell me? I know he works in a car dealership."

"No. There's something else."

By this time, she seemed bored. She began to slowly swing back and forth. She threw her head back like she was paying no attention to anything I was saying or about to say.

I took another deep breath. Then haltingly, I began to explain about her mom and my dad and how I saw them together in the red T-Bird. When I finally got it out, she stopped abruptly and sat up in the swing.

"What are you saying?"

"I'm saying…well, I'm saying…they're seeing each other."

"Why…because they were in the car together? She was probably helping my stepfather with a sale. That was all it was. Ridiculous!"

This wasn't turning out well. I had no choice. I had to tell her everything.

"No…it wasn't like that. He's not buying a car. They were…they were…"

I couldn't say it. I didn't know why…it just wouldn't come out.

"You know…they were…"

She jumped off the swing and stood up.

"Liar!"

I stood up and faced her.

"I'm not lying."

"Yes you are. Liar! Liar! Liar! I can't believe you would say that about my…"

I'd suddenly had enough of Upper Zoo behavior. I wasn't the liar, and I didn't like being called that. I interrupted her and let the truth spill out in a single sentence.

"Stop! *Your* mother was kissing *my* father in a red Thunderbird in the alley next to the drug store, and I saw them there…two times… with my own eyes…and my brother Billy saw them too!"

She got up and walked away from me, just like she did in the lunchroom.

"You're doing it again."

"Doing what? I'm going in."

I ran after her and pulled her around by the arm.

"Gwen..."

She yanked her arm free.

"Let go of me!"

She turned toward me. In the moonlight, I could see silver tears beginning to form in her eyes and stream down her face.

"Don't you *ever* touch me...don't *ever....!*"

I couldn't let that go.

"I touched you the day I first really saw your face. You didn't say that *then*. I...pulled your hair back...and there you were...more beautiful than I could ever have imagined."

"What are you talking about? You never did that."

"Yes I did. I did that," I insisted.

Apparently she didn't remember that either. I felt like I was in a strange universe talking to someone who only looked like Gwen.

"You cried. Remember?"

"You're completely off your nut."

She began to leave again.

"Don't leave now...don't..."

She turned around and shouted at me.

"I hate you! I hate you! And I hate your father just because he's your father! I hope Robey kills you...and him too!"

Where did that come from?

"What are you talking about?"

She stepped up to me and jabbed her finger over and over in the direction of my heart, like she was discharging a loaded pistol.

"I'll tell you what I'm talking about. He said there was a man...a man who saw my mother besides his dad. He called my mother a bad name. He said he'd *kill* the man if he found out who it was. My mother told him he was crazy. He *is* crazy. There *is* no man. He's a liar just like you are. His dad...he...he hit him when he said it...and...he...hit my mother, too. I hate all of you! I hate everybody! My mom would never do anything like that!"

She stamped her feet.

"It's a lie! It's a bald-faced lie!"

I was trying to grasp what she had just told me. Did she say Robey accused Margaret of cheating?

"Did you say Robey thinks your mother is seeing someone besides your stepfather?"

"You heard me…the liar…just like you."

"And…you mean your stepfather hit her like he hit you and put marks on your…your neck?"

Suddenly, Gwen turned back to me with the look I had seen when we first talked in the lunchroom in the beginning of the year.

"Well, not exactly. That's our secret. Remember? You promised."

She stared directly at me and then took a very deep breath. Maybe the other Gwen was back.

"Remember?"

"Of course I remember," I whispered. I wasn't about to tell her I shared it with Billy and Clarence. She reached out and took my hand, leading me back to the swings.

"I'm…I'm sorry. Let's sit back down on the swings, Jonathan. I don't really hate you. In fact, I like you."

We sat down. She began to swing slowly again, now and then twisting and then swaying to and fro. No words were exchanged, just the sound of the chain creaking as it swung and turned on the hooks. The moon shone against her profile as she moved and reflected different aspects of her exquisite face; her forehead, nose, lips, chin.

Then, even as I watched her swinging with her hair silver in the moonlight and her royal robes wrapped around her, a sense of foreboding began to replace my quiet reverie. What if she told Robey about my father? She could be just crazy enough to say something to him. It seemed like she didn't remember some things and didn't forget others. I didn't want to break the precious silence, but I knew I had to.

"Gwen…umm…about my father…"

"I don't want to talk about him now."

I didn't want to either, but I had to.

"Okay. But…maybe you shouldn't mention anything to Robey… or his father…or his mother…or anyone. I mean, you know, he could hurt someone…I mean Robey could."

"I don't want to talk about it."

"Please. Can't that be our secret, too?"

She sat up in the swing again.

"Okay. That'll be our secret…if you say so."

She looked over at me for a short second and then sprung up and ran all the way home, the train of her silk robe swaying just above her fluffy pink bedroom slippers. I could just see her disappear behind the door and close it with just a soft clicking sound.

I headed for home, trying to comfort myself that Robey would never find out about Dad. The poison of the Upper Zoo world may have already spread to my life at home, but I had to believe there was an antidote in keeping the worlds as separate as possible now.

By the time I got home, it was almost midnight. I quietly crept upstairs and slipped into bed. As I lay there, a deep sadness swept over me. It was not for myself. It was for Gwen. I didn't know what was wrong with her, but I knew something was. I drifted off to sleep with the sense that Gwen would always be strangely sick in some way. Some day I hoped to be out of the Upper Zoo and rid of it for good. Even if I never *applied myself,* as Mom would say, I was pretty sure I wouldn't be stuck in that elevator between floors forever. But I wondered if Gwen would be in some kind of zoo for the rest of her life…in a cage with thick bars. These were profound drifting off to sleep thoughts, and they took a long time to fade out. By the morning, they were gone.

I got up late. I looked out of my bedroom window at 10 o'clock and saw Robert Rogers mowing his lawn. He looked so normal. His father walked out of the front door with a pair of shears. He looked normal, too. I watched them as they worked together like the best of friends to make their front yard look beautiful.

All year I hadn't allowed myself to think about what Robert Rogers thought of me. I hardly ever ran into him at school and just ignored him on the bus. We were in two separate worlds. But now I gave in to my deepest feelings of shame and disgrace. The words came to me as the truth I'd been denying. *He thinks you're a dumb retard, and his parents do too. Didn't his mother tell yours you'd always be a dumb failure? And she was right.*

I continued to watch him mow the rows neatly while his father trimmed the hedges. The summer was almost over, and the grass wasn't very high. But the Rogers family was neat about everything they did. Even their Jewish last name was neat and tight and clean. It wasn't any longer than ours, but it seemed more normal. We seemed closer to the strange great uncle that I hardly knew, with his yarmulke and yellow teeth and accent. It seemed to me like their family and everyone in their synagogue went all the way back to George Washington…fully American…and normal. Maybe Robey was right about Jews after all…except that he was in the Upper Zoo, and nothing in the Upper Zoo seemed like it could be right.

There was a knock on my bedroom door. I knew it was Billy.

"Yeh?"

He came in.

"What is it, Billy?"

"I have something to tell you. You're not going to like it."

He hesitated for a second like a man with privileged information that only he knew. But he finally relented and relayed it.

"Robey was here yesterday. I would've told you earlier, but you slept so late. Were you up late?"

My heart jumped in my chest, though I didn't want Billy to see it. I tried to act as normal as I could.

"Yeh."

"What were you doing?"

I snapped back.

"None of your business."

I knew Billy didn't like me snapping at him like that. But he was used to it by now, so he didn't even blink.

"Fine. Anyway, he was here."

"Did he…did he say what he wanted?"

"No. He just wanted to see you."

He left the room, obviously irritated. I didn't care. I just wanted to know why Robey took the time and effort come all the way over to my house to see me. And that question weighed on me all day. Why? He couldn't possibly suspect anything, could he?

Finally, about 5 P.M, after a day of lying around eating and watching useless game shows and of overriding anxiety, there was a knock at the front door. I opened it to the familiar towering figure and a slap on my back. He was in front of me, and still my back felt the sting. I couldn't quite figure out how he did it. But that was Robey…full of surprises from out of nowhere.

"Friend! Jonathan, old buddy."

"Hi Robey," I squeaked out with great effort.

It was very important to hide my pounding heart. He reached out and squeezed my shoulder until it hurt and then became very resolute.

"We've got to talk. Can I come in?"

"Well…"

He walked past me without hesitating. Mom walked out of the kitchen toward us.

"Umm…Mom…this is Robey."

She was stiff, trying to hide her disapproval as I was trying to hide the throbbing.

"Nice to meet you."

She reached out a formal hand and shook his mechanically. I could tell Robey wanted to get down to business, but he had to put on his *almost* Eddie Haskell affectation that I'd seen at Clarence's.

"Nice to meet you, Mrs. Richman. Sorry to intrude. Jonathan, can we talk in your room?"

I didn't want Robey in my room. But he turned from Mom and, like he'd been there at thousand times, walked right up the stairs and into it.

"Beach Boys. Nice poster."

"Thanks," I mumbled as I caught up with him.

"I Get Around. Nice song."

At that moment I had no interest in the Beach Boys.

"Thanks."

"Good taste."

I wasn't in the mood for flattery.

"Thanks. What is it, Robey? What do you want?"

He got right down to business.

"You've been seeing Clarence."

"So? Big deal."

He leaned in and spoke low.

"It *is* a big deal. Me and the boys taught him another lesson to… to remind him to keep his place. Capiche?"

"Okay. So?"

It wasn't really okay. I cared about Clarence. But I just wanted to end the conversation. Robey, however, hadn't yet made his point.

"He said you saw him…under questioning from us, of course."

I knew more about Robey now than he knew I did. I was convinced he was dangerous. I wanted him as a friend less than ever. And I wanted him out of my house. So I tried to give short answers.

"So?"

"We had an understanding."

"*You* had an understanding."

Robey repeated his standard mantra.

"It's not safe for you to see him…not safe with me…or Michael and Ted. Capiche?"

"Is that a threat?"

"Yes it is."

I was actually relieved that he wasn't at my house to look for Dad, though he didn't realize that. Anything else seemed like the smallest of small potatoes. So I was actually pretty relaxed.

"Then I'll have to live with it."

I walked toward the bedroom door.

"I'm not finished. He knows my address. He threatened me, telling me my own address, the retard. Do you know it?"

"What?"

He pointed his finger in my face.

"Don't play with me, Richman...my address. Do you know it?"

I knew why Robey was surprised. How could Clarence know his address?

"I guess...I know about where you live...about..."

My heart started to pound again.

"Did you tell him? Did you?"

"No."

I was quick with that one. He responded by coming in even closer.

"He couldn't know it unless someone told him. He's too retarded. It had to be you, Richman."

He hardly ever called me by my last name. He had done it twice in a row. He was *really* angry now. But I was telling the truth and I stuck to it.

"It wasn't me."

"I don't want anyone to know where I live, Richman. Got it?"

"Why?"

Of course I knew why, but I was curious what he would say.

"That's for me to know and you to find out. Capiche? How does the retard know?"

The answer was easy, and I spoke it confidently.

"He knows where everyone in both classes lives. He only had to glance at the sheet for a split second as it sat on the teacher's desk in 8G at the beginning of the year, and he knows everything. He knows every word of a Hardy Boys book after reading it once...and probably the whole Bible. He's what they call an idiot savant...the doctors call it autistic. That's how he knows."

I was proud of myself for knowing something Robey didn't.

"I *know* he's an idiot, Richman. And you're lying, covering for him. He couldn't know my address."

He grabbed my collar. It suddenly it dawned on me how much smarter Clarence was than Robey. He finally no longer impressed me, only repulsed me. After a few seconds, he let go of my collar and pointed his finger at my face.

"You stay away from him, or we'll take care of you like we took care of him…and worse. You want to be my friend, you listen to what I say."

He opened the door and headed down toward the living room and the front door. Just then, Dad entered. Now they were both in the same space, not five feet from each other. I noticed that Robey got a good look at him as he left. That made me more uncomfortable than the whole bedroom confrontation. Dad turned and watched him leave.

"Who the hell is he?"

"Nobody. Just a kid from my class."

"Figures. He couldn't introduce himself?"

I wanted to talk to Dad less than I wanted to talk to Robey. I continued with short answers.

"He had to leave."

"What kind of manners does he have? He's a jerk."

"Yes, he is."

He passed me by and headed for the kitchen. If I were starving, I wouldn't have walked in there. I didn't want to be anywhere near him.

I may have gotten up late that day, but I was ready to go to sleep by 8 that evening. Dad left as usual. I secretly took a sandwich into my bedroom, telling Mom I didn't feel like dinner. The summer should have been a time of vacation and rest. But it wasn't. The world around me was on a collision course. And all my emotional energy went toward trying to avoid it.

# CHAPTER 23

By the next morning, I had made up my mind. It came to me in the middle of the night between fits of anxious sleeping and waking. The smartest person I knew was in the bowels of the Lower Zoo. Billy was right. There were different kinds of smart. In fact, I surmised, maybe everyone in the world was smart in different ways, though I wasn't sure of that. At least I knew one thing—Clarence was smarter than me, maybe even smarter than Robert Rogers. He knew things regular people didn't know...not only about books and sheets on teachers' desks, but about people.

Billy tried to know those things, and sometimes he was right. But Clarence had him beat. He was *wise*. I'd heard that word used in Hebrew school about some Jewish old people from a long time ago whose names I could never remember...except somebody named Hillel, and of course about those three guys during Christmas... whoever they were. But I realized that no matter how many wise people there were in the world at any given time, Clarence was one of them. And I wanted to tell him my dilemma.

I thought about going to Clarence's house again, but then I had another idea. What if Clarence came to my house? I could give him cookies and let him talk to Billy. Billy knew more about Clarence than anyone I knew, except Clarence's mother. I could put up with the Edison lectures. And I didn't care what Mom thought. I wanted to host Clarence at my house.

Not having the memory Clarence had, I looked up Carlson in the phone book again and found the number. I dialed a phone number I wouldn't remember a minute later, though Clarence would remember my number his whole life. That was smart! I hesitated as I stood in the kitchen holding the phone in my hand, almost hanging up as it started to ring. Why did I want to have Clarence at my house? Would he make a fool of himself? What if he did something retarded? And what would I say to his refrigerator mother about the visit when she picked up the phone?

"Umm…hello?"

"Yes, can I help you?"

"Umm…is Clarence home? I'd like to speak to him."

There was a pause. Then…

"Who is this?"

She sounded suspicious.

"Umm…it's Jonathan Richman."

"Oh, hi Jonathan. He can't come to the phone now."

I could hear the edge in her tone. Probably not too many people called to actually talk to Clarence on the phone…maybe no one.

"Well…"

I knew I had to ask her if he could come over or hang up the phone. And if I hung up the phone, I probably would never be able to visit Clarence at his house again. Whatever the refrigerator part of her was all about—if that doctor was right and there *was* a refrigerator part—I was sure it would shut me out cold if I hung up.

"Umm…"

"Yes?"

"Umm…I wondered if Clarence could come to my house for some cookies and to…"

I winced as I said the next word, but she couldn't tell.

"…to *play.*"

"When? I think he'd love that."

Her tone brightened. She seemed to really like the idea.

"Today…today would be good."

"Okay. What time?"

I wanted to feed him cookies, but not lunch. I'd have to ask Mom to prepare lunch if he came too early, and I didn't want to do that.

"Umm…about one o'clock? I mean, after lunch…about one or one-thirty."

"He'll be there. What's your address?"

I was tempted to tell her to ask Clarence to give her my address. But I didn't. I just gave it to her, and she said he'd be there and hung up. The only words that came to my mind were *mission accomplished.* Like so many phrases I knew, that came from some movie. But it seemed more than appropriate now. I had wanted Clarence to visit, and he was coming over in just a few hours. All I had to do was put out some cookies and wait.

I got dressed at noon and had a small lunch at 12:30. At exactly 1:28, a car pulled up outside and Clarence, wearing a red sock hat over his bowl haircut even in late summer, got out and loped up the walkway to the front door. I wanted Mom to answer the door so I could get that part out of the way. I let it ring and watched from by bedroom door as she came down the stairs and opened the door a crack.

"Yes?"

"I'm…I'm…Clarence…Clarence…Carlson…ClarenceCarlson."

He said it proudly, like he was introducing himself at an inaugural ball. And he rocked more than usual. I guessed he was nervous. I was nervous too, and began to twirl my curls at my bedroom door. Mom seemed taken aback by the visit and was at a loss for words. She paused for a few seconds and then said, "Oh."

"I'm here to see Jonathan…Jonathan Richman…of 2235 Garden…2235 Garden…Street. This…this is…2235…Garden…"

He was in the middle of carefully repeating the address when she let him in. I couldn't see her face, but I knew she had the same look of disapproval that she'd had when Robey visited...only probably worse. Then she tilted her head as if it was the only way he could see her and spoke very slowly and deliberately.

"Yes. This—is—where—he—lives. Would—you—like—to—see—him? Do—you—un—der—stand?"

I couldn't take it anymore. I walked up between them and interrupted.

"Okay. I'll take it from here."

Mom put her hands on her hips and straightened her head from its tilted position.

"Did you invite this boy?"

"Yes I did, Mom. His name is Clarence, Mom. *His name is Clarence.* Clarence, this is my mother."

He saw the cookies across the room and just nodded his head toward her as part of his overall rocking before heading for them. He seemed more motivated to eat one of ours than he had been in his own house.

"Oh, I see you like cookies," she spoke at a more regular pace. I figured she forgot to speak slowly for the moment. Clarence laughed as he approached the plate in the dining room. I had only heard him laugh once before and, as awkward as it sounded, I liked it. I wanted Mom to like it too. She turned to me. The look of disapproval was clear.

"Well...I guess you want to be Clarence's friend."

"I *am* Clarence's friend."

"I think...that's good. It's very kind of you."

I was genuinely angry now, which I rarely was with Mom. I had been particularly sensitive to her recently, because I knew she was suffering about Dad's girlfriend Margaret...who I still had a hard time thinking of as Gwen's mother. But now I couldn't help myself.

"It's kind of *him*. It's kind of *him*, Mom."

Then I spoke to her like an executive would to his secretary.

"I'll be in my room. Come with me, Clarence."

I walked over to Clarence and led him by the shirtsleeve up to my room. With his other hand he took the whole plate of cookies as he loped behind me. I slammed the door deliberately after him as a message to Mom.

"Wait a minute."

I walked out and knocked on Billy's door.

"Billy, come into my room. I have someone here I want you to meet."

When I got back to my room, Clarence had climbed up on my bed and stood with his nose almost touching the Beach Boys poster. Suddenly he started bouncing up and down and flailing his hands like I hadn't seen since the first time Robey approached him in the school cafeteria…but even more so. I stood there shocked and dismayed. Then to make matters worse, he started squawking uncontrollably. What was this wise man doing, acting like this?

"Mike Love…Brian Wilson…I…I…love…I love you…Carl and Dennis…Carl and Dennis…Al Jardine! Carl and Dennis…Al Jardine… Mike Love…Brian Wilson…Carl and Dennis…Al Jardine! Jardine! Jardeeeene! Al Jardeeeene! I want you Beach Beach Beach Boys!"

He started tearing at the poster. I screamed at him, something I'd never done.

"What are you doing? Stop it! Stop doing that, Clarence! Now!"

I got up on the bed and tried to pull him away from the now torn poster.

"Mine," he demanded in his high-pitched whine. "Beach Boys are mine!"

He grabbed my shoulder with both hands and pulled me onto the mattress. He was a lot stronger than I expected. We lay there together on the mattress. Then he quickly pulled away from me, and I tried to stand up and pull him up in the process. But we both fell back on the mattress while he continued his high-pitched squawk.

"Mike Loooove, I loooove you. Brian, I'm tryin'. Jardeeeene makes the sceeeene."

Billy walked in. I didn't want Mom to hear us, though I knew she could anyway.

"Shut the door…fast."

She yelled from the kitchen.

"What's going on up there?"

"Nothing," I yelled back. By that time, we were both standing on the bed. I continued to scold Clarence.

"See what you've done? Now just be quiet. Be quiet!"

Clarence fell down on the bed again and tried to pull the mattress around him. Billy looked as surprised as I was when Clarence first grabbed the poster.

"What's he doing on the bed?"

"I don't know. Don't just stand there. Get him off it!"

Billy got on the bed and tried to grab Clarence. But Clarence's rocking got more intense, and like a fisherman with a feisty bass, Billy couldn't get a firm hold. Clarence and I came dangerously close to butting our heads as his flew to and fro, looking like it might fly off any second.

Finally, after what seemed like forever, he began to slow down and stopped squawking. Apparently, he ran out of energy. He had just enough left, however, to reach out and grab the model car with the terrible robin's egg paint job off my dresser.

"1958 Impala Impala…let's play. I love the 1958 Impala. LOVE it! My favorite…favorite."

As he pulled the car toward him it fell out of his hand and, with the crack of its brittle plastic parts, broke into several pieces on the floor. He suddenly froze, surprised by what he'd done.

"Oh-oh."

I didn't care about the car. I'd gotten tired of both it and its lumpy brushed-on paint job. But Clarence's behavior was very upsetting. I turned to Billy.

"Okay, genius. What's going on with him?"

"He's out of his comfort zone…his routine. This is all new to him."

"Is that so? Well, I thought he knew every word in the Bible. Doesn't it say in there somewhere not to steal? Like in the Ten Commandments? Look at my poster! He kept saying 'mine.' Well it isn't his."

I turned and faced Clarence.

"It's *mine*, Clarence. It's *mine*! And see how you've torn it? Look what you've done to it!"

Clarence was now whimpering. He climbed off the bed and stood up, rocking his usual way. Billy, who was still standing on the bed, continued.

"To him it wasn't stealing. He recognized the Beach Boys. So to him the poster was his too. It was something he shared with you. Right, Clarence?"

"I...I...I...sorry...I'm sorry...I'm...bad Clarence. Bad Clarence. Sorry. Sorry. I *love* the beach Boys. I LOVE them. I get around. I get around, Jonathan."

He began hitting himself...hard, pounding one shoulder with the other fist. That was too much to take.

"Cut that out. Stop it! Stop being retarded. Behave yourself."

I grabbed his wrists, holding them. He looked like he was going to butt heads with me for sure this time. But then he seemed to think better of it and just looked at me with darting but pleading eyes. He pulled away.

"I *love* them. I LOVE the Beach Boys. I get around. I get around!"

That struck me as funny, and I giggled.

"I can see that. I can see you get around."

His voice took on a pleading tone.

"Can I hear 'I Get Around'? I want to hear 'I Get Around.'"

"No. You can't. You've been bad. So you can't."

I'd never treated him like a baby before, though Billy didn't know that. I turned to Billy again.

"Well, I see the *idiot* part now...with my own eyes..."

Billy interrupted and spoke to Clarence.

"Clarence, I'm Billy. I'm Jonathan's brother."

Billy put his hand on Clarence's shoulder. Immediately, Clarence pulled away and then started rocking in Billy's direction.

"Billy...fifth grade...Jonathan's brother...2235 Garden Street. Billy Richman."

"That's right."

"Incredible," I whispered to myself. Then I brought up the reason I invited him over in the first place.

"All right. Clarence, I just wanted to say that you were right. Robey *does* live at 105 Green Tree Street."

"105 Green Tree Street...Robey Romero...Gwen Anderson...105 Green Tree Street. I know that. I know that."

"Right...that's right. He lives there, like you said. I'm sorry I doubted you."

I turned to Billy again.

"Now Billy, it's really important that Robey not see Dad with Gwen's mother. We've got to make sure that doesn't happen."

"What are you talking about? Why?"

"Because Gwen Anderson's mother is..."

I could feel an ache in my stomach as I revealed for the first time what I'd discovered over the past few days.

"...is...is...she's Margaret...and she's also...Robey's father's wife...believe it or not."

Billy was clearly shocked by the news. He collapsed, sitting on the side of the bed.

"Oh my goodness. Even Edison couldn't invent this."

"No, I guess he couldn't. Listen to me. Robey says he's gonna kill whoever it is she's cheating with. He knows she's cheating somehow, and..."

I no longer expected anything much from Clarence. My estimation of him had gone from idiot to wise man and back to idiot again. So I was focused completely on Billy. I had no idea that Clarence was taking in the whole thing.

"He picks on weak…Robey…on weak…weak…weakest…evil… evil picks on that…"

I was tired of dealing with Clarence…at least for the time being.

"Okay, Clarence, please. I'm busy now. We'll play later."

He became strangely persistent.

"No! No!"

I was ready to tell him to shut up again. But Billy picked up on something.

"Listen to him. He's trying to say something."

I had forgotten the other side of Clarence, the side I had originally wanted Billy to see…the wise side. Now his words seemed like just a distraction.

"No he isn't, Billy. He's just mumbling. I know when he's making sense and when he's not, and he's not making sense."

"Yes he is. Ask him."

"All right…whatever you say."

Clarence was doing his usual rocking and swaying. Impatient, I tried to get his attention.

"What is it, Clarence? What are you trying to say? Billy said you're trying to tell us something."

He spoke slowly, his voice lowering a few octaves.

"'…because your adversary the devil, as a roaring lion, walketh about, seeking whom he may devour.' First Peter…First Peter five… five, eight."

There was that Bible voice again, speaking from some other place. I had to explain it to Billy.

"Not that again. I think that's the Bible…from the New Testament, probably. He's done that before."

Billy responded in agreement.

"Of course it's the Bible. I don't think that's in our Bible, the Tanach. But it sounds like the Bible, like the New Testament.

He turned to Clarence.

"What are you saying, Clarence?"

I jumped in with my knowledge of Clarence's book memorization gift.

"Look, he knows the whole thing by heart...and the Hardy Boys books too, by the way. He just...well, he just starts."

Indeed, that got him started. And he recited from a Hardy Boys book.

"Hardy Boys...*The Tower Treasure*...Chapter One...Frank and Joe Hardy clutched the grips of their motorcycles...no, I don't want to...don't want Hardy Boys...no...not now...First Peter...First Peter Five..."

"Just like that," I said, gesturing Clarence's way. Billy, however, continued to pursue things further.

"What are you trying to say, Clarence? Is it about Robey?"

"About Robey...yes...definitely...about Robey...Robey...Romero..."

He spelled it out.

"R...O...B...E...Y."

Now even I was becoming interested. I turned back to Clarence.

"What about him? What are you saying?"

"Picks on weak...like...like...Jews...like weak Jews...remember. Remember? Drug store...remember?"

"Yes, I remember."

Billy was understandably confused. He pressed his glasses to his face as if to gain understanding.

"What's he talking about now? He's lost me."

I explained about the conversation Robey and I had at the drug store and how I had shared it with Clarence.

"Evil...weak...picks on...like...like..."

Billy continued to draw him out, gesturing with his hands.

"Like what, Clarence? Like what?"

Clarence pointed at his own heart.

"Like me..."

"Brilliant," I whispered again.

"Like...like..."

"Like what?" Billy asked.

"Like...like..."

His finger pointed right at Billy.

"Like you...not your...your...father...you...*you*."

We stood there speechless for several seconds. Then he finished with a flourish.

"He...he...Robey...Robey likes to...he like to break things... weak things...like my soup...French fries in my soup. He likes to break things...like Billy...like French fries...in my soup."

We were silent again. Clarence had spoken. The wise idiot had shared his wisdom, for whatever it was worth.

When Clarence's mother came to the door to get Clarence, Mom answered. If she was upset about the sounds she heard from my bedroom, she didn't say anything. And neither did I. But I could see she was somewhat put out, her mouth tightening and her eyes glaring at me in a "You know what I told you" expression. She did bring herself to say a few words directly to Clarence before he left.

"Do you have everything?"

"Everything...yes...but...the Beach Boys...that's his...Jonathan's...I'm leaving...leaving...thanks for the...the cookies. They were good."

"You're welcome."

I was glad he thanked her. For some reason I still wanted her to be impressed with him. But then he suddenly darted away from her and loped quickly out in his usual oblivious manner, running ahead of his mother.

"Well..." she said with obvious embarrassment, "thank you for having Clarence. Did everything work out okay? Wait up, Clarence!"

Just then, Billy entered the room.

"Yes," all three of us said at once.

"Well...I'm glad."

He ran out into the yard, and she backed out onto the front porch like she was leaving the presence of the queen of England. When the door closed, Mom turned to me.

"What was that all about…Beach Boys?"

"Nothing."

That night lying in bed, I reviewed the day. It had been exciting to say the least. Then my thoughts turned once again to Dad. I felt like everything was upside down. I was the father and he was the child. I knew things he didn't know, and I was trying to protect him from himself.

"Dad should be in 8H, not me," I whispered out loud. "Maybe if he felt the sting of Robey's thumbtacks, he'd stop seeing Robey's mother…step-mother…Gwen's mother…beautiful Gwen's beautiful, ugly mother."

I felt like the stuck elevator was getting crowded, like the room in the ship in *A Night at the Opera* that I'd seen the year before on the Late Show. Only in the movie they all fell out at once, and we were all still stuck in there…Robey, and Clarence, and Billy, and Gwen, and her mother, and Robey's father, and Mom…and Dad. Yes, he was stuck in there too, and he didn't even know it; stuck in the stupid Zoo…stuck between floors with everyone else, and he didn't know it.

Then it occurred to me that the whole world might be stuck between floors in that elevator. And maybe that's what kept everyone from being as smart as they really were…whatever kind of smart that was. So maybe we were all different kinds of idiot…idiot…what was that word? That's right…*savants*, that's what they call it…savants- idiots who were smart…and were stuck. Maybe everyone was stuck. Maybe everyone was a Clarence, only he was the only one who knew it. Maybe that's where his wisdom came from. Maybe that was the gift from his Jesus that he talked about, the gift that meant so much to him.

Sometime after midnight, I drifted to sleep with all those thoughts swirling in my mind. As often occurred when I woke up, I couldn't remember my dreams from the night before. But this time the thoughts were the first things that came to my mind.

# CHAPTER 24

WHEN I WAS YOUNGER, A nice bike ride early on a warm, sunny summer day was a treat. That morning it was more of an escape from the thoughts of the night before. I dressed quickly, ran downstairs, and was out the door by 8 A.M.

I liked riding on vaguely familiar streets and exploring neighborhoods near mine that I'd only passed through in a car or on foot. I spent almost two hours gliding past duplexes and ranch homes, two-story moderns and old Cape Cods. I didn't know the names of those in the houses, but I knew the houses. And none of them were as rundown as Gwen's house…Robey's house. Most of them were well-kept. They had flowerbeds and rose gardens, trimmed hedges, and freshly painted shutters. How many of them also had people in them who were stuck between floors, trapped in cages like I was?

I pulled on both hand breaks and screeched to a halt. I had to stop thinking those thoughts. My mind wanted to untangle a whole year and all the tangled up connections in it—mothers, fathers, stepmothers, stepfathers, classmates—I needed a break. I hopped back on the bike seat and began to pedal again. I knew I was headed back toward the center of town as I rode through one of those small suburban neighborhoods. My hands and feet were strangely drawn that way, even though I had planned to leave the city behind, so to speak, and hit the wide open spaces.

I saw the car dealership coming toward me in the distance. I recognized the two cars instantly...the big black car and the red T-Bird. As I neared it and coasted by the showroom, I could see Margaret through the glass. She seemed to be walking briskly near the front of the store almost as fast as I was riding. Without even thinking, I rode around the corner and put my bike down behind the showroom building. I rounded the corner and walked in. I dreaded hearing the bell that reminded me of the dentist's office but, oddly, no one seemed to notice. The two salesmen who were in the front were focused on Margaret, whom I could now see had a swollen black eye. She was angrily pacing between them like a caged bird.

"Is he in the back? Get him out here!"

One of the salesmen put both hands up with his palms toward her and spoke quietly but firmly.

"This isn't the place for this, Margaret. This is a business."

She shouted right in his face.

"Shut your mouth, Joe. Get away from me, you two!"

He snapped back.

"Margaret!"

She stamped her foot and turned to the other salesman.

"Just get him out here, Steve. Now!"

They closed ranks around her, reminding me of Robey's iron filings. As they closed in, she started screaming wildly.

"Get his ass out here right now! Get off me...both of you. Don't either of you touch me!"

They both instantly backed off at once.

"We're not touching you," the one named Steve said. "Calm down."

When Robey's father suddenly came storming out of the back of the store, the shock of his rage rattled me. When I recovered, I figured it was time to leave. But I couldn't even if I wanted to, because Margaret and the two salesmen were pretty much blocking the main doors now. So I thought quickly. There was a bright blue Corvair next to me, and I ducked into it, pulling the door closed. I didn't want to shut it altogether and call attention to myself, so I left it open just a crack. But as it happened, I could also hear what was going on in the showroom. The new-car glue smell hit me as I ducked down underneath the dashboard on the front passenger side. I fought not to gag.

"What are you doing here? Go home."

I recognized the voice I had last heard at Gwen's house. He was angry now, just as he was then.

"You've got a lot of nerve. Look what you did to my eye. You two jerks are witnesses."

"Leave them out of this."

Her voice got even louder, and she began to shriek.

"I want a divorce! I want a divorce! You can't hit me like that, you…"

"You deserved it."

"You son of a…I'll take you to the cleaners. You'll have *nothing* when I'm finished with you!"

"You won't get a dime," he said with a vicious growl.

Steve interjected in a light playful tone, probably calculated to bring the level down.

"'Cause he doesn't *have* a dime. He hasn't sold a car in…"

Robey's father's voice boomed back at him and shook me again.

"Shut your mouth, Steve. Stay out of it or I'll rip your throat out."

Steve responded in a cowering voice. "Sorry Dom. I was just kidding."

I'd never heard Robey's father's name before. It was strange, exotic, like Robey's.

"Listen, you whore. I know what you've been doing. And your slut daughter is just like you. Like mother, like daughter."

"How dare you call Gwenny that!"

"The truth hurts, doesn't it!" Dom bellowed back.

Now I knew where Robey got that word for Gwen. I wanted to jump out of the car and tell Dom off. But of course I couldn't. As one of them grabbed the other and they struggled, I could hear gasping and groaning. After several seconds, Dom barked at his iron filings.

"Hold her, boys. Get her off me!"

Then I heard the crack of a slap and a high-pitched scream. I almost jumped and shook the car, but I clung to the floor and tried not to breathe.

"Get off me, you two apes. Let me go! How *dare* you talk about Gwen that way! She's a good girl."

"She's a slut. Let her go, boys."

She wasn't finished with her tirade.

"Yeh? Your son…he's just like you…a pig…a violent filthy pig! He'd better stay away from my daughter. He'd better stay away!"

He laughed scornfully.

"She's too ugly for him. She better stay away from *him!*"

"Shut up, you two! Someone's coming," I heard Steve say. The bell rang.

"Can I help you?" he said softly, but with a hint of tension in his voice.

"I'm just looking. I'm interested in the Corvair. I saw a little ad, a movie GM put out about it…about ten minutes long. It looks like a great car."

"I know *just* the ad. I've seen it myself."

The tension in his voice was gone. He seemed so polished…even right after he was holding Margaret while Dom slapped her…at least it sounded like that's what happened.

"It's quite a road hugger, and the safest car that GM has ever produced. It's very well-built. I'm Steve."

"I'm Ted."

I heard the rustling sound of shirtsleeves as they shook hands.

"We have one over here, a beautiful blue model. Did you notice the rear engine in the ad?"

"Yes, I did."

"You get more traction that way. And there's plenty of room under the front hood for luggage. Check it out."

I heard the front hood lift. My heart was going faster than on the second floor of Gwen's house. Then the hood slammed down, shaking the whole car with me in it. I thought, *It couldn't be that well-built.*

"Nice."

"Check out the passenger compartment. You won't believe how roomy it is."

Now it *was* time to leave. I knew they were all on the street side of the car, which was the passenger side. I couldn't go out that door, which was the one slightly open. So I turned the handle on the driver side door as quietly as I could and scrambled out, leaving it open. I ran low, like I'd seen Groucho do in *A Night at the Opera.* I passed the salesmen's cubicles and strode into the back of the store, past an open office. I could hear a man inside say to another man, "Romero's fired. Tell him to get his things and get out."

I ran out a back door and through the service area. The sound of drills and hammers filled the space, and I could see several mechanics at work on cars in different stages of repair. A bay door was open to the parking lot, and I cleared that in a split second. I was finally free. I quickly retrieved my bike from the back of the building.

As I rode away, I knew I didn't want to go home. I wasn't in the mood to face Mom and Billy, and especially Dad...if by chance he was there. Instead, I felt drawn once again to Clarence's house. Even though he had ripped my Beach Boys poster and acted like a crazy loon, his insanity seemed better than the pain in Mom's eyes. I was ready for some childish Lego playing...and Mrs. Carlson's cake or cookies. Clarence's house was just the thing for me that late summer afternoon.

As I had hoped, the soft off-white almost pink carpet of Clarence's living room was indeed the perfect place to forget everything and act like a little boy without a care in the world. We worked together to build what we called a skyscraper. It was a rectangular structure with a complex multicolored scheme; and the bigger it got, the more it seemed to please Clarence. I had learned by observation that a certain kind of rocking and smiling indicated deep satisfaction. And when he did this while seated on the floor, he resembled a happy toddler, which I had no problem with that day. At least he wasn't grabbing posters and swinging his head wildly.

Everything was peaceful, and the events of the past few hours were the last things I wanted to think about. But I felt I wouldn't be totally content with my milk, chocolate chip cookies, and Legos until I released the tension of the day with a few quick comments…spoken more to myself than Clarence.

"Everybody's cheating on somebody…my dad, Gwen's mom… everybody. It's like a soap opera. I'm not even supposed to think about these things at this age."

That was the kind of kid's comment that adults either laugh about because it's funny or cry about because it's true. But Clarence, who was busy building, and from whom I once again didn't expect a response, did neither.

"'For jealousy *is* the rage of a man: therefore he will not spare in the day of vengeance. He will not regard any ransom; neither will he rest content, though thou givest many gifts.'"

He spoke the verse in that other voice, which I could never quite get used to.

"What in the world is that supposed to mean, Clarence?"

He didn't answer me. Instead, without any introduction to warn me, he began praying. At least that's what I thought it was. I'd never heard anything like it. It wasn't out of a book or memorized like the Bible verses or even the Hardy Boys. It was from somewhere inside Clarence that I'd never been introduced to. And it was accompanied by faster rocking and faster speaking than I'd seen or heard before. It began with "Jesus...Jesus," which caught me off guard.

"I pray...I mean I *really* pray for Mr. Richman and Mrs. Romero, and Mr. Romero. Will you *pleeeese* hear me and forgive them?"

I was amazed again for the umpteenth time. He got the names *exactly* right. What's more, he seemed to understand all the relationships. And there was something else. What was it? Then I suddenly realized what it was. Where was the stuttering and repeating of words? Where was the halting and hesitating? It seemed to be replaced by a high-pitched intensity that was nothing like the flat tones I was used to hearing from him. It was like there were three Clarences...the autistic stutterer, the remote loud speaker, and the high-pitched desperate yearner. I was taken aback as he continued.

"Most of all...*pleeeese* forgive Robey. You said you were a doctor. Fix him because he needs fixing. I need fixing, too. And you fix me because you *looove* me. Yes, you *looove* me...and I *looove* you."

The way he said love was long and whining, and it made me uncomfortable. It was similar to the way he said Mike Love of the Beach Boys' name. But it was, at the same time, from somewhere else altogether. And his rocking reminded me more of my great uncle when he prayed than Clarence when he was just being Clarence.

Now I really wanted to leave. I regretted that I'd come. But he continued...this time with a list that reminded me of the old Romper Room show I watched on TV when I was four, when the teacher would *see* different children through her magic mirror...something that embarrassed me even then, because somehow I knew it was fake. How could she really see us? But though I was embarrassed now too, this surely didn't seem to be fake. It seemed to be very real.

"And I forgive Robey for pushing my French fries into my soup and being really mean to me like people were to you a long time ago... and James who pushed me off the swing, and Barbara, and Cathy who laughed at me, and Jonathan when he called me a name, but he's my friend who plays Legos with me and likes the Beach Boys...and... and...and..."

Was he now going back to repeating and halting, with all the "ands"?

And what was it with all of this forgiving this person and that person…and me? I had been hoping he didn't remember that time I called him a name. After all, I couldn't remember what I called him. But then again, he seemed to remember everything he ever saw or read.

"And…and…and my father…I forgive my father…yes, I do that. So *pleeease* forgive Mrs. Romero and Mr. Richman for their sin…and Mr. Romero too, for the bad things he did."

I was actually moved somewhere inside me by all of this sincere forgiving, though I didn't want to admit it. But it also made me nervous. Would he start swinging his head wildly and grabbing for things again?

"Okay, Clarence. Maybe I should leave now."

I got up and he followed suit, following me like a puppy dog and almost running into me. I was finished, but apparently he wasn't.

"And protect Jonathan's brother, Billy, from whatever Robey wants to do, because you are the *Grrreaaat* Shepherd who protects the flock, and you're watching over Billy…to protect him, too. Pleeease bring him through it better than ever."

I'd had enough. Was Clarence wise or just plain crazy? He was, in fact, starting to scare me now.

"He'll be fine, Clarence…just fine. Billy will be fine," I said walking toward the door.

"Yes…yes…he will…he will…he will be…okay…okay now… now he will…he will be…in the end…all things…all things…will be…in the…end…the end."

I nodded and tried to convince Clarence…*and myself.*

"Right. You said it. *The end.* I've got to leave, Clarence. It's getting late."

"Another…another cookie?"

"No thanks."

He rocked to and fro a bit faster.

"We could…we could build…a…another sky…scraper."

"No…no…that's okay."

"Jonathan?"

"What?"

I wasn't used to Clarence speaking my name to me or asking me something and then waiting for an answer. I had never once known him to do that. After his surprising question, he just stood there for what seemed like a minute. But it was probably just several seconds. I repeated myself, though still not expecting a coherent answer remotely like a real conversation.

"What, Clarence?"

He seemed to rock in my direction.

"Umm…I really…I really…really like you. You're…you're a… really…really good friend."

Even though Clarence wasn't looking at me (in fact, he was looking every other direction), I knew he was speaking directly *to* me…more directly than he ever had. Then he did something else I'd never seen him do. He reached out to me with his arms and attempted to hug me even as he continued rocking. He fell short and just put his arms over my shoulders, in a kind of more benevolent Robey gesture; only he wasn't tall and draping his frame over me. He simply aimed for my shoulders and then pulled me to himself, putting his head on my chest very briefly. Then he pulled away. I somehow realized that he had done something very unusual and difficult for him. But I knew it was very important; not only for him, but for me.

"Thank you, Clarence," I said, as I stood there, careful for some reason not to respond with a corresponding embrace. I knew he wouldn't like that. But I knew what he *would* like.

"Thank you. I like you too. You're a good friend."

He kind of looked at me for a split second, and a little smile appeared at the corners of his mouth.

"You…you…you go. It's…it's late."

I realized how genuine and thoughtful that small statement was. "Yes, it is. I'll see you soon."

I meant that. Friends see each other at some interval, and we were friends. That was clear.

Riding home on my bike in the golden waning hours of a cloudless, summer day, I thought about how I never would have met Clarence if I weren't in the Upper Zoo. I wouldn't have paid attention to him, except to notice him out of the very corner of my eye, loping into some mysterious classroom for retarded kids that I would never want to know anything about. If I were Robert Rogers, I would never know his extraordinary almost miraculous memory, his Bible voice, or oddly heart-stirring prayers…or his surprising love.

And I wouldn't have met Gwen, with her changeableness and strange forgetfulness…and her sad, exquisite, sensitive, and even tragic beauty. I would have seen her disappear with her curtain of hair into a classroom I'd never enter or want to enter. And I'd go about my business in a classroom with Robert Rogers and all the other *normal* people. But I wouldn't know her, or Clarence…or get to know Robey so close up…close enough to see the rage…and the fear.

# CHAPTER 25

My bicycle seemed to have a mind of its own that evening. It carried me through Clarence's tree-lined neighborhood and beyond. It floated past shrinking houses and narrowing front yards. It coasted down gentle grades and pedaled up slowly rising hills, from slightly recognizable blocks to very recognizable corners. And it finally pointed me toward the deteriorated structure with which I had become so familiar.

I stood next to my bike one house down and across the street…just a stone's throw from the little park we visited in the dim moonlight… watching the thin edge of sunlight slowly recede behind the house. I stood there for ten minutes while darkness was falling, and was about to pedal off toward home when I heard crying and the slamming of a front door. I knew instantly it was Gwen. I hopped on my bike and rode over. She had run to the edge of the yard and was crying convulsively. Her tears were falling onto her light brown dress, which was clearly ripped near the collar.

I threw the bike down and entered the yard. As she came close, she let out a short scream. I had surprised her.

"It's just me…Jonathan. I was riding by. What's the matter?"

As she came close, I could see that her hair was once again hanging like a straggly curtain over her face. It wasn't as long or full as it once was, so it couldn't hide her eyes as well. But her face was still hidden. And her tears had soaked through the thick strands, causing them to cling to her cheeks like seaweed. When I saw her, my heart sank.

"He...he...no more...he...I can't say it...I'm so...ashamed... dirty...you'd hate me if you knew. I'm a slut...he's right! I want to die. I want to die!"

She didn't have to say any more. My naive mind got enough of a picture. He lost his job, came home angry, and treated her like the slut he called her.

"Get on my bike. You can go side-saddle."

She paused and then giggled slightly through her tears.

"I don't want to die *that* way."

"Get on. I'll be careful. I promise."

I had no idea where I was going to take her. I simply knew that this wasn't a pretend hero's daydream. This was the real deal. I was going to save Gwen from Dom, and Margaret, and Robey, and the whole sordid life she had been forced to live. I was going to rescue her, and stop him...somehow. I didn't know how, but somehow. At any rate, I would take her away on my bike, and we'd figure the rest out later.

How much of this was actually just a desire to be Gwen's hero— even I couldn't tell. But I did believe, though without any evidence, that I could somehow help her by taking her away from the house. And that was all that mattered.

It was during the slow wobbly ride, with Gwen more or less in my unsteady arms as I steered the bike, that she shared more. This was spoken very close to my right ear, because there was no other way she could speak to me from a sidesaddle position.

"He got fired. He was so angry when he walked in. There was no one there, no one but me. He came into my room, pushing things around. He was cursing, saying all kinds of horrible things about my mother and me, calling me names and...and bad things...worse things. Maybe he's right. Maybe I *am* what he says I am . Maybe it's my fault.

But I *tried* to get away. I *did*. He told me I wanted him. I pushed him. I told him to *get off me*, get away from me. He never listens. He never does. But I pushed him harder than ever, as hard as I could. I never did that before. I never pushed him like that. He fell and I heard his head hit the desk chair...*crack*. Then he got up and started slapping me...he was...hitting...and hitting...slapping...and...trying to pull my dress off and..."

Pure rage began to rise in me. I pedaled faster and faster. My heart was racing. I could feel it in my temple and through my wrists. And I could hear Clarence's strange and mysterious prayer voice inside my head saying, *Pleeease forgive Mr. Romero. Pleeease.* It sounded completely ridiculous now. I just wanted to hurt Mr. Romero...and Robey too. I wanted to kick them like Robey and the iron filings kicked me. I wanted to kill them...yes, to kill them. I wanted them dead so they couldn't hurt Gwen ever again.

But of course, I knew I couldn't do that. So what could I do? How could I protect Gwen from this vicious evil man and his evil son? I suddenly pulled on the hand breaks and stopped up short on the bike. Gwen practically fell off, and screamed out a tremendous shriek followed by an angry growl.

"What are you doing? You idiot! You almost threw me off the bike!"

"We're going to the police."

"Are you completely crazy? We can't do that. I told you. It's our secret. He...he told me not to tell. He said he'd...we can't!"

I straddled my bike and stood my ground.

"We are. Get back on."

"It's too far."

"It's not that far. I want you to come with me. We have to stop them."

She paused for several seconds to think about what I was saying. Then slowly, without comment, she climbed back on. I started pedaling again and gradually picked up speed until we attained some semblance of balance. She groaned in my ear, clearly in pain.

"Please let's just get there. This bike is killing me."

I knew she was uncomfortable, but the bike was faster than walking, and we had to get to the police station. We said nothing the rest of the way. Finally, we arrived on Main Street and passed the drug store. As we pulled up to the station a block or so away, a few policemen were outside. One of them eyed us up and down.

"You know that's not safe, son. One or both of you could get hurt."

"Yes, sir. Can you watch the bike?"

Before he had a chance to answer we hopped off, dropping the bike like an old pile of junk, and flew up the steps into the station. There were two cops standing around in front of the intake desk with another behind it. He spoke up.

"Yeh?"

Gwen just wanted to leave. She tugged at my shirtsleeve.

"Let's go, Jonathan."

One of the policemen spoke up.

"What's the problem, son?"

I took a deep breath and spoke.

"I...we...I..."

The other one spoke. He had a paunch like Dad did, I thought probably from too many donuts in the morning.

"Yeh? Well, we're here to help. So how can we help you two?"

Just then, the cop from outside came in and whispered something in his ear. He turned back to me. Notwithstanding the paunch like Dad's, he seemed like the nicest of them all, so I directed my plea to him.

"Sir...her stepfather...he...he hit her...and..."

Gwen became more insistent, pulling my arm and trying to drag me toward the door.

"Let's go, Jonathan. Let's leave."

I pulled her back toward the policeman.

"Wait Gwen. As I was saying, he threatened my father...he threatened to come over and..."

The policeman straightened up and focused all of his public guardian's attention on me.

"What? Who threatened your father? What's his name?"

I summoned up courage and spoke.

"Dom...Dom Romero."

He looked at me cross-eyed like I was totally insane.

"What? The car salesman? Are you kidding?"

"No sir," I responded as earnestly as I could.

He burst into raucous laughter, holding his donut belly and almost losing his cap. When he had composed himself, he began to lecture me.

"Look, son, he's a real nice man. He wouldn't hurt your father. He wouldn't hurt a fly. I know him. I know him real well...*real well*. See, I bought a real nice car from him a few years ago...a Chevy...a *real* nice car."

I didn't care if it was a Rolls Royce. I had to make him understand. Gwen was no help. She had given up trying to shut me up or drag me out. She just stood there with her hair not quite covering her eyes, which I could see were closed. I tried talking to the cop again.

"But her stepfather said..."

"People say all kinds of things, son" the policeman butted in. "Yep, it was a real nice Chevy...a used Impala...drives like a jet, a solid car. He's a nice man, son."

I switched to trying to explain what Dom was doing to Gwen, but I didn't have the words.

"He hit her...he...he...I don't know...he..."

Gwen opened her eyes wide and stamped her foot hard on the concrete floor.

"Stop, Jonathan."

"Wait, Gwen. We have to tell him."

The policemen took on an irritated I've-had-enough expression.

"Listen kid, if my daughter went around in a Beatnik Beatle-type yeh-yeh-yeh haircut like that, where you couldn't even see her eyes, and rode sidesaddle on a boy's bike with him in the middle of the damn…excuse me…darn street…"

"Yes sir, but…"

He looked down at me dismissively and continued.

"Well, I might have to set my daughter straight if she did that. You know what I mean? And I might have to discipline her friend, too. Sometimes kids need discipline. Get the point, son?"

"But my father…he said he'd get my father…"

The cop behind the desk spoke up.

"We can't just go by hearsay, son. You know what hearsay is?"

Now I was being quizzed like I was in the Upper Zoo. But if I played along, maybe I could get them to understand what was happening.

"I don't know. I think so."

He leaned back in his chair and joined his hands behind his head.

"Well let me tell you what it means, son. It means if *he* hasn't done anything, *we* can't do anything. So go home and have a good talk with your fathers…or stepfathers, as the case may be…"

"Yeh, as the case may be," one of the others chimed in. "And pick up your bike. You can't just throw it *anywhere*. There are places for parking it."

"But…he…to her…he…"

"Go home, kid. And walk the girl home. Don't put her on your bike. And…call us if there's any *real* trouble. Okay? We're busy."

"But…"

One of them shoved us toward the door.

"We're busy. Goodbye."

We left. I walked over and picked up the bike. When we had walked down the street about a block, I stopped.

"They were a great help. Hop on."

Gwen hesitated.

"But the man said we shouldn't ride…"

"Just get on. We've got to warn my dad…not that he'll even be home. But still…get on."

Resigned and exhausted, she surrendered and got on the bike. I found my balance as I slowly pedaled and we wobbled away. She whispered into my ear in a trembling and fearful voice.

"It was our secret. You promised."

I didn't respond to her complaint. I only held her more tightly so she wouldn't fall off. For a moment I felt a little like the father she didn't have. I wanted to keep her safe, and I wished I could carry her to safety forever and beyond.

"You promised," she repeated with greater conviction.

I thought to myself, *I kept my promise when we talked with those cops. They didn't hear much from me that made any sense, and believed less.* But I didn't say anything.

Because we were riding slowly and it was getting dark, it took a long time to get to my house. It was almost nine o'clock by the time we got there. Mom was standing at the door waiting for me. She looked very upset. Her hands were on her hips and she spoke the first words slowly and deliberately, sort of like Mr. Schott.

"Where—have—you—been? Where's Billy? Isn't he with you?"

"No."

"No?"

She said that with greater alarm. I shook my head no for emphasis.

"Well then, where is he?"

"I don't know," I pleaded innocently. She noticed Gwen for the first time.

"Who's this?"

"This is Gwen."

She seemed distracted by her concern for Billy, but asked about her anyway.

"Gwen who?

"Gwen Anderson."

Gwen just stood there and said nothing.

"Oh. Where is she from?" Mom said halfheartedly.

"From my class...at school."

"Oh."

Even though Mom was distracted, I could sense the old disapproval. This was another person I should feel sorry for, but not be friends with…and it was also a girl, which made things more complicated. But she did notice Gwen's distress, and remarked about it seemingly more out of obligation than concern.

"Is she okay? She looks like she's been crying."

I'd had it with her third person interrogations.

"Why don't you ask *her?*"

But she didn't ask Gwen anything. Instead she laid down the law.

"She needs to go home, Jonathan. It's getting late."

Then she returned to her interrogation, like I was withholding information from her.

"*Where* is Billy?"

"I told you, I don't know."

"What do you mean, you don't know. I thought he was with you. I mean you came home so late. I thought he was with you."

I felt like Cain being grilled about Abel, which we'd just read about in Hebrew school.

"He's not."

Then suddenly, I began to worry too. Where was he?

"Did you check his room?"

"Yes, of course I did," she said.

"Did you check everywhere? The basement…everywhere?"

She was clearly getting more agitated as she sensed my concern.

"He's not in the house. I checked everywhere."

I left Gwen in the doorway and ran around the house to the back yard. I could just faintly hear Mom say to her, "Come in and call your parents." But my focus that moment was elsewhere. I began to scream at the top of my lungs.

"Billy! Billy!"

I don't know why I ran to the back yard. Certainly screaming into the trees and the back yards of neighbors behind us would be less effective than shouting up and down the street in front of the house… not that there was great sense in that either.

"Billy! Billy! Billy!"

I heard a slight rustling in the tall bushes that were up against the back patio. Whatever squirrel I disturbed would have to put up with my more important task. And that went for the neighbors who might complain too.

"Billy! Billly!"

When the squirrel began to moan, I realized it wasn't a squirrel. I ran over to the bush and tried to separate the branches. This time I whispered, almost afraid of my own voice.

"Billy? Billy?"

I heard the moan again. I ran to the front of the house.

"Mom! Mom!"

She was inside with Gwen. I almost kicked the screen door in.

"Mom! The back yard! The bushes! Get a flashlight. Put on the patio lights! Hurry."

"What is it?"

"Just hurry!"

Mom ran around, obeying my orders, flicking the lights on from the inside of the house.

"Come on Gwen," I shouted.

We ran around to the back. The patio lights, which we almost never used except for the rare summer party, created a warm glow. I grabbed the flashlight and added to the light, shining it into the tall, thick bush where the moan came from.

There, crumpled and tangled in the back of a bush against the wall, was Billy. The first thing the light exposed was his torn tee shirt. Then I scanned his body from one end to the other. There were what looked like deep gashes and numerous cuts and a good deal of fresh and caked blood. I was almost positive this was the work of Robey and the iron filings. Who else could it be? It had to be.

"Billy. Are you okay?"

He spoke in a weak, thin, wavering voice.

"What's...what's it...look...like?"

Just then Mom became somewhat hysterical. She paced in a circle rapidly like she was chasing the perpetrator. Then she came close and called into the bush.

"Billy…Billy, can you move? Billy!"

"I don't think so. My head…it hurts."

I knew she wanted to hold him, but the bush was too thick. She tried to comfort him from a few feet away, like the mother of an earthquake victim buried under a few feet of rubble.

"Oh, Billy. You'll be okay. We're here, baby. We're here. Just…just rest…don't move. We'll get you…baby…my baby."

She sobbed quietly. Actually, it was more of a whimper. I knew she was controlling herself, not wanting to worry him.

He moaned again. It was a long, slow, painful moan. I pushed the branches aside the best I could. He was trapped, lying out of my reach on the wall side of the bush. I fought through the branches until I got as close to him as I could. But I couldn't get right next to him. The foliage and number of branches with thorns kept me back. I could now clearly see the red blood in the beam of the flashlight. I turned around to Mom and Gwen.

"Call an ambulance!"

Mom, who had been pacing and quietly saying Billy's name over, suddenly came to her senses and ran into the house. I could hear Gwen quietly weeping several feet away. Now was my chance to ask Billy the most obvious question.

"What happened, Billy?"

Billy gasped out the answer.

"Robey…Robey."

"Yes, Billy? What did he do?"

"Jonathan…Jonathan…"

Tears came to my eyes when he called my name.

"I'm here, Billy. We'll get you out of there. Hey, if it wasn't for Edison, we wouldn't have found you. See? The flashlight."

I wiggled the flashlight in my hand.

"Sorry, Billy. I'm really sorry…for everything. I'm sorry for the way I…I don't know…the way I treated you all last year. I was *so* wrong. I was *so* wrong, Billy. Billy?"

He was silent. I couldn't hear anything, even breathing.

"Billy? Billy?"

It seemed to take an eternity for the siren to wail in the distance. I heard it increase until the sound of the vehicle itself and the shutting doors could be heard in the driveway. I shined the flashlight on two rescue workers as they ran into the back yard.

"Turn it off! You're blinding us! We have our own. Where is he?"

I pointed to where Billy was.

"There."

He shined his much-more-effective flashlight.

"What the hell? We'll have to cut the damn tree down."

"It's a bush…a big, fat bush," the other one said.

"That's even worse. Get the frickin' tree cutters."

The other one ran to the front yard and came back with some kind of long shears. I guessed they must have used them to cut tree limbs. But they weren't great for the bush, which was more like a thick hedge. After several minutes of "frickin'" and "damn," I could see them finally reach Billy.

"Son, you all right? We're gonna take you out of here."

There was no answer.

"Get some oxygen over here, slowpoke. Come on!"

They seemed to me a bit like Laurel and Hardy, but without the weight problem, since they were both as skinny as toothpicks. As I watched them, I wasn't very encouraged. But I supposed they had to know what they were doing. My heart pounded and ached all at one time. Mom and I kept calling Billy's name out, but he didn't say anything in response.

"Billy! Billy! Billy!"

"Hurry!" one of the workers shouted. "John, get the stretcher."

One of them ran to get it. I could see what I figured was an oxygen mask being put over Billy's face.

"Pulse?"

"Yeh. Just."

"Breathing?"

There was a pause. Then...

"Just. Looks like he fainted from the blood loss, or worse... definitely could be worse."

"Okay. Let's get him out of here."

They rolled him onto the stretcher, which they'd laid next to the hedge, and picked him up together.

"Let's get out of here."

"I'm coming along," my mother said in a panicked voice.

"Fine," one of the ambulance workers said.

They disappeared around the corner with the stretcher. I heard the doors of the ambulance slam and the siren screech as it drove away. Soon there was just the sound of summer crickets and Gwen's sniffling. I stood there next to her.

"It's all my fault," she whimpered.

"What are you talking about?"

"If Robey and his father didn't live with us, none of this would have happened. It's all because of me that they're there. It's all my fault. I want to die."

She began to weep like she had in her front yard. I didn't know what to do. I took her by the shoulders and looked into the wet strands of hair in front of her eyes.

"Please stop...please. We've got to think. Billy might be...I mean, he might not be okay. Robey's out there...and your stepdad. We have to think, Gwen. We've got to think. So please, stop!"

Suddenly, while my hands were on her shoulders, she put her head on *my* shoulder while a new flood of tears poured out. I could feel them, mixed with mucus, soaking through my tee shirt. I wanted to wipe it off, but I knew I couldn't. Instinctively, I started patting her on the back with one of my hands.

"There, there. It's okay, Gwenny. It'll be okay, Gwenny."

I didn't expect to call her by the name her mother did, but it just came out that way.

"I'll take care of you. Don't be afraid. Everything will be okay."

I couldn't believe that my brother might be dead and here I was trying to comfort Gwen Anderson, who was dripping tears and mucus all over me. I had to admit that normally I liked comforting Gwen, but this was the wrong time. I stopped patting her back and drew back. She began to catch her breath like a baby calming down after a crying spell.

"Shhh. Shhh," I whispered.

She took over a minute to calm down. Finally, she stood there and tried to take deep breaths. When she had composed herself, she spoke.

"You're…you're…you're my only friend…the only one…who doesn't hate me."

I had to say something, so I said the first thing I could think of. I meant it, but I also wanted to move on.

"That's not true, Gwen. No one hates you. Listen…umm…wipe your face, and get on my bike. We'll go to your house and try to see your mother. Okay?"

I gave her a napkin I'd stuffed in my pocket that morning. She blew her nose in it and put it in her own pocket.

"There, now let's go."

She looked around her at the darkness of the night.

"It's…it's too dark."

"We'll use the headlight. Come on."

She hesitated.

"Come on. We can't just stay here."

"Okay. Whatever you say."

She got on the bike and once again we wobbled off. Riding at night was more difficult than I had assumed, with only the light of a small flashlight bulb backed up by two silver, size C Eveready batteries. Even though there was more traffic on the highway into town, the headlights and light poles, traffic lights, and illuminated storefronts were helpful guides. I just had to avoid the police station. We got off the bike and turned off the headlight while we passed it, walking to the other side of the street.

When we rode by the closed drug store, I instinctively glanced down the alley. That had become a habit, even when I knew there would be no sports car there. And I didn't expect it this time. But something *was* there.

"Shhh…get off, Gwen."

"Hey…stop the bike first."

I impatiently dragged my feet to slow us down.

"I will, on the other side of the alley. Keep your head down. And don't even breathe."

I knew she had no idea why I said that. We got off the bike on the other side of the alley and stood by the wall of the building. I was just feet from what I knew might be Margaret's car. I had seen the dim glint of the street lamp reflected on its fender. I whispered in Gwen's ear.

"I think your mother and my father are in that alley."

She didn't follow my whispering lead, but instead expressed her disbelief in a loud protest.

"You're crazy. Take me home…right now!"

"Shhh."

"I told you, take me home, Jonathan."

"Shhh."

The second "Shhh" didn't come from me. It came from the alley. A female voice spoke up.

"Who's there?"

The other voice…a male…jumped in.

"Shut up."

I turned the bike into the alley like a gunslinger with his six-shooter and aimed the now weakening headlight on the car. The outline of a T-Bird appeared, though it looked more gray than red in the dark. I turned to Gwen.

"Well? Was I right?"

The male voice spoke again.

"Turn that damn light off."

"No, Dad."

There was a short pause before recognition.

"Jonathan?"

The presence of Margaret was now undeniable, even though the bike headlight could hardly penetrate the dark alley.

"Mom?" Gwen asked with a trembling voice.

This time there was no pause.

"Gwen?"

Gwen spoke into the darkness.

"What...what are you doing here, Mom? What are you doing in this alley?"

Margaret's voice rang out.

"What are *you* doing here? You should be home. It's late. And what are you doing with *a boy?*"

Gwen tried to defend herself.

"I...I...don't know...we're...his brother Billy...Robey..."

Anger rose in me like a thermometer in a wild fire. I finally asked Margaret the question I couldn't ask her in the dentist's office.

"What are *you* doing here with my father? And what are *you* doing here, Dad?

Margaret shot back.

"Don't you dare talk to your elders that way!"

"Elders? Elders? *You lowest of the Lower Zoo scum!* I hate both of you!"

My open fury took on a martial tone, and I started bossing them around like an FBI agent.

"Get out of the car! Get...out...of...the...car! Now! Both of you!"

Dad found his boldness as well.

"Yeh, we'll get out of the car and beat the crap out of you! Get home before I do just that!"

I snapped the headlight out of its holder and walked into the alley. I could hear Gwen's footsteps following me. I stepped right next to the car door and shined the dim, yellow light on my father and then Margaret.

"Robey came over to our house and beat up Billy because of you two. He's probably dead. Now get out of the car!"

I didn't really think Billy was dead. Even though he didn't respond when I called him, the paramedics said he was still breathing. And anyway, I just couldn't imagine Billy being dead. But not knowing much about his actual condition, I wanted to be dramatic and heap as much guilt on Dad as possible. He got out of the car, followed by Margaret. For the first time, I could see the worried look on his face in the yellow glow of the headlight.

"Where is he?"

"I don't know…the hospital."

He turned to Margaret.

"I'd better go. I'll call you."

He disappeared into the night. I looked at Margaret in the glow of the headlight. I had never been this close to her. I knew she couldn't see my eyes, though I could see hers fairly well. So I felt I had the advantage. Gwen began to whimper again. I spoke to Margaret.

"Do you know Gwen's secret?"

"What are you talking about? What secret?"

I felt a sharp kick to my shin.

"Ouch! What are you doing, Gwen?"

"Shut up, Jonathan. You're making that up so you can bother me."

My anger turned to Gwen.

"That's not true. How can you say that? Tell her! Tell her!"

Gwen punched me hard on the arm, though I didn't think Margaret could see it in the dark anymore than she saw the shin kick. The punch just made me more resolute.

"Tell her. Tell her how Dom hurt you…what he did to you. Tell her!"

"He didn't do anything, Mom. You know Dom. He's all threats."

*Just which Gwen is this?* I wondered. I had to think of something. I quickly decided to bring in some clear evidence.

"What about the marks? Show her those marks. Look."

I shined the pitiful little headlight on Gwen.

"What, a few scratches? What are you talking about?"

She turned to her mother.

"Mom, this boy Jonathan here is bothering me. Please...tell him to stop it. He made me ride on his bike in the dark with his arms around me. He's always following me. I don't like him. Can we go home? Please?"

I was fuming by this point.

"You're lying! You told me he hurt you! You told me your secret! Why are you doing this? You said he...he...touched you...you told me that! Tell her!"

I turned the headlight toward Margaret. She looked straight into it. From the black of night, Gwen protested.

"That's not true, Mom. He's making it all up!"

Margaret suddenly took on a sympathetic motherly tone.

"I believe you, Gwenny. You wouldn't let that happen. Dom wouldn't touch you. He's rotten to the core, the SOB. But he wouldn't touch you like that. You'd tell me if he did, wouldn't you? You'd tell me."

"Of course I would, Mom. Get Jonathan away from me. He's a creep. He threw things at my window in the middle of the night and almost broke it. He won't leave me alone. He scares me."

I was completely confused now. All I could think to do was to turn to Margaret and change the subject to her affair with Dad.

"Yeh, well you didn't tell Gwen about my dad, did you...and how you kissed him right here in this alley? You didn't say *anything!*"

"That's a lie! We were...just talking business...which is none of *your* business. But my daughter *is* *my* business. Did you hurt my daughter? What did you do to her? Are you following her?"

She moved in closer.

"Are you bothering her? I'll call the police. I'll go over to that phone booth right now and call them."

She pointed to the phone booth as she moved in closer, so close I could almost feel her breath.

"You're out way past your bedtime, little boy. They're just down the street, and they'll come and get you!"

I thought about the police station and riding my bike with Gwen sidesaddle...and their good friend Dom Romero, the car salesman. Now she had me on the defensive.

"I...I...no...no. I'm not. I'm not. I'm not bothering her. Honestly I'm not."

"He is *so*, Mom. He bothers me. I don't like him. He's a creep. Let's go home...now."

"Yes, honey. Let's go home. Stay away from my daughter. If I see you near our house, I'll call the police."

Gwen got in the car. I snapped the light back into its holder. As Margaret started the engine, I slowly rode away into the night. I didn't know what I knew and what I didn't know, and I was too numb and worn down to try to figure it out. The headlight grew dimmer and dimmer as the batteries began to wear down. Finally it went out altogether, like an extinguished flame.

I tried to navigate my way in the dark from one street to the next. Finally, I recognized my street in the light of one street lamp. When I got home I saw that there were a few lights on. When I got inside, no one seemed to be there. I called out several times, but no one answered. I went straight to my room with no idea how Billy was and went quickly to sleep.

# CHAPTER 26

I AWOKE TO BILLY'S VOICE. When I opened my eyes, I realized it wasn't really his voice. It was a dream, and he was still talking right up until the time I woke up. We were arguing about whether everyone really was smart in different ways. I said that for one thing, it wasn't true in Gwen's case. I finally realized that she was just dumb.

All of this took place in a back yard that was supposed to be hers, and the whole time I was afraid her mother would look out the kitchen window and call the police. But of course, as in many dreams, it wasn't her back yard. It wasn't *anyone's* back yard. I had created it as I slept and placed bushes everywhere similar to the one we found Billy under.

And when I woke up, Billy had just been saying "You're wrong. She has a great gift, but it's trapped." I was just getting ready to tell him that Gwen was trapped because she was an animal fit only for the Upper Zoo. I would have said it loudly, but as it turned out I didn't say it at all. Then suddenly I remembered where Billy was, or at least where he had been the night before.

I lay in my bed for maybe a minute, staring at Clarence's rip in the Beach Boys poster. Why did he do that? I knew what Billy said, but was it actually true that just being in a new place would make him rip the poster, smash my model car, and almost crack skulls with me? There certainly was a lot about Clarence I didn't understand.

I turned and looked at the clock. I expected to see maybe 7:30. But I guessed two hours early. It was 9:30. I called for Mom. There was no answer. I sprung up and headed downstairs. The blinds were open, which was normal for 9:30. But I knew instinctively that they had never been pulled the night before. She probably hadn't even come home. Dishes in the sink confirmed my suspicion.

I pulled on a tee shirt and shorts and was back on my bike within ten minutes. The hospital was on the other side of town. There was a light, late summer breeze in my favor, and the rapid RPMs of my pedals brought me there in record time, perhaps twenty minutes. At about 10, I stood breathless before the information desk. I barely got the words out.

"Billy...Billy Richman. Is he here?"

The woman at the desk scanned the names in a loose-leaf book. I couldn't help but think of Clarence. He would know Billy's room number after a quick glance and never forget it for the rest of his life. But he would also sway and act like he was retarded while she, with her little pillbox hat and pearl necklace, looked like the First Lady responding to a reporter's question...well, like Jackie Kennedy...not like Lady Bird Johnson. She interrupted my thoughts, glancing up from the loose-leaf book only briefly.

"It's family only, little boy. I'm sorry...no friends at this time."

"I'm not a little boy. I'm his brother...his *big* brother. I'm his big brother."

"Oh. I see. Well, only adults can visit the Intensive Care Unit."

"The *what?*"

Obviously put out by my ignorance, she repeated herself, pronouncing each word like an elementary school teacher on a bad day.

"The—Intensive—Care—Unit."

I had no idea what that was. But I knew what the words intensive and care meant, and it didn't sound good.

"Is he okay?"

She looked up at me with dull green eyes. For the first time she looked me over.

"Look, I don't have that information, but…it says critical here, which could mean a lot of things."

"Could you call and find out?"

"Yes…I suppose I could call the floor. Are your parents with him?

"Yes…my mother."

"Your mother, then. I'll call now."

She dialed the phone and said a lot of "I see's." Then she hung up.

"They'll be right down."

I thought, *They? Was Dad with her?* The receptionist asked me to take a seat in the waiting area. As I sat down, I was thinking about how Billy was and at the same time wondering whether my bike was in a safe place. The elevator across the hall opened and, to my surprise, Mom and Dad stepped out. They must have been on their way down already.

I hadn't seen Mom and Dad together outside the house since the restaurant, and it felt strange to watch them walking next to each other. But I could see more than that as they drew close. I could see Mom's tears and broken heart all coming out of her eyes at the same time. And I could see something in Dad's eyes like a dingy lamp in a damp, dark chamber. I guessed that he now knew who Robey's father was, and who his stepmother was. I didn't know how he knew it, but I just figured he did. The cobwebs of ignorance weren't totally gone, but they were definitely visible. Mom reached out and gave me a tight hug. She was clutching several crumpled tissues in her left hand.

"You can't see Billy just yet. We asked for permission. They're asking the doctor. Okay?"

"Yeh…I guess so," I shrugged, trying not to appear afraid.

I still didn't know what was going on. Dad wouldn't look at me. So I wasn't going to find out anything from him. I wondered if I should just wait and find out whenever Mom wanted to tell me. But I was starting to feel my heart speed up like bad news was around the corner, and I wanted to get it over with and find out what the news was.

"Mom?"

She turned and looked at me, even though her eyes kept filling with tears.

"Yes, Jonathan?"

"What's going on?"

She hesitated, searching for words.

"Well…"

I didn't get my answer, as the receptionist interrupted her.

"He can go up."

Mom took me by the hand and led me to the elevator. Dad trailed behind. Once the elevator was closed and we were alone inside, she spoke…squeezing my hand as if to comfort me and allay my fears.

"He's sleeping…sort of."

"Sort of?"

She didn't respond. Apparently, she thought what she said was enough to prepare me for seeing him. But I wanted more information.

"Mom?"

"Yes, dear?"

I tried the most direct approach I could think of.

"How's Billy? I want to know."

She looked at me as my father watched the floors pass by on the lighted dial above us. Then she sighed deeply and spoke again, this time more seriously.

"Not so good. He's in what they call a coma. A bone in his arm is broken, and there's a little break in his leg…actually, his ankle. They will heal. He'll be fine. He'll be able to walk."

She paused. I knew there was more.

"And?"

She began to tear up again.

"And…his head…his brain…it's a little bit…big right now. So… he's sleeping. But he'll wake up. And when he does, he'll want to see you very much. But right now, he's sleeping…sort of."

"His brain is…a little big? What does *that* mean?"

It sounded like something out of Frankenstein. What had *really* happened, and what was Billy feeling? I began to feel nauseous, combined with the sense that I was still dreaming, that I'd never woken up that morning. Mom tried to answer my question.

"It means…"

Dad turned away from looking at the lights and toward me.

"Stop asking questions."

Anger flashed in me again, and I spoke to him abruptly.

"It's your fault. It's all your fault!"

Mom stepped between us as the elevator opened.

"Stop it. We have to see Billy. Both of you stop it!"

Why didn't she just agree with me? I knew I was right. She must have known it too.

We walked down a hall with light green walls. I could see in patients' rooms as I passed them. All I could think of was *ouch*. I had never heard anyone crying out in pain from hospital rooms before. It strangely embarrassed and startled me. I tried to look straight ahead so I wouldn't meet anyone's eyes and no one's eyes would meet mine. Mom told me Billy was at the end of the hall in a corner room.

Finally, we arrived at the door. As we entered, I could hear machines of some sort of buzzing and clicking. He lay in a bed in the middle of the room with his eyes closed, a fat tube in his mouth, and a thin tube in his nose. I just stared at him. He looked quiet, but I knew he must have been crying like the other patients…on the inside. No wonder he didn't answer me from the bush.

*He probably wouldn't hear me now,* I thought, *and he also probably didn't hear me when I said I was sorry for everything then.* But even if he *could* hear me, I couldn't repeat it now in front of my parents, especially Dad. Mom spoke up, her voice trembling.

"You can take his hand. And you can talk to him. The doctor said it's good to talk to him."

"Okay."

As awkward as I felt, I took Billy's hand. It was limp. How many times had I arm and thumb wrestled with that hand, making sure I won. It crossed my mind that I could win even faster if I tried now. That was a crazy thought, so I put it aside and leaned over him. I wanted to ask him about Robey and the iron filings, but I knew that wouldn't be pleasant, and I wanted to be as pleasant as possible. So I invoked Saint Edison.

"Umm…Billy…umm…you know Thomas Edison? Remember him?"

My mother whimpered and my father groaned.

"You love Thomas Edison. Umm…when you wake up, I want you to tell me all about him…because I…I love to hear you tell me about Thomas Edison. You could talk about him all day, and I'd ask for more."

Tears began to streak down my face.

"So please wake up so we can talk about Edison and how he invented all those things. Please?"

My voice began to shake like Mom's. I dropped his hand and walked out. Mom followed me. I spoke without turning around.

"I'm going to take my bike home. It's right outside, and I don't want anyone to take it."

Mom knew I didn't care about the bike. She took my hand in hers again and squeezed it.

"Jonathan…Billy may be a little different when he wakes up. He may talk a little different. We have to…we have to be patient."

Her words stunned me. Was she holding something back from me?

"You mean *if* he wakes up. He's gonna die, isn't he? Don't lie to me, Mom! You always lie about everything to make me feel better. If he's gonna die, I want to know. I'm not a little baby anymore."

She drew closer and squeezed my hand harder.

"I'm not lying, Jonathan. I promise. I know things have been hard, with Dad doing those wrong things and not being there for you, and with you being in that class…and that boy Robey. The police are looking for him…but…I'm not lying, Jonathan. The doctor says Billy has a good chance of waking up and getting better. It'll just take time."

"Will he…" I was afraid to ask the question. "Will he be like Clarence?"

She was emphatic, shaking her head.

"No. No, he'll never be like Clarence. Clarence is abnormal. He's not like Billy. And Billy will never be like him."

I knew I had to tell her my feelings about Clarence now or I never would. I let go of her hand and looked at her, demanding her full attention.

"Then he's a good abnormal, Mom. And he knows how to pray. He prays to Jesus, Mom, and it's really kind of funny to hear. But he does it. And he knows the whole Bible by heart, and a lot of other books, like the Hardy Boys. It's true. He's not like those mean Christians Mrs. Moliver talks about in Hebrew school. He's nice. And he's kind of special, Mom, and I like him. He's not retarded. He's smart…in a different way. That's what Billy says, and he's right. Billy's right. So I'm going to ask him to pray for him. I'm going to ask Clarence to pray for Billy. I'm going right over to Clarence's and asking him to pray."

She reached out her other hand, still clutching a few tissues, and gently touched mine.

"I think you should do that, Jonathan. Billy needs all the prayer he can get. And…and…"

"What, Mom?"

Tears streaked down her cheeks, and she wiped them with the tissues.

"I like Clarence, too. I'm…I'm glad he's your friend."

We stood a few feet apart, both quietly crying. I didn't want to hug her in the hospital patient floor hallway like I had downstairs, with all those people looking out of their rooms at us. So I just stood there until I didn't know what more to say.

"Okay. Well, I'm leaving now. I'll…I'll see you soon."

"Okay. Be careful going home."

"Okay."

I slowly walked down the hall. I looked back and Mom was gone, back in the room with Dad and Billy. I took the elevator down to the main floor and walked past the receptionist at the desk. When I got to my bike, I found it hadn't been touched. I grabbed it and rode away.

It felt a bit strange asking Clarence if he'd pray to Jesus to help Billy. But then again, a lot of things about Clarence were strange. He could stutter and stumble and rip my Beach Boys poster. And yet he knew things other people didn't know. And he saw things other people didn't see. He was the only person I wanted to see that morning. I arrived by 11. It took a long time for his mother to answer the door.

"Clarence is still in bed. Maybe you should come back later."

"Well…it's…it's about my brother. I want to tell him something about my brother."

"What about your brother?"

I didn't want to tell her the details. I just wanted to see Clarence.

"Umm…just something. Can I wait outside?"

"Well…it may be a little while."

"I'll wait outside then."

She looked at me like I was a little off. But I had to talk to Clarence and ask him to pray one of those prayers for Billy, and I'd wait as long as it took. I walked out of the house and sat on the front step next to my bike. His mother saw that I was determined to stay. She explained a bit more about why Clarence slept so late.

"He was up late last night. Sometimes he doesn't sleep well…just sometimes. He gets up and can't get back to sleep. But I'm sure he'll be getting up soon. I'll check on him in a bit."

She gently closed the door behind me. I looked at my bike in the summer sun and thought of Billy and our close times, our bike rides, our model building, our Frisbee throwing. I began to wonder what I could have done to protect him. How could I have stopped Robey? Why did I ever even want to be Robey's friend? What would he do next to hurt the people I loved and cared about?

I began to picture Robey as the lion of the Upper Zoo, tearing his prey, destroying the other animals in their cages. But he was also like King Kong on the loose, destroying everything in his path. I had just seen that movie on the Early Show. Only with Robey, there didn't seem to be anyone there to rescue people—no biplanes buzzing around him with their machine guns blazing until he fell from his high and death-defying position.

Ten minutes of this meditation must have gone by. I had no idea whether Clarence was still sleeping or getting dressed. I stood up, wondering if I should knock on the door or just get on my bike and leave. I turned toward the street. That's when I saw someone who walked suspiciously like Robey in the distance. He was still so small, I didn't know if it was a mirage or real. Whatever it was, it was about a block and a half away and coming toward me with a swagger just like his.

I realized I could quickly hop on my bike and ride the other way. But then he would still be on the loose like King Kong, and he had just hurt Billy so bad his brain was big. I thought maybe I should go back in the house and call the police. So I turned around and tried to open the door. It was locked. I began to knock and call out to Clarence's mother as quietly as I could.

"Mrs. Carlson, Mrs. Carlson…please, please come and open the door."

He was getting closer. I could see that it was indeed Robey and not a mirage. At a half a block, he saw me. There was no escaping now. He shouted loud enough for me to hear.

"Hey, Jonathan. What are you doing there?"

I didn't answer. Instead I knocked a little louder. He came closer, now a quarter of a block away.

"Hey, Jonathan. You're just the man I want to see…after I see Clarence. But what are you doing at his house? You *know* what I told you."

I knocked really loud now. He was walking faster and was just a few houses away. My heart was racing. Suddenly the door opened, and I forced my way in, shutting and locking it behind me with shaky hands. Mrs. Carlson stared at me, her hands on her hips.

"What are you doing?"

"Nothing. Please don't open the door."

She wasn't about to just accept that. After all, this was her house.

"Why not?"

"Please just don't."

She kept her hands on her hips and acted like she could do what she wanted. But she also didn't open the door.

"Well anyway, he's getting dressed now. He was really glad you waited. So am I. You turned out to be a good friend, Jonathan. You'll never know what that means to me."

"Umm...no. *He's* the good friend. But..."

I would have loved to continue the conversation, but this wasn't a great time. Instead, I had one more request.

"Umm...could you by any chance call the police and...umm...tell them that the kid who beat up Billy Richman is at the door?"

"No he's not. I was just out there with you. You must be seeing things, Jonathan."

"He *will* be. Please just call."

Clarence loped into the hallway, his hair wet and plastered down like a shiny, black porcelain bowl and his stained white tee shirt sticking out of his pants. I turned toward him.

"You were right, Clarence. Robey got Billy. He's on his way here now."

"'Surely he will deliver thee from the snare of the fowler.'"

There was the voice. But I wasn't in the mood for it.

"'A thousand shall fall at thy side, and ten thousand at thy right hand; *but* it shall not come near thee.'"

"Yeh, well it's near now, Clarence."

There was a knock at the door. I turned once again to Mrs. Carlson.

"Please Mrs. Carlson...the police."

She hesitated, but thankfully still didn't answer the door. I realized I had to completely fill Clarence in on what happened.

"Clarence, he beat up Billy like you said. He's in the hospital and he's not waking up. Robey's here, at the door."

The knock became more persistent. And a voice could be heard from outside the house.

"Mrs. Carlson, will you tell the boys to step out here? I just want to tell them something."

Mrs. Carlson recognized the voice.

"That *is* Robey, isn't it?"

"Yes, Mrs. Carlson. It is. Please call the police."

The voice got louder.

"We just have to straighten some things out, guys. You see, I believe in people keeping their word. It says that in the Bible. And when they break their word, there are consequences. We talked about making things clear. There are two zoos for a reason. Let's talk things over."

Suddenly, my anger superseded my fear.

"You hurt my brother. Go away!"

My face reddened and I shouted. "Go away! Go away! Leave us alone!"

The door spoke again.

"Your father hurt my father. Remember at the drug store I said there were good Jews and bad Jews? Your father is a bad Jew, and someone has to pay. I must defend my father. That's justice, and there must be justice. I sat on the tack. I paid. He must pay. Capiche? Is this your bike? It is, isn't it, Jonathan?"

Suddenly, through the living room window we could see the bike sail through the air and land with a crunch on the driveway. *That* finally got Mrs. Carlson's attention. There was a quiet nervousness in her voice.

"Oh my. Stay calm. He really *is* sick, isn't he? I'll call the authorities now."

She picked up the phone and dialed. It seemed like suspended animation before she gave someone her address and hung up. Then Clarence loped for the door. I ran over to stop him.

"What are you doing?"

"'Yea, though I walk through the valley of the shadow of death, I will fear no evil: for thou *art* with me; thy rod and thy staff they comfort me. Thou preparest a table before me in the presence of mine enemies: thou anointest my head with oil; my cup runneth over.'"

He unlocked the door and stepped out onto the front porch with no hesitation. Then he shut it behind him. I tried to open it, but I couldn't.

"It's stuck. It's stuck, Mrs. Carlson. I can't open it."

"What are you talking about? Let me try."

She tried and fared no better than me. She kept pulling as she turned to me.

"It's not locked. I don't understand it. Open the window over there in the living room and find out what's going on."

I raced over to the living room window and pulled it up. A light breeze blew through the screen. I could see Robey press Clarence up against the door. Clarence had one hand behind him and it was holding the doorknob, his knuckles white. Then Robey pulled his fist back and punched Clarence in the chest. He did it a second time and hit him in the stomach. Clarence released a dull aching sound from his throat, and his breathing quickened. One hand was flying all over the place, as was his head. But his other hand tightened its grip on the knob and the knuckles turned even whiter. Robey was more enraged than I'd ever seen him.

"Move aside, retarded freak. I don't want to have to kill you to get inside. Capiche?"

"Yes…yes…okay…Robey…right…"

But Clarence didn't budge. I wanted to call out, but suddenly I lost my voice. A jolt of fear that Robey would kick the screen out and come after me paralyzed me. And right then and there, I hated myself for it.

Mrs. Carlson called to me frantically from behind.

"What's going on?"

I couldn't say anything. Nothing came out of my mouth. She became very agitated.

"Where, oh where are the police?"

I kept looking at the porch. Robey pulled his arm back for another punch, a harder punch. He was about to release it when a sonorous and thunderous voice came from the very deepest part of Clarence.

"'And I will bless them that bless thee, Israel, and curse him that curseth thee: and in thee shall all families of the earth be blessed,' Genesis 12. 'Ye worship ye know not what: we know what we worship: for salvation is of the Jews,' John 4. 'What advantage then hath the Jew? or what profit is there of circumcision? Much every way: chiefly, because that unto them were committed the oracles of God,' Romans 3."

Robey stood there frozen, his hand ready for the punch like a Roman statue in mid-stride. Clarence spoke again, his hand still firmly gripping the doorknob.

"You…you will…you will…go…will go…"

Now he was hesitating and halting even more than usual.

To…a…to a place…a place…a place where…where people with broken minds…broken…minds…go. You will…you will…go there for a long time…not a jail…there…and you can get…get…help…"

"You're the one with the broken mind, retard. And people need to see the difference between the retards and the normal people. Now step aside!"

Clarence held his ground. I suddenly realized that he was protecting us…his mother and me. He was protecting us with his life.

There was a faint sound of a siren in the distance. And it was getting closer, as Robey had when he walked toward us from a block and a half away. That seemed like hours ago now. Robey could hear the siren too, and got one last punch into Clarence's stomach. He fell to the pavement, releasing the doorknob, just as the cruiser pulled up the driveway. Two of my policeman friends from the station got out as I opened the front door.

"There he is!"

They took hold of Robey, and one of them grabbed his ear, pulling it. Then he let go of the ear, but not of Robey. He put him in a headlock.

"What's a matter with you? You're an embarrassment to your father. He's such a good man, and look at you!"

Robey tried to free himself, screaming and growling.

"Yeh, you rotten cops! You're as rotten as he is, with that slut Gwen in her room in middle of the night. You think I didn't hear him with her? With Gwenny Gwenny Gwen Gwen. She and her slutty mother, they ruined his life! They ruined my father's life, and they have to pay. And you're all just like him. All of you copper boys! You have to pay too. Capiche? Capiche!"

As tall and powerful as Robey was, they easily cuffed him and threw him in the back of the cruiser like a Raggedy Andy doll, slamming the door shut behind him. Only this time he didn't have a smile on his face like he did in Mr. Schott's class. He had a scowl, and he kept screaming. But no one could hear him, and he couldn't hear the police as they talked to him from outside the car.

"Shut up, punk. Kids like you make this job a drag."

"You said it," the other cop said.

Clarence had gotten up from the ground.

"You okay, kid?" the one with the donut paunch asked.

"Fine...okay...I'm fine...yes...I'm...I'm...fine, sir officer sir."

The policeman turned to Mrs. Carlson.

"Ma'am, he's talking a little strange. Maybe he ought to be checked out. We can call an ambulance."

"He's fine. He always talks like that."

He took off his hat and scratched his head.

"Okay, Ma'am, if you say so. Only, could you three come down to the station? We need some eyewitness information."

"We'll be down...in a bit."

The other policeman looked at my bike lying in the driveway.

"That bike's got a problem, son. I told you not to ride with that girl. Now it doesn't look so good."

"Yes sir. I'll take care of it."

They got into the cruiser and drove off. Clarence's mother gave him a quick hug. He pulled back, as I'd seen him do many times before. She shed tears and breathed sighs of relief, but he just stood there and rocked.

"Why did you hold the door closed like that? We wanted to help you, but you just stood there like a...like a..."

Clarence interrupted.

"...a refrigerator...a refrigerator...I was like refrigerator...like a refrigerator...like you."

He laughed as only Clarence could laugh, like a toddler when being thrown in the air, like he didn't care what anyone thought.

# CHAPTER 27

Finally, the summer came to an end. I never asked Mom if she knew what class I would be in when school started. Even if she *did* know, I didn't want to hear it. I'd find out soon enough. And anyway, if I *did* end up in the Upper Zoo again, at least Robey wouldn't be there.

Clarence had once again spoken the truth. With Mom and Dad in the courtroom, along with Mrs. Carlson, some judge with a black robe told Robey and his father that he was going someplace for "emotionally disturbed" teenagers. And it was somewhere far away. So that was that. I didn't end up having to talk about what I saw under our bush or on Clarence's porch while Robey was in the courtroom. And he didn't say anything in the courtroom while I was there. If he looked at me, I didn't know it. I never looked in his direction.

That courtroom was also the last time I saw my parents go somewhere together. Mom filed for divorce just before school started. Dad moved out that same week.

I lay in bed the night before school started, trying to piece together the fragmented few months that had been my summer. During that time, I found out all about Dad and Gwen's mother. And then I ended up seeing both Dad and Gwen disappear in one way or another.

I almost lost Billy too...the brother I'd ignored almost the whole year. His brain shrunk to its regular size again. And eventually he came home from the hospital, though not until my school year had already started. But he didn't go to the same school he went to the year before, the elementary school where I had also attended years ago. He went to a new school, a school where Clarence also now attended. The teachers told Mom it would probably only be for a few years, after convincing her Billy needed it.

After Billy came home from the hospital, I discovered a level of love in my heart for him I hadn't known before. He repeated things a lot now, and it wasn't only about Edison. It was about everything…like what he was eating or what we did during the weekend. But that was okay. I just loved hearing his voice. He could repeat things as much as he wanted. And sometimes he would come out with the wisest things, just like in the old days before he was beat up. He'd be in the middle of some mundane thing, and he'd come up with a gem. In fact, I couldn't tell who was wiser when that happened, Billy or Clarence. And I wondered how many other kids like that went to their school.

Billy and I would take long walks. He really enjoyed taking long walks now. And I never said no when he asked to take one. I finally realized that he had always looked up to me, even when I was in the Upper Zoo. But now he didn't hold back telling me how smart and gifted I was, over and over. And then he would tell me again. But the hugs were the greatest thing. They were long and childlike, and I was thankful for each and every one of them.

As I lay in my bed the night before ninth grade started, I thought about Mom. I felt most sorry for her. Something in her seemed to die when Billy ended up in the hospital with his brain problem. And the divorce just seemed to put the nail in the coffin. I tried to comfort her, but I wasn't very good at it. At least she let me be friends with Clarence. And that worked out pretty well, because she arranged something with Clarence's mother to take Clarence and Billy to school together. It turned out their school had no buses.

The next day was the first one that felt a little bit like fall. I had to wear a light jacket, which I threw on at the last second right after grabbing a hot Pop Tart from the toaster. I was still chewing it when I hugged Mom and ran out of the house to catch the bus. There was Robert Rogers, getting on just ahead of me. I ignored him, as I had the whole year before. And I sat on my usual inside seat, leaning against the window the whole time.

As usual, I'd been sent the room number in the mail just before school. As I walked down the hall toward it, I noticed that Robert Rogers was going the same direction. And when he walked into the room, I knew that I wasn't in the Upper Zoo anymore. The elevator had started again from between the two floors and had let me out in regular old ninth grade. The cages had been opened, and I was in the real world...*if indeed this was the real world.*

I entered the class. I realized that this was my homeroom and that I would have perhaps five teachers and not just two. I knew that I would have lots of homework and all kinds of papers and exams. I really wanted to keep up this year to make Mom happy. I hoped I would. She had been so sad. But those thoughts faded when I looked around.

Robert took a seat on one side of the room, so I took a seat on the other. At first, I thought maybe I wouldn't know hardly any of the other kids. Maybe some of the kids from the last year were in a ninth grade Upper Zoo. But then Gwen walked in, with her hair looking cute and shiny, perfectly framing her face again. She was laughing about something with another girl also from last year's class. I was surprised to see her looking so happy and beautiful once more, but then again I had heard that her mother had left Dom and moved with her somewhere else in town. I was sure that would make her happy. I couldn't tell whether she saw me, but she must have because she so clearly avoided me. And I realized then and there that I would probably avoid her the whole year.

I looked around again and saw one of the iron filings...Michael. He seemed like a regular kid without Robey there, like a filing without a magnet. And then I saw Ted, the other filing, on the other side of the room. If I didn't know better, I would think they didn't know each other. Clearly, the magnet was missing. And just as clearly, they didn't want anything to do with me. I knew they wouldn't bother me all year, so I didn't care whether they had anything to do with beating up Billy. Maybe I should have cared, but I didn't. They were like bees without stingers, cats without claws.

The girl with the imperfect nose was there, and so was chubby Marcus. After I saw them, I wondered who *did* end up in the Upper Zoo. I should have figured it out, because Clarence was in a special school that helped kids like him. But it took the rest of the day for it to dawn on me, and Mom confirmed it that evening. There *was* no Upper Zoo in ninth grade. They had just thrown us in with everyone else, and now it seemed that the eighth grade Upper Zoo was just a dream.

That evening, I looked at all the schoolbooks on my dresser. They seemed so thick and full of words…Algebra, World History, Chemistry. They looked so serious, not like the tinker toy models in Mr. Garner's class. That night's homework was just as serious. There were several reading assignments in my notebook. That evening at home, I wanted to just bury my head in my pillow and go to sleep even though it was only 7 p.m. But I remembered Mom and opened the history book. I had no interest in the Byzantine Empire, but I read the first paragraph.

I only stopped long enough before the second paragraph to think about Clarence's thunderous words of advice to me when I told him I was going to visit Dad at his apartment the Saturday before. I didn't want to go. I had nothing to say to him, and I didn't feel like he had anything to say to me. But I couldn't ignore that voice that came through Clarence from somewhere else. No one could…not even Robey that late summer day on his porch. Clarence rocked back and forth in his usual way as the words came out.

"Father, forgive both our fathers, for they know not what they do."

I figured they were Jesus' words, and I knew they were from the Bible. I was wise enough to know that if Clarence spoke them, they were worth remembering.

# ABOUT MICHAEL ROBERT WOLF

Michael Wolf has led Beth Messiah Messianic Jewish Synagogue in Cincinnati, Ohio, for the past 33 years. He is past president of the Messianic Jewish Alliance of America and presently serves on their executive committee. He has produced several children's video movies and is presently working with Kingdom Pictures on an independent film he wrote called *Sound of the Spirit*, due to be released early in 2012.

# In the right hands, This Book will Change Lives!

Most of the people who need this message will not be looking for this book. To change their lives, you need to put a copy of this book in their hands.

> *But others (seeds) fell into good ground, and brought forth fruit, some a hundred-fold, some sixty-fold, some thirty-fold* (Matthew 13:8).

Our ministry is constantly seeking methods to find the good ground, the people who need this anointed message to change their lives. Will you help us reach these people?

> *Remember this—a farmer who plants only a few seeds will get a small crop. But the one who plants generously will get a generous crop* (2 Corinthians 9:6).

## EXTEND THIS MINISTRY BY SOWING
### 3 BOOKS, 5 BOOKS, 10 BOOKS, OR MORE TODAY,
#### AND BECOME A LIFE CHANGER!

Thank you,

Don Nori Sr., Founder
Destiny Image
Since 1982